Michael Alty

Michael boldly and courageously goes where no author has gone before. He writes his books combining modern contemporary poetry with humorous verse and important historical recollections; integrating satire with strange fiction and, together with his ability to introduce controversial judgement contributed by alien local radio presenters, he faces the unbending task of dismissing his adversaries with words consisting of two or more syllables.

Lancaster Grill

Michael Alty

Published 2018 by arima publishing

www.arimapublishing.com

ISBN 978 1 84549 728 6
© Michael Alty 2018

Printed and bound in the United Kingdom

Typeset in Garamond

Swirl is an imprint of arima publishing.

arima publishing
ASK House, Northgate Avenue
Bury St Edmunds, Suffolk IP32 6BB
t: (+44) 01284 700321

www.arimapublishing.com

Chapter One

The celebration day had arrived. It was Friday 14th August 2015, and progressed with a loving smile when Harold Rigby put one foot in front of the other and rose from his marital bed in the same way he had done for the past forty-four years of marriage to his wife, Mabel, and apart from him being away for several weeks in Saudi Arabia working for BAE Systems, he always brought her a cup of tea before toddling off to work on foot less than a mile along the main road. The exception to all of this was he was now retired and didn't have to share with others the same ordeal of having to get up early to install the same avionic equipment into multi-million pound jet fighter aircraft. 'Ah, I can remember happiness.' Harold said, after spending many years sharing several feet of ground space with one of his colleagues. 'Ah, BAE Systems,' others would say with a sigh, 'they are one of the world's leading toy manufacturers, second only to *Triang* and *Hornby 00* train sets' when a regular tippler in the local pub so eloquently described the situation from just a few yards away. The confusion, relating to Harold's loving relationship towards the company had waned over the years promulgated by prolonged strikes and redundancy notices being handed out to employees who found it difficult to arrive at the clock on time during a spell of cold mornings.

Mabel, however, still received her cup of tea without having to hear the kitchen door bang shut, echoing throughout the house every time he left to go to work. The forty-fourth Ruby Wedding Anniversary was to take place that evening at their home, a semi-detached dormer-bungalow at No 23 Calder Vale Avenue, Freckleton, a pretty, rural village on the outskirts of Preston in Lancashire.

It was then, just under a year when Harold walked out of the main gate at BAE Systems for the last time having surrendered his identity pass, a clocking in and out swipe card and the keys to his personal locker which was situated in hangar number three.

After a few pleasantries had taken place and the usual ritual of him having to give a speech of no less than three-hundred words to his colleagues in order to receive a non-obligatory bouquet of flowers wrapped in translucent cellophane paper, he proceeded to walk the few yards to the main entrance under escort, lest he decided to uninvitingly stray into an office to give someone a black eye for refusing to give him a voluntary redundancy package fifteen years previously. With tears in his eyes, he found it difficult to focus, and to tell the time on his gold watch which had been presented to him in the May of that year for his loyal and devoted service to the company over the past twenty-five years. The money he was about to receive in pension was to be of little significance and was of minor compensation for all the mornings he had to trudge to work in all weathers; "walking to work in the dark and coming home in the dark is a real bundle of fun",' he used to say. "I only wish I could cut a hole in the factory's wire fence because it would shorten my journey by half, but then I could be run down by a rocket-assisted Tornado when it hurtles down the runway at one hundred and fifty miles an hour before it and I take-off".

The highlight that day was when a Typhoon Eurofighter aircraft flew past making one hell of a noise as Harold waved goodbye to the heavily pock-marked Group 4 Security guy, Brian Ferguson behind the barrier, whose face was covered with more holes than a SODEXO chip basket or a John McEnroe see-through tennis racket. Harold Rigby retired at the age of sixty-five from his job as an electrician at BAE Systems at Warton Aerodrome in May 2014.

Harold and Mabel met in 1960 at a Mat Jolly Holiday Camp in Morecombe when they were eleven years of age, and if it wasn't for a progressive barn dance in the camp ballroom they would never have been together all these years. They were married at the Holy Trinity Anglican church in Freckleton, Lytham Road, Preston on Saturday 14th August 1971 by the Right Reverend William Henry Thomas, the local clergyman in the diocese of Blackburn, Lancashire.

Harold Rigby is a born and bred Freckletonian and the son of his late father, Roland, a pork pie and sausage roll manufacturer in Preston. Mabel for all her sins is a '*Plastic Scouser*', a posh out of town type of person from Ormskirk Road in Southport and is the daughter of eighty-nine-year-old, Bert Hatton, an ex-petrol station owner from Kirkby,

Liverpool.

The celebratory proceedings began at six-thirty when their four children, Doreen, Jean, Emily and George arrived with carts full of grandchildren who are called, Howard, Raymond, Patsy, Lillian, Warren, Janet and Susan, and not to upset the local populous their next-door neighbours, Fred and Nora Barnes and Bernadette Cartmell, were cordially invited. Agh, Freckleton, the only place I know that can deep-fry Mars Bars and serve them with chips as long as your arm.

Nora Barnes was the first to arrive having deflated the circular blue and white plastic paddling pool which she uses to drown unruly children who scream their heads off five days a week. It is of little consequence to tell you that the council imposed a hose pipe ban the previous day; the water however, came from somewhere, but certainly did not fall from the sky. She is now a registered child minder following her employment as a traffic warden and has more lines on her face than Preston railway station after being hit on the head by a brick in Preston's oldest and most prestigious legal area, Winkley Square.

Her long-suffering husband, Fred Barnes, however, is totally impervious towards all of this because his daytime job is controlled by how many people he can fit inside his ambulance before speeding off to take them to the Royal Victoria Hospital in Blackpool.

Mrs Cartmell, our neighbour in the adjoining house is seventy-two, and has been a widow-woman for three years. She, for all *her* sins was a district nurse and operated from the Infirmary in Lytham St Annes. Bernadette couldn't wait for her retirement day to arrive because her patient list was increased considerably when a model train was de-railed on the town's village green causing extensive damage to a Porsche Carrera, a miniature 1940's fire engine and an ice cream van. It was interesting to hear that during the same day, a hardware shelf became disconnected from the wall in Woolworths, crashing down on to the floor. A woman had to undergo a major surgical operation to remove two wooden spoons and a saucepan from the top of her head.

Her husband, Joseph Cartmell, a local market gardener, died of a heart attack in 2012, leaving her with a legacy of two sacks of potatoes, three boxes of tomatoes, a plastic banana and a rubber cucumber. It was several years earlier a British Aerospace Tornado flew over the village and broke the sound barrier shattering their double-glazed windows, cloches and his greenhouse glass on a small plot of land situated to the north of Freckleton village.

Joseph didn't get over the ordeal of having to replace all those panes of dirty old sheets of Perspex and glass, especially when a stray pig from next door decided to walk over a bed of strawberries just before the annual Freckleton, Warton and Wray Green 'Club' carnival days when one could see more bunting flying than during the Queen's Diamond Jubilee celebrations in 2012.

Mrs Bernadette Cartmell, a red haired Irish woman with looks that could turn milk sour, and a smile to promulgate and bring to an end the Iraq war, came to the door having walked less than twenty-five feet away from her house next door. The woman who could be turned upside down and used as a 'Swan Vestas' match, was clutching a gift-wrapped box which one could have easily mistaken for being an explosive device because of the long dangly bits of ribbon which looked similar to red, green and blue electrical wire. However, in metaphor, it had Carrick-Fergus stamped all over it and after the bomb disposal expert, Mabel, had submerged the package in water, it was eventually opened to find circular blocks of pink perfumed soap.

Her generosity was inspired some time ago when she chased a lowly duck down her drive when it became diverted from a dried-up pond on a village green some three miles outside of Freckleton.

The postman, John Hogarth, arrived at his usual time, eight-thirty am, delivering lots of letters, cards and brown paper packages tied up with string. One of the presents Harold and Mabel received had come all the way from Seattle in America, it was a miniature clock with a plastic dome and a pendulum which rotated backward and forwards to the tune, "Anniversary Waltz", the tune was played every time a greeting card, depicting Ronald Regan, was pressed as he climbed up on to his high horse. Another present to be thrown into their Christmas recycle bin was a state of the art tin opener which was made in China; the instructions weren't very clear, and it took Harold just over three and a half hours to figure them out and how to open a tin of Morrison's baked beans and sausage without losing a few fingers in the process.

Andrew Whittle, the village pop man, the deliverer of soft drinks and crisps became the hero of the day when gallons of orange sugary liquid was brought in litre bottles to their home in Calder Vale Avenue. The lavatory had ceased to function when a rubbery thing called a grommet had, over a period, corroded, allowing a constant flow of water into the cistern. The over-flow pipe jutting out into the drive was now gushing water, reminiscent of the time Harold and Mabel went to the village pub, The Coach and Horses, to celebrate his retirement; 'goodbye cruel world' he said when he returned from being alone for ten minutes inside one of Freckleton's better chapels of silent repose.

The problems continued when Harold realized the two brass stop taps had ceased up because of an unnecessary lick of white paint which had been daubed between the octagonal metal nuts screwed around the pipe, and so he was finding the whole situation extremely difficult to cope with. Andrew Whittle, however, saved the day by leaping into action from his lorry with a twelve-inch monkey wrench to stop the water cascading down the drive preventing the possibility of subsidence or being reported to the council for breaking a hose pipe ban. Needless to say, the following day the heavens opened, and it began to rain buckets, and didn't let up for weeks. It was Mabel who asked Harold later 'why do people call an adjustable spanner a monkey wrench?' Only to be told, 'when I worked for BAE Systems, there were a lot of monkeys using them.'

'And why, may I ask, did they have to leave a tally on a shadow board to obtain a monkey wrench?' Mabel asked, inquisitively.

'It is because of safety at the workplace, it was not so long ago, a shop floor worker lost a cheese and pickle sandwich, contained in a plastic container. They were later found inside a pilot's vanity glove box together with a copy of the 'Daily Sport'.'

'Did the pilot eat the sandwich, Harold?'

'I shouldn't have thought so, Mabel, it had been there for at least six months.'

At five-thirty pm, the caterers arrived, Margaret Smith, Joe Langford and Alan Plumley from Lytham St Annes. There was enough food to feed an army, in particular, 42 Royal Marine Commando, who were about to drop in within the hour. Harold's son, George Rigby, is a forty-six-year-old 'Green Beret' an ex Warrant Officer and veteran of Northern Ireland, Iraq, Afghanistan and other campaigns of somewhat notoriety. He was awarded the BEM, the British Empire Medal in 2013 for his outstanding roll, latterly as a RQMS, the battalion's Regimental Quartermaster Sergeant, excelling at golf, especially on Wednesday afternoons. George is now a manager and in charge of Naval Barrack Services in Portsmouth, a sort of, you can go, and I can go to 'IKEA' type of job, putting things up and taking things down in servicemen's married quarters, that sort of thing.

His forty-three-year-old wife Abigail and their children, nineteen-year-old Patsy, eighteen-year-old, Lillian and twenty-one-year-old, Warren who are all at Bristol University. Warren is hoping he will follow in his father's footsteps when he graduates from university and become a Royal Marines officer, and unlike George, won't be blown off course during weekend manoeuvres, uninvitingly using a Sainsbury's car park as a military drop-zone. Patsy and Lillian incidentally, have designs on becoming television and radio presenters following the vocation of their mother, Abigail, who spent a number of years working for the British Broadcasting Service in London before The BBC World Service collapsed around everyone's ears on the eighteenth of February 2008. It was reported that a Masai warrior, who was trying to emulate Sebastian Coe, was using a clockwork radio in the flat and arid desert wastes of Kenya when he was cut-off from the outside world, and the dulcet tones of Alan Johnston, the journalist and radio foreign correspondent, went off the air for the last time. Another incident was when an Eskimo became equally annoyed trying to clock-up eight score draws on Littlewoods Pools one Saturday afternoon somewhere in the Arctic Circle. Quinn the Eskimo was found sitting by a hole in the snow suffering from acute frostbite holding a pencil in one hand and his football coupon in the other.

'Ah, rapprochement; re-establishment of friendly relations with the neighbours,' Harold said, tongue in cheek. 'What a load of unadulterated bullshit and hypocritical garbage; that Fred Barnes is doing his unlevel best to destroy the facia of our house by stuffing Wrigley's peppermint chewing gum inside a wasp nest, and as for Bernadette Cartmell, our other next door neighbour, she will insist on playing songs by the popularized Irish singer, Val Doonican at a very high volume which interferes with the dog's sleeping pattern. Prince, our golden Labrador goes crazy every time he hears "Paddy McGinty's Goat" and I draw the line when I hear the not so popular song, "Delaney's Donkey" bellowing out from Bernadette's sixteenth century Elizabethan record player when it scratches and penetrates through our wafer-thin walls. Oh, how I wish I had a magic carpet, so it could fly me back to Middleton Towers Holiday Camp in Morecambe.' he sighed. 'Come back David Whitfield, all is forgiven.'

The distinct smell of Lancashire 'Hot Pot', a kind of stew, not dissimilar to Mabel's Liverpudlian *Scouse*, consisting of succulent neck of lamb, carrots, onions, potatoes in rich tasting gravy, was now permeating all around the kitchen, escaping towards the front door of the house. The stew is usually served with red cabbage and a puff-pastry triangle, the smell is enough to put one into heaven, but then, in an instant one can be put into heaven and the next into hell.

An Anniversary fruit cake was delivered minus the candles because the Swiss Patisserie had forgotten the amount of years Mabel and Harold had been together. The caterers recommended the local Spar shop and said they did a good line in candles, especially during power cuts, brightening up darkened coal holes, that sort of thing.

The drive was now as dry as a bone and the up-and-over garage door was open, revealing Harold's shiny black Ford Môndial motorcar, and Mabel's rickety and old ladies three-speed Raleigh bicycle, complete with a wicker shopping basket tied on to the handlebars.

'I will go down into the village and buy the candles, Harold; we don't want the cake to look like the 'Church of the Holy Family', do we?'

'That is very kind of you Mabel, I didn't want to venture out in the car this afternoon because I thought that by the time I get back from the Spar shop, the engine wouldn't have had enough time to warm up.'

'But first, can you fix the chain on my bike?' she said with an uncaring expression.

'Yes dear, and is there anything else you would like me to do before our guests arrive, like, set up the barbeque and help the caterers to set fire to the bungalow or, stand guard over the Jameson's Irish whiskey bottle before Bernadette Cartmell decides to give us and our guests a rendition of "When Irish Eyes Are Smiling".

'Well, Harold, I can remember our Wedding Anniversary last year when you walked into the house through the French windows from being out in the garden.'

'How the hell was I to know they were closed at the time?'

'We don't want another repetition of that, do we, Harold, and you should set an example to our guests and take a little more water with it.'

'Perhaps, you would like me to sit on the front door step and drink lemonade and eat a packet of cheese and onion crisps.'

'That would be a good idea, Harold, and then perhaps you could lose weight because the only exercise you get these days is to put your foot down on the accelerator pedal.'

'Does this woman never let up?' Harold thought after re-positioning the chain around the cog wheel and seeing grease and oil dripping from his fingers.

'I won't be long, dear.' Mabel said, looking back after pushing her bike a couple of revolutions along the drive towards the two-tone, black and rust double wrought-iron gates.

'Watch out for the tractors, parachutists and low-flying aircraft, dear; the RAF's aerobatic display team "The Red Arrows" apparently, are returning from a display in Southport this afternoon and we don't want you to get lost underneath all that multi-coloured smoke, do we?'

'Would you like to help with the barbeque, Mr Rigby?' Margaret Smith said as she adjusted her white French Chefs hat to the prone unsupported position on the top of her head to emulate a "Ready Steady Cook".

'No, I think I will stay away from barbeques this year, Margaret, because of what happened at our last Anniversary celebration party.'

'You mean when you were put in charge of char-grilling the sausages and beef burgers in the garden.' Margaret said coughing when smoke from the charcoal burning BBQ began to rise into the atmosphere where the smell of manure and avionic gas is considered to be common. 'I can remember it began to rain heavily,' she continued to say. 'And you, having to run into the house to shelter from the downpour.'

'Well, Michael Fish, will insist in getting the weather forecast wrong.' Harold said, insisting it was him who was instrumental and responsible for uprooting trees and ruining people's barbeques.

'According to the weather forecast, we are in for a few spots of rain tomorrow.' Margaret so knowledgably went on. 'Nothing to worry about though; we have to do the catering for the teachers at King Edwards School in Blackpool tomorrow afternoon, and that will be fun won't it?' she added.

'Yes, really funny.' Harold said, being reminded of the time he was an apprentice, working for Nicholson's the electrician's in Blackpool and, along with two of his mates had to re-wire nearly a thousand square metres of the school's draconian stone building with its back facing the Irish Sea.

'I went to Saint Mary's School for Girls.' Margaret said smugly. 'It is the girls' exclusive grammar school next to King Teds.' she added.

'Yes, I do know that school.' Harold replied with a little boy grin on his not so little boy face. 'That lot used to hang around Fairhaven Lake wearing black pleated skirts, blue blazers and white socks twisted around their ankles. I can also remember their leather satchels slung behind their backs to accentuate a kind of naivety, not knowing that one day they might end up serving sausages and beef burgers behind a barbeque.'

'Another banger, if you don't mind, Joe.' Margaret demanded when she felt miffed at Harold's remarks which were totally uncalled for.

Harold thought then, that out of shear vindictiveness, she could arrange for Alan Plumley to spike a beef burger with hot chilli sauce, enough to blow his brains out from underneath a green beanie hat with an embroidered military badge emblazoned upon it. He was hoping that his son, George would be impressed at the gesture of him wearing the much sort after bonnet which was covered in oil and grease stains and now only fit to be put on to a bonfire or into a dustbin.

It was exactly six o'clock when the guests began to arrive.

'Good afternoon Mrs Barnes, had a nice day in the garden?' Harold said looking at a bottle of 'Blue Nun' table wine she was about to present and was once described on a television Food and Drink programme as cats' pee.

Fred Barnes followed in her wake carrying a basket of fruit wrapped in crinkly translucent cellophane paper, all of which could have been nicked from the Royal Victoria Hospital in Blackpool.

'Good afternoon, Fred, had any accidents today?' Harold said, standing by the side door to show them both into the kitchen.

'Only a couple of call-outs today, nothing to get excited about; one was Patrick Fiddler, the fruit and vegetable man from Lytham High Street, he went down with a stroke after chucking half of his rotting stuff away, it is amazing what goes off in this heat.' giving Harold cause for worry when he clocked Bernadette Cartmell walking towards his front gates with a rather suspicious looking package.

'Who was the other emergency patient, Fred?'

'Oh, it was on the Golden Mile, one of Gipsy Rose Lea's customers, a holiday-maker tripped and fell over her step after she had told her fortune, she had predicted that she was going to stay in good health, at least for the time being.'

'Good afternoon Mrs Cartmell, had a nice day?' Harold said, knowing she would start her blarney at any second.

'Ah, for sure it is the evening, I'm sure it is the evening, and if it wasn't for the evening we wouldn't have the night, and if it wasn't for the night we wouldn't have the morning or indeed the afternoon.' she went on in amazement.

'Don't be too sure about that.' Harold muttered underneath his breath.

'Has anyone else arrived yet, I'm sure there is because there's a van parked outside my house and it is blocking the drive.'

'Tell me, Mrs Cartmell,' Harold asked. 'Why did Tommy Snape, the meals on wheels man, run down your drive at lunchtime waving his hands in the air?'

'Oh, for sure that was because I hit him with a tin tray when he placed another plate of fish and rice pudding down on to the kitchen table; for sure this is the second time I have eaten trout this week, if I eat any more trout this week I will look like one.'

'You know, Mrs Cartmell, there are people in Africa who would give their right arm to have trout twice a week.'

'Oh, for sure, I'm sure there are, Mr Rigby, and when I was a nursing sister working in Libya,' Bernadette said. 'there were natives who had been caught poaching and tickling trout, they had to give their right arms, but unfortunately I wasn't in any position to sew them back on again.'

'Just go into the house, Mrs Cartmell and talk amongst yourselves.'

Not to add anymore arms and legs to the conversation, Harold was out on a limb. He mentioned to Mabel later that the slithers of Scottish smoked salmon displayed on a silver entrée dish were relatively safe, away from Bernadette Cartmell's idea of refreshments but could easily turn into a personal banquet when she sees the Lancashire hot pot looking identical to Irish stew.

As predicted, George was the next to arrive with his wife Abigail, their two daughters Patsy and Lillian, their one and only son Warren, and Bobby, the incontinent Yorkshire terrier. It was just after six when their Land Rover, a second-hand 'Discovery', and now covered in highway dust, pulled up outside Bernadette Cartmell's house after George and Abigail had negotiated the traffic for six hours travelling on the M3, M4, M5 and M6 motorways. They were all to be staying for the weekend at the County Hotel in Lytham St Annes, a reasonably priced Inn with an adjoining pub which is frequented daily by solicitors, show business people, retired lifeboat men and coxswains who, continually went out to rescue English Electric Test Pilots when they precariously ejected through glass canopies of prototype aircraft and touchdown in the Irish Sea.

Bobby, the ten-year-old mini-Yorkshire Terrier was not so popular one

Sunday afternoon when he cocked his leg up to have a pee against a portrait of the Rock Star, Garry Glitter, which an artist was hoping to sell in an exhibition outside the hotel for a couple of pounds; needless to say, the painting was ruined and taken off display.

The next to follow in their wake was thirty-eight-year-old Ms Emily Rigby who is still looking for a man to share the rest of her life with after filling her day working as a gym mistress at a school in Garstang which is northbound, on the way to the Grand Duchy of Lancaster, a town heavily fortified with a Norman castle. There is only one way in and one way out and some would say around the ramparts one goes in but, in metaphor, they never come out. And, following on behind her were Harold and Mabel's twin daughters, forty-year-old Doreen and Jean, who had arrived separately from Preston and Blackpool with their husbands, Barry and James, along with their teenage children, Howard, Raymond, Janet and Susan.

Doreen is a housewife and married to a police sergeant, Barry Garston, who has a steady job based at Hutton training monkeys to become police officers; their two sons, fifteen-year-old Howard and Raymond whose sixteenth birthday had been on the Thursday of the previous week have designs on becoming members of one of Britain's under-rated SWAT teams when Preston North End football club loses when they play against Aston Villa. Their two sons both attend the highly acclaimed Hutton Grammar School just a few yards away from the Police training college.

Jean, a qualified dental nurse is married to a dentist in Blackpool called Doctor James S.R Wilson; his name, odd as it may seem, is named after a famous brand of toothpaste and he is a doctor of dentistry and a keen extractor of people's money, especially when they break their teeth on synthetic sugary confection, such as Blackpool rock, mint humbugs and multi-coloured gumballs dispensed from an upright glass container, all of which are sold without license freely along the promenade.

They have two children, sixteen-year-old Janet and fourteen-year-old Susan; they are both keen football supporters and attend a girl's grammar school in Cleveleys.

The mobile phone which had become an extension to Harold's right arm rang out loudly to the tune of "Jingle Bells" confusing his guests to the point of and having them think it was Christmas and not a wedding anniversary party.

'Where are the nuts?' George asked looking over at a six-foot collapsible table with plates of egg and cress sandwiches, chocolate cakes, iced buns and a strawberry flan placed accurately in the centre.

'Shut up George.' Abigail said softly, poking him gently in his ribcage.

It was Mabel to say that after buying the decorative candles the chain came of her bicycle and asking Harold if he could arrange for someone to bring her and the bike back home from the village.

Abigail suggested they go in the Land Rover to collect her, and when she said to George he was to drive he became somewhat irate and replied by saying:

'We have just driven three hundred and fifty bloody miles to get to this party and I am beginning to lose my appetite rather quickly.'

'Come on, George, another mile isn't going to make such a difference to your petrol allowance, and if it makes you feel any better, I will go while you and the others are occupied stuffing your faces.'

'No, I will go and fetch her.' George said with anger in his voice. 'It's the least I can do having driven all the way from sunny Portsmouth.'

'Thank you, Abigail,' Harold said with a sigh and a pathetic looking smile. 'And do you know, what you have achieved in two minutes had taken me and Mabel eighteen years, but that was before the Royal Marines took over and made him into a man.'

'Why, wasn't he a man before?' Abigail asked, beginning to cough when another waft of grey smoke began to escape down the drive. 'I often wondered why there were a couple of boxes of black pantyhose in the bottom drawer of the dressing table in the bedroom of our spacious married quarter in Gosport.'

'Ah, he had to wear those when he went out on manoeuvres during cold nights.' Harold said, putting things to right.'

'But, that doesn't explain why a frilly lace handkerchief with a shamrock was hidden inside his combat jacket shortly after he came back from Northern Ireland.'

'I can't explain that one, Abigail, it certainly is beyond my expectations of him. I am sure you can always take it in hand when he starts to get out of hand.'

'Do you mean use it as a weapon or to blow my nose in.' she said, taking another sip of *Perrier* water to aid the coughing.

'But, beware of the powder marks on it.' Harold remarked.

'You mean the person who gave it to him had a compact?' Abigail asked curiously.

'No, I wasn't referring to that sort of powder Abigail; I mean the kind that blows up.'

Joe Langford, the catering assistant who was next in the hot seat, chargrilling sausages, beef burgers and jacket potatoes. 'Come and get um.' he said with great enthusiasm redirecting the five-thousand away from the three loaves and five fishes; the Scottish smoked salmon which seemed to be disappearing rather rapidly. 'Roll up, roll up and try one of my hotdogs.' he continued to shout as if he were still frying well-burnt onions on the Pleasure Beach in Blackpool.

'Give it a rest, Joe.' the catering boss, Margaret Smith said to him. 'If you don't improve you may just find yourself back on the Golden Mile keeping the laughing clown company.

'Yes ma'am,' Joe replied with an air of sarcasm. 'Come and get your Lancashire Hot Pot here.' he continued to holler, lifting a lid from a stainless-steel container in order to stir the mashed-up contents with a deep stainless-steel ladle.

Susan Wilson, commonly known as 'Flat Pack Sue' from B&Q, elected to have one of Joe's hotdogs, a well-burnt banger inside a bun. They were similar to Mrs Cartmell in shape, flat around the bottom, flat around the top and squidgy around the edges; caramelized onions, tomato ketchup and hot *Coleman's* mustard oozing out from the sides. Susan had, for the most part spent a good part of her school holidays purporting to be a warehouse assistant, working for B&Q, the 'Do it Yourself' store in Blackpool; it was on a work experience basis and she had gained a reputation of being a joke because of her bright red and blue streaky hair which contrasted with some of the vinyl flooring and rolls of wallpaper.

'Those should be good for your teeth.' her father said to her when he decided to be a party pooper and take one of the triangular egg and cress sandwiches, a prelude to having a generous piece of strawberry and fruit flan. 'And when are you going to get your hair cut, Susan, you look like a *Mohican* Red Indian.' he added.

'I know, dad, and when I hover around in B&Q pretending to work, I can easily blend in with some of the colours in the background and then none of the staff can see me.'

It was at this low point Mabel came back from shopping on her bicycle which had been miraculously fixed by Jack Fenton, a local builder's merchant in the village.

'What is everyone staring at, hasn't anyone seen a woman in charge of a bicycle before?' she said, pushing the machine which should be in a museum of antiquities.

'George isn't going to like this when he finds out that he is down in the village trying to find you.' Harold said hesitantly.

'He can always call me on his mobile or alternatively, I can always call him on mine.' Mabel said with a sigh.

'You mean, this one, mum.' Abigail replied, removing George's phone from her day bag, knowing he would now have to utilize a public telephone box to locate her whereabouts.

'Well, these things do happen, and how the hell was I to know that help was at hand when the chain came off on the village green.'

'You rode your bike the back way from the village green to Calder Vale Avenue?' Abigail asked curiously.

'Yes,' Mabel said, is that a crime?'

'No, no, it's just that George wouldn't be in any position to see you if he is driving on the main road.'

'Oh, I wasn't thinking straight, I just thought it would be a good idea if I were to cut a few corners on my way home.'

'I don't think he will be able to use the telephone box to phone your mobile, mum, because I've just found his address book inside his jacket pocket.' Abigail said, adding more oil to the chip pan fire.

'Well, he can always phone here, he knows the telephone number off by heart, especially during his younger days when he needed money to play the slots.' Harold said, giving away precious secrets.

'I can tell you of a time when George and I were courting.' Abigail put in. He told me he was in the (SBS), the Special Boat Service belonging to the Royal Marines. We went to the Lake District town of Bowness in Cumbria, and I was suitably impressed when George hired a rowing boat and took me to one of the small islands on Lake Windermere. When we arrived, we got out of the boat and went for a stroll in the woods. I can recall it was a hot summer's day and so we discarded some of our clothes and him teaching me how to light a fire on the top of the water. We eventually went back to where we thought we had left the boat only to find it had gone missing.'

'What do you mean, gone missing?' Mabel asked.

'Well, the boat hire company tied a long length of string to the back, and it was systematically pulled to the mainland. The situation became even worse; our clothes were scattered on the back seat of the boat.'

'How on earth did you manage to get back to Bowness?' Harold asked intriguingly.

'George was sending Morse code signals with the aid of a mirror; a motor boat powered by two, one-point seven litre Johnson outboard motors, and an inboard screw, eventually came out to rescue us. And, there's more, the last straw was when the skipper of the boat handed over two 'Popeye' beach towels to cover our bodies.'

'Oh, that was very kind of him; were you wet?' Mabel asked, preparing to make her way over to the 'Hot Pot' table.

'What the hell do you think you're playing at?' George said to his mother ten minutes later, 'While you lot have been feeding your faces, I've been swanning around the village looking for you for well over half-an-hour, and the Land Rover, if I may say, doesn't run on its own you know. Anyway, I found your bike outside the Spar shop after the lady told me you were having problems with the chain; I will get it out from the back of the car.'

'Don't bother, George,' Mabel said looking puzzled. That bicycle you have brought home with you doesn't belong to me, it belongs to Mrs Clayton; mine is in the garage.'

'Bloody Hell, can't anyone get it right first time around here?'

The music which was specially chosen for the occasion bellowed out noisily from a couple of twin loudspeakers. Max Bygraves was singing "Daisy Daisy" and his bicycle made for two, followed by Anita Harris singing the "Anniversary Waltz" as George hastily made a quick exit before speeding off in the car towards Freckleton village.

Chapter Two

The continuation of the Anniversary party at No 23 Calder Vale Avenue

The disc jockey, Barry Gibson, arrived with his equipment at seven just in time for the anniversary cake to appear from the kitchen. It was an enormous task for Margaret Smith to find space for the forty-four candles to be placed around the pastel pink and blue decorative petals, artistically made from icing sugar.

'And now, ladies and gentlemen, by special request we have for the happy couple a song which we are all too familiar with, especially when one overstays one's welcome at the Pickwick Tavern on a Saturday evening. The song, written and sung by the prolific and much acclaimed singer and songwriter, Randy Newman, appropriately is called err.....'

"I WANT TO SEE YOU SMILE"

I was born to make you smile.
I think you're just my style.
Everywhere I go.
Telling' everyone I know.
Baby I love to see you smile.

Don't want to take a trip to China.
Don't want to sail up the Nile.
Wouldn't want to get too far.
From where you are
'Cause I love to see you smile.

Like a sink without a faucet.
Like a watch without a dial.
What would I do if I didn't have you?
I love to see you smile.

In the summer, in the springtime
The winter or the fall.
The only place I want to be
Is where I can see you smile at me?

In a world that's full of trouble.
You make it all worthwhile.
What would I do if I didn't have you?
I love to see you smile.
I love to see you smile.

George arrived back at Calder Vale with the bicycle still in the back of the Land Rover.

'What is the matter this time, George? Have you got a fetish with machines on two wheels of late?' Abigail asked curiously when she stared at a shiny black pedal town-bike with 'brand new' stamped all over it. 'I have heard that pedestrians, and motorists in particular, go around London removing chains and seats from bicycles in order to stop them from dangerously weaving their way in and out of the traffic.' she added.

'Just watch it, Abigail; if you don't stop this aggravating sarcasm, you may find yourself careering down Beechnut Drive on two wheels, and believe me, it won't be on a bike.'

'You can't take a joke, George; that's your trouble.'

'Tell me, George.' Abigail said when the lines on her forehead began to look like waves on a sand dune. 'Why is Mrs Clayton's bicycle still in the back of the Land Rover?'

'It is because when I returned to the village, the Spar shop was closed for a short family break.'

'Well, in that case, George, you will just have to deliver it to Mrs Clayton's house in Ribblesdale Avenue.' Mabel said with a sigh.

The next record to be placed on the well-scratched and much-used turntable which started its life in a discotheque inside Noah's Ark, was a song sung written by Henry Cooper and called "Shadow boxing in the Dark".

'When do the dancing girls come on?' George said to his father who was now busy stuffing his face with rich fruit cake.

'Oh, that will be in a few moments when my grandchildren take over the entire garden to rearrange the flower beds.' Harold replied, pre-empting another visit to the property by the local gardener, Les Barnes.

'And by the way, dad, will I be entitled to a 'doggy bag' once I've off-loaded the bike in Ribblesdale Avenue because the house is beginning to look like a Sunday afternoon visit to McDonald's.' George asked, continuing with his requests.

'There's something wrong with the toilet, granddad.' Susan, the epitome of a googly-eyed gook said, holding what looked like an aluminium handle in her hand.

'You are supposed to sit on the toilet, Susan, not perform bloody handstands on the damn thing.' he said knowing he would have to either install a thunder box in the garden shed or ask the neighbours to come to his rescue by allowing everyone and their dogs to utilize theirs.

'Do you realize, dad.' George said. 'It is well over twenty years since I last rode a bicycle, and I think I'm going to enjoy riding down Ribblesdale Avenue this evening, especially when 'The Coach and Horses' pub is just a stone's-throw away. I would sooner be drunk in charge of a bike than a Land Rover Discovery.' he added wisely.

'So, you are going to return Mrs Clayton's bike after you have been to the pub, are you?' Abigail asked concertedly.

'Well, I might.'

'And what, may I ask is wrong with all the beer, wine and spirits here.' Mabel said stomping her feet in time to Errol Smith singing the 'Hot Chocolate' song "You Sexy Thing".

'Listen, mother, in one way or another, I've been on my feet all day and have not been given the chance to settle down and relax. And as for your contraption you call a bicycle; it would concern me not if I were never to see one ever again.'

George, by nature of agreement, soft-pedalled the bicycle to Mrs Clayton's house with the idea of arriving at the pub on foot, but all of this changed when Irene, one of the village librarians told him the bike didn't belong to her and that she had a similar one in the garden shed.

The Coach and Horses

Bring me a Flagon of thy finest Ale Wench

For my thirst I must indeed quench

Bring me Tobacco and a Clay Pipe
Then bring me a platter of your Honeycomb Tripe
For to light of my Pipe
Bring a long Taper
Then bring me a copy of today's Pickwick Paper
For the Mush in the corner some Cheese and a Flagon
Before we all board the next Stage Coach Wagon.

It was music to the devil's ears, and he wasn't disappointed when the local bobby, police Sergeant David Pennington who belongs to Kirkham police station made an entrance into the pub and asked who owned the bicycle which was parked outside. George made the biggest of mistakes by conceding and admitting that the bicycle belonged to him.

'Would you like to accompany me to the police station?' Sergeant Pennington asked, giving George the impression that there wasn't any choice in the matter. 'There is a lady outside who says it belongs to her and it was stolen from outside a shop late this afternoon.

'But first I would like to phone my mother who I'm going to strangle when I am released from your prison in Kirkham.' George said angrily.

'Now, there is no need for that, sir.' Pennington replied feeling his way around a leather belt to find a pair of handcuffs.

'And so, this is what one gets if one does someone a favour.' George said to Pennington before his statement fell on stony ground.

'I wouldn't call stealing someone's bike as doing them a favour.'

'Oh, come on, I've just driven three hundred and fifty miles from Portsmouth in a Land Rover Discovery, I'm hardly going to steal a lady's bike from outside a bloody Spar shop, am I sergeant.....?'

'How did you know it was stolen from outside a SPAR shop?' Pennington said, asking the most obvious question.

'Well it wouldn't have been inside would it, sergeant?'

'That's him, constable,' Mrs Barton, a local farmer's wife said excitedly, knowing she had done much to solve the worst case of theft in the last fifty years, equal and on a par with the Brinx Matt robbery in London, and to capture one of the most ardent of criminals in the western world.

'That's him constable, I saw him putting my bike into the back of a green Land Rover which looked to me as though it needed a good clean.'

'Are you referring to the bicycle or your mouth missus?' George said despairingly.

'He's the rudest man, I have ever met, constable.' Mrs Dorothy Barton mistakenly said.

'I am a sergeant, Mrs Barton, police sergeant David Pennington, if you don't mind, madam.' he said to correct her eyesight problem.

'Arrest that man and lock him up.' she went on showing off her farmyard refinement...

'Okay Mrs Barton, we will do our best.'

'Do you realize sergeant,' George put in angrily. 'I am an ex-Warrant Officer and a member of the 42 Royal Marine Commando Services Club in Portsmouth and I was awarded the British Empire Medal in 2012 for my dedicated service to Queen and country.'

'Well why didn't you tell me when we were in the pub, George, and please call me David?' Sergeant Pennington said, bending down to lick his boots. 'I could have bought you a pint.' he added with a smile.

'Oh, no, I'm not falling for that one; drunk while in charge of a bicycle.' George said sarcastically.

'Thanks for telling me the circumstances as to how you came to remove Mrs Barton's bike from the steps of the Spar shop, it has been a gross misunderstanding.' Sergeant Pennington said and continuing with his apologies. 'I will take you home in the car and that will be fun, won't it?'

'Yes, very funny, very funny indeed, and by the way, do you know of any plumbers around here, preferably one that doesn't deliver soft drinks.'

'Hello, hello, hello, what is going on here?' Pennington asked, sounding like PC49 Jack Warner, 'Good Evening All.' continuing with his stupid repertoire of historical television garbage.

'It is my mother and father's wedding anniversary.' George told him when they pulled up outside No 23 Calder Vale Avenue. 'They have been married for forty-four years. Would you like to come into the house for a sandwich and a piece of cake, that's if there is any left after the Rigby family and their guests have eaten through half a ton of food?'

'I know a good joke, dad.' Susan said as soon as they went in, admiring sergeant Pennington's brand-new blue peaked cap emblazoned with a Lancashire Police Constabulary badge placed in the centre, 'What song did Jack Warner sing under the blue lamp?'

'I don't know, Susan, what did he sing?'

'It was called, "And the Beat goes on".'

'I used to wear one of those funny helmets with a superfluous arrangement of silvery bits, but every time I chased away unruly supporters on Preston North End's football ground the bloody thing kept falling off. And now, I wear one of these chequered hats, they are far more user friendly and easier to clean.'

'After you have explained to my mother and father about the bicycle,' George said, turning to look at Pennington. 'And before you re-arrest me for grievous bodily harm, I will introduce you to my sister Doreen who is married to police sergeant Barry Garston; he is a police training instructor and if you pardon the pun, he has been stationed at Hutton Police College since Sir Robert Peel established the Metropolitan Police Force in 1829. And apparently, Robert Peel, having been born in Bury, Lancashire knew more about black puddings than Michael Jackson's fan club.'

'There is no need to introduce him to me, George because Barry and I attended the same school in Kirkham, and he never forgave me for gluing-up the lid on his wooden desk.

'I thought you guys were supposed to be pillars of the community?' George curiously said to him.

'Well, some of us are yes, but, others do go off the rails from time to time, especially at the police Christmas party when they are caught sitting on top of the Xerox photo copying machine with their pants down.'

'It's as serious as that, is it, Sergeant Pennington?'

'Yes, I'm afraid it is George, I suppose one can expect that these days. Anyway, I must go back to the station and fill in a negative report before finishing my shift to see "Crime Watch" on television.'

'You never know, I may be on it, pinching an odd bicycle or someone's bottom.' George replied.

'See you around.' Pennington said getting back into a blue, white and yellow police car.

'Not if I can help it.' George said under his breath.

'Oh, and by the way, who is Michael Jackson, and which football team did he play for?' Sergeant Pennington asked poking his head out from the driver's seat window.

'He was just someone who was famous for a while and just happened to buy the rights to Lennon and McCartney's songs for several million dollars.' George replied, not knowing that there were people on the planet who hadn't heard of Michael Jackson.

'And where the hell have you been until this time, George?' Abigail asked having just returned from a public convenience next door.

'I have been to London to see the Queen, and what did I do when I got back? I had to put up with a load of flak.'

'That's enough of that, George, and what was that police car doing outside the house?'

'Oh, that was Dave Pennington, the village bobby; he just called in for a cup of tea, an egg, watercress and mayonnaise sandwich, and of course, a piece of anniversary cake.'

'I see you've got rid of the bike then?' she said, continuing with the third degree.

'Oh, yes, it was no problem, Abigail; Mrs Clayton was very appreciative when I explained the circumstances as to how it fell into my hands.'

'Well, how come, a Mrs Dorothy Barton phoned the house half-an-hour ago to apologise, and thank you for returning her bike.'

'Would you like a piece of cake, Abigail?'

'Just how big is this bloody cake, George?'

'It is fairly big, fairly big.'

'Listen, George, who is that I can hear singing in the background?'

'It sounds remarkably like Bernadette Cartmell; she is giving a rendition of "Danny Boy".' he said when he at last opened up a tin of Heineken lager. 'I think she may have found the Jameson's Irish whiskey bottle on the kitchen table.' he added.

'I think someone should go and take her home, she is becoming an embarrassment.' Abigail suggested.

'Not before I have been.' George said bobbing up and down like a demented fool.

'You know, Abigail, the little boy's room, and I don't want to be caught with my trousers down, I have seen that thing she's got hanging over her mantelpiece; I think it is made from willow, and is called a Shillelagh, a Gaelic cudgel capable of unparallel destruction.

'Well, you better hurry-up because everyone may get the same idea.' Abigail said, giving George the idea she was smiling.

The party continued in a happy mood with Barry Gibson giving it plenty on his mobile jukebox with the usual wrap crap everyone has to contend with these days instead of listening to Noel Edmonds on 208 metres medium wave, radio Luxemburg, and the BBCs Jean Metcalf on Sunday lunchtime's presenting, "Family Favourites" on a 'Benkson' transistor radio, the batteries lasting as long as a Vimto penny ice-lolly.

The popular wrap-crap group, "The Black-eyed Peas" were talking their way through something that sounded like "I don't know what I'm talking about when I'm living with you".

'Tell me Granddad,' Susan asked inquisitively, 'has Barry intentionally changed the tempo of the music by playing Jonny Ray, singing "Smoke Gets in Your Eyes", and what was it really like when you and my grandma first met in Mat Jollies holiday camp in Morecambe?'

Chapter Three

'It all started Susan, when my mum and dad, your great grandparents, took me to a Mat Jolly holiday camp in Morecambe. I seem to remember it all too well, as if it were only yesterday, all those years ago.

'The year was 1958, and I was just a mere slip of a lad; nine years of age and a little wet behind the ears having been chucked in at the deep end of the camp's swimming pool on a number of occasions by teddy boys and an entertaining 'Jolly humbug' who purported to be Neptune and was hell bent on seeing me drown. I can recall wearing my first pair of long casual trousers, an expandable snake belt, Clarke's sandals, fluorescent socks and a pastel blue shirt made of a drip-dry nylon fabric; the baseball cap which I pulled up from an ornate stone wishing-well depicted 'The Chicago Bulls' and rested on the back of my head for an entire week.

The music which daily bellowed out peacefully from several twin loudspeakers scattered around the camp included: the late big bandleader's Ray Conniff and Bert Kampfert and the singers, Cliff Richard and "The Shadows", Tommy Steele, Paul Anka and the late, Johnnie Ray were just a few celebrities of that period to fill the air. It is appropriate I can recall hearing Johnnie Ray, and just like this evening he was singing "Smoke gets up your Nose".'

'There is this guy who works for B&Q, granddad, he is camp, he has a slack wrist and is in charge of ball cocks, padlocks and chains; that type of thing. And, by the way, the song, sung by Johnnie Ray is called "Smoke gets in your Eyes".

'The term camp is often applied, Susan, to the holiday camp in which the residents live in chalets and bungalows and eat in restaurants; this type of camp is run on hotel lines with servants to clean the living quarters and perform other essential duties, leaving the residents free to enjoy the recreational and sporting facilities provided. Jolly's holiday camps were well-known in Britain after the Second World War, noted for restoring the joy and happiness which somehow seemed to have disappeared. Here the word 'camp' is used in its broadest sense since facilities provided are more in keeping with those of a hotel. The signposts give some idea of the range of these facilities i.e., sun terraces, chalets, reception, indoor bowls, dining hall, ballroom, theatre, launderette, car park, cocktail lounge etc, etc. The two camps at Morecambe and Blackpool were designed to cater especially for families with young children.'

'It all sounds great, granddad; far out.' Susan said, listening intensively like a Sunday school pupil sitting on the lawn with her legs crossed, munching her way through a packet of cheese and onion crisps.

'And while we are talking about great-grandparents, Susan, your great granddad after having his breakfast every morning went into Morecambe fishing from the end of a stone jetty having hired a rod and tackle from a shop in Bare Lane; I have often wondered why he went on holiday with my mum because he was always worrying about the business in Preston and his sausage rolls and pork pies going off. Meanwhile, I used to put my hand inside the largest box of Kellogg's cornflakes you have ever seen to find a small plastic submarine with an aperture which one filled with soda, so it could rise to the surface inside a glass jug filled with water. And then there were the 'hoofer doofers', the ballroom dancing couple, Samantha and Nicholas Taylor, the regular floor-sliding 'Glitter' and 'Jitter' buggers, who kept my mother occupied for hours dancing to the "Cha, Cha, Cha" an irritating tune called, "Wheels", and if that wasn't enough she was to disgrace herself participating in the Miss Mannequin competition inside the 'Astra Theatre' where a wooden parquetry fruit bowl could be won, together with the ultimate prize of having to travel hundreds of miles to claim a free complementary holiday in the middle of winter. It was of little wonder why my father went fishing and didn't come back to the camp until the early hours.

'This sounds interesting, granddad; when do UB40 come on to the scene?' Susan asked.

'Well, that comes later, when all the 'Humbuggers' get the sack.' Harold replied waiting impatiently to get back to the story.

'Who were the humbuggers, granddad?'

'They were the participating staff, so called because of their peculiar

Vaudeville style of dress; orange, yellow and white striped blazers, straw boaters with matching band, white shirts, yellow ties and white casual trousers. The women who were also called 'Jolly Babies' wore the same as the men except for an extremely short white pleated skirt, or skimpy bra, white shorts, white socks and plimsolls.'

'Was this before or after the January sale in Marks & Spencer, granddad?'

'Susan, will you please let me continue.'

'Yes granddad, when do the choc ices come around?' she asked with an air of sarcasm.

'The entertainments manager and chief organiser of this bunch of bananas was called 'buggerlugs', Bert Symonds a Baldrick type of character who had big ears, wore round National Health spectacles and a black Breton beret.'

'And where did 'Noddy' come in to all of this, granddad?'

'All in good time, Susan, be patient, he comes into the story later when I tell you about the fancy dress competition.'

'The names of Mat Jolly's two North of England holiday camps were called 'Jollies'; one situated in Morecambe and the other twenty-two miles down the coast in Blackpool.'

'Yes, I do know where Blackpool is, granddad; I live there if you have forgotten.'

'These two establishments were well-named after the owner, Matthew Jolly, who was a North of England business man and entrepreneur, and like you Susan, had the privilege to live in a big house in St Annes. One of my favourite pastime occupations was to watch the resident 'all-in wrestlers', Jack, the Pirate and Rory, the Rogue in the Astra theatre; their regular job when they weren't removing stubbed out fag ends from their backsides was to bend pipes, maintain the plumbing and unblock drains around the camp.'

'Well, granddad, it has been a great party.' Susan said, sadly. 'But unfortunately, it looks like my mum, dad and my sister, Janet are all preparing to go home, I will leave you to reminisce on your own.'

'It is a great pity you can't listen to the rest of the tale, Susan; you would have enjoyed the bit about me and Cyril lighting fires on the beach and our faces becoming black as the ace of spades from the smoke rising up from the well-burnt jacket potatoes.'

'Who was Cyril, granddad?'

'Oh, he was from the Wirral, a place across the River Mersey in Liverpool; a likeable young man who wore short pants and was careless with boxes of matches. I wrote a poem about him when I returned home, and it read:

'Cyril from the Wirral'
A holiday camp was all I had
Every year when I was a lad
My mum and dad took me there
It was their intention
For me to relieve some of my tension
I spent most of my time on the beach
Lighting fires out of arm's reach
Roasting potatoes and a bottle of pop
It was better than any 'Chip Shop'
My friend Cyril was really keen
To spot a Japanese submarine
Lurking on the shore late at night
He sent coded messages
With a 'Pifco' torchlight
He covered up his ears and waited for the 'boom'
As a torpedo headed for the ballroom
He had this thing that it was a kinda false
To prance around to a last waltz
For him it was a strange fascination
To add to his imagination
It gave me the greatest of pleasure
Watching him dig for unwanted treasure
One day again, he was acting the fool
When suddenly he fell into the paddling pool

There was no way of holding him down
He said he could swim and wouldn't drown
After a week I was at my wits end
I needed to find a girlfriend
It was so sad, it was all too much
We never did keep in touch

'That was really good, granddad; it was enough to bring a tear to a glass eye.' Susan said, aching to get away.

'Yes, your grandma says I could have been another poet laureate, you know, like Andrew Emulsion.'

'Don't you mean, Andrew Motion, granddad?'

'Agh yes, I always thought he was a bit of a drip.'

After everyone had gone home to bed and the fiddler had fled, Harold was sitting on a decorative green wrought-iron bench seat by the ornamental fishpond having flash conversations with Arnold, the garden gnome; his fishing rod and tackle dangling over the yellow and red bordered water lilies. The candles which were meant to illuminate the lawn had all but one gone out, it was now dark and the moon so full with its shadowy craters of grey and brilliant white light.

'Aren't you ever going to go to bed?' Mabel said as she crept up behind the two of them in her brand-new red 'Rob Roy' tartan dressing gown which had come all the way from bonnie Scotland and delivered especially for her anniversary by DHL carriers.

'Mabel, how many times have I told you not to creep up on me like that, Arnold and I could have easily fallen into the pond.'

'It could be worse.' she said, removing a half-empty Grouse whisky bottle away from his possession. 'Instead of the pond it could have been the wishing well at Mat Jollies' holiday camp in Morecambe.'

'Have you ever thought that when we first met doing the progressive barn dance at Mat Jollies, Mabel, and where everyone had to clap before moving on to the next person, things may have been quite different if you had gone backwards instead of forwards.'

'Yes, I do realize that, Harold, and furthermore, if we were to go back forty-four years to our honeymoon at Middleton Towers, you could have found yourself latching on to that tart who won the beauty competition, the scrubber of the week award; you know, the one who paraded around the pool with a number sixty-nine tattooed on her back. And, by the way, Harold I am not a person, I'm your wife.'

'Well, I don't suppose the resident social cycle, bicycle and go-kart manager, Brian "Screw Loose" Blackburn was complaining, the man who was in charge of the 'Jalopies' the peddling "Tarts in Carts".' Harold said with a cheeky grin.

'I can remember the wonderful time we had when we first met, Harold; it was on the Monday evening of our holiday at Mat Jollies. You gave me sixpence to buy a bottle of Coca-Cola and a straw, but when I returned you had disappeared only to surface the following morning inside the Hoedown Club where they had the 'The Wild West Show' with Billy Saddles, the resident gun-slinging compere. I can also recall the song with which everyone had to melodiously join in; it was called: "Oh, We're off to see the Wild West Show", the elephant and the kangaroo hoo hoo, never mind the weather just as long as we're together, we're off to see the wild west show. Roll up, roll up see the 'Hokey cokey bird',' Billy would say, and then we in the audience would reply: 'The hokey cokey bird?' Yes, the 'hokey cokey bird', every time it puts its left leg out it would shout: oh, hokcy, cokcy, cokcy, and wc'rc off to see the Wild West show everyone would sing before waiting for the next verse.'

'Well, it made a change from that hideous song, "Heidi, Heidi, Hi, Hodi Hodi Ho, Heedi, Heedi He, Hodi, Hodi, Hodi Ho".' Harold said when he stepped on a green plastic frog which had been thrown over the fence by one of the children from number twenty-one Calder Vale Avenue, next door.

'Tell me, Harold, where did you get to during that evening; I was so looking forward to having the "Last Waltz" with you.'

'Oh, I was caught by my mum having a smoke around the back of the ballroom; she was outside looking for my dad at the time. He came back to the camp drunk holding a bucket- full of fish, and when I asked him about the chips, I immediately received a slap around the head. And, as for last waltzes, how many are we supposed to have?'

'Just as many, as I would like, Harold, and don't forget our anniversary ends at midnight tonight and you may just go to bed nursing another sore head. And what is that noise I can hear?'

'It's 'Kermit' the green plastic frog; he's sensitive to vibrations, high pitch noises, and he croaks every time a car goes by; it belongs to one of those little brats from next door.'

'Likely story,' Mabel said, looking for three AA batteries which had long since dropped out from its bottom.

The sweet chimes of midnight rang out from their recently acquired anniversary clock.

'If we don't go to bed soon, Harold, we may feel the worse for wear in the morning and you won't be able to take Prince out for his morning walk.' Mabel said, now feeling cold above the knees.

'Can you remember the time when we had Rupert, the King Charles spaniel, Mabel? He used to *sit* in front of the television and watch the bespectacled dog trainer, Barbara Woodhouse, she would insist on saying *sit* every five minutes, but that became intolerable when I had to clean up the mess on the sofa.'

'I wonder what happened to Barbara Woodhouse?' Mabel asked.

'She died from rabies when one hundred and one Dalmatians having watched several episodes of her nonsensical programmes followed her home from the studio.'

'Oh, how awful; such bad luck.' she put in.

'Well, six million viewers didn't seem to think so at the time. The police helicopter is busy tonight Mabel, the beam from the search light is illuminating the pond and is taking over the last flicker of life remaining in a burnt-out candle.'

'I heard from my friend, Alison Hornby, that the police helicopter has a sophisticated infra- red system and dependent on the colours which show up, they can detect drugs, bank robbers, and look through people's bedroom and bathroom windows.' Mabel so knowledgably conveyed.

'Have they no respect for their privacy, and can it detect frogs that croak during the night?' Harold replied.

'Big brother is watching you.' she said, standing under a circle of light similar to a Mr Bean Movie.

'The person in the helicopter is not my brother; my brother-in-law, as you well know, Mabel, lives in Seattle, America.'

'They are only doing their job, Harold.'

'Doing their job.' he replied, putting two fingers up towards the rota blades; I can remember one dark night when a police helicopter, based at Warton, followed me all the way home from BAE Sports and Social Club in Mill Lane, I drew the line when I dropped my keys to the bungalow and a laser beam showed me where to find them.'

'Are we never going to go to bed, Harold; I bet the tadpoles, newts, goldfish and Coy carp in the pond are asleep by now.'

'Talking about tadpoles,' Harold said, throwing Kermit back over the fence where he knew it belonged. 'I once read a poem in the *'The Sun'*, and it went something like this:

The Tadpole

"A tadpole went into a photo booth

Sat on a stool feeling smooth and kinda cool

He pushed a button to change his fizzogg

And came out looking like a frog"

It was all a matter of *Frognosis*, and *Frognosis* being not frognetically correct in France.'

'I always thought that newspaper to be raunchy, far too extreme and politically sensitive.' Mabel said looking forward to reading a copy of that morning's *'Daily Mirror'*.

'Yes, I thought so as well, Mabel, because one lunchtime after I had torn the pants off Samantha Fox who was flaunting herself inside page three, I settled down to a good afternoons work.'

'You, don't mean.....'

'Yes.' Harold said with a smile as wide as the River Ribble estuary; 'she was keeping my fish and chips warm.'

Chapter Four

Middleton Towers holiday camp Morecambe, Lancashire July 1958

To continue the story, Harold and Mabel, following the lengthy discussion in their garden at No 23 Calder Vale Avenue and sipping two generous cups of the sleep-inducing drink 'Ovaltine', they finally went to bed at one am that morning.

Harold, soon after his head touched the pillow continued to digress into his past, particularly from where he left off when he was describing Mat Jollies holiday camp to his granddaughter, Susan, who had to prematurely leave his company because of a severe headache.

And this was how it all started.....

Harold recalled the eleven forty-five steam train from Lancaster pulling into Bare Lane railway station in Morecambe just after midday, where an open-top double-decker bus was parked on the forecourt, waiting to take a multitude of passengers up towards Regent Road before careering along the promenade to enjoy the sights of the Lake District across the picturesque, albeit treacherous bay.

He remembered a couple of the holiday camp 'all-rounders'; a Mat Jolly regular fit bugger called Mike Brindle and an athletically built 'Jolly Baby' called Deborah Hall, who were both waiting on the platform holding clipboards to pencil in who had, or, who had not arrived.

Mike and Deborah were wearing orange, yellow and white striped blazers, straw boaters with a matching hat band, white shirts, yellow tie and, except for Uncle Mike, who was wearing heavily starched white casual trousers, Auntie Debbie wore a short snow white pleated skirt, blouse, tennis socks and plimsolls. The participating staff were generally called 'Humbugs' because of their peculiar, chic, Vaudeville style of dress; their badge an 'JH', Jolly Holidays, was embroidered in yellow on a maroon background and emblazoned on to the top handkerchief pocket. These two celebrities were immediately attacked by attention seekers, creeps and ankle-biters waving recently acquired autograph books with signatures of a North Western Railway ticket inspector, a buffet bar waitress and a Preston Railway Station toilet cleaner who just about managed to scroll their names inside the first couple of pages.

Harold remembered his mother and father pushing him up the spiral staircase at the rear of a red London bus with no door and minus a conductor; his eleven-year-old sister, Veronica, following on behind in her Sunday best outfit, a long floral dress, ankle socks and a black elasticised 'Waspie belt'. There was a roll down sign in large white letters above the driver's cab displaying where the bus was going just in case the passengers had forgotten.

Sitting with his sister on the backseat that had stainless steel rails, they could see the town with its nineteen-thirty's style cylindrical type of architecture, in particular, Morecambe's *Art Deco* Midland Hotel, the swimming pool, stadium and the nearby recreation grounds where miniature replicas of a red 1940 fire engine and a racing green British Leyland single-decker bus would take holiday-makers for a ride in the gardens for two shillings and sixpence. He could also recall, the aromatic smell wafting down the promenade from a '*Bruciano*' Italian owned coffee shop, and a restaurant which displayed steak pie, cottage pie and Lancashire Hot Pot behind a steamed-up window; the delicious smells emanating from the suet crust pastry became part of the general seaside atmosphere, adding to the pungent smell of Irish sea food; cockles, mussels, oysters, prawns and, of course, the famous Morecambe Bay potted shrimps.

The fairground was in evidence on the left-hand side of the road facing the sea and Margery, Harold's mother was never the same again after she came out from the hall of mirrors during our first visit into town. She was four feet eleven and three-quarters when she went in, and five feet eight and a half when she tried to exit the door; meanwhile, his father had been fishing on the end of the 'Stone Jetty' since nine-thirty that morning and was in no position to assist her, also the black "Kiss Me Quick" hat she was wearing had grown several inches in circumference and had fallen down around her red bulbous face.

The bus was now turning into a road which led towards the uplands of Heysham, a quaint medieval village by the sea which boasts one of the smallest churches in England and is called St Peters. A Viking explorer was known to have phoned up the vicar on his mobile to ask him as to what time does the service begin?' The clergyman replied by asking him at what time can he turn up in his '*drakkar*' long ship?'

Another feature of this twee village was that of a pub and a shop which sold quart glasses of nettle beer outside on the cobbled pavement; the gravity and alcohol volume being minus zero similar to fizzy lemonade. It was here at Heysham Head, a sort of play area Harold, Veronica and their classmates were taken to on school one-day outings and given the opportunity to express themselves on a stage while the teachers let their hair down before disappearing to the village inn. On one occasion, Harold won a prize for singing one of Cliff Richard's famous songs called, "Living Doll"; he was presented with a pair of plastic binoculars, a toy balloon, and a paper bag full of sweets. He could recall spending sixpence on a bottle of scent contained in a small cardboard box which had been dispensed from a machine inside a penny arcade. The fragrant smell escaping from the bottle was of Lily of the Valley and destined for his mother when he arrived home late that afternoon. Harold also brought home a slim stick of Morecambe rock to give to his father; it resembled a shaving stick with silver paper wrapped around its base; his father the next day complained about him having to scrape away sugar from underneath his chin.

The journey by bus continued along the top road.

"Rock'n' Rolling Riding
All along the bay
All bound for Middleton Towers
Many Miles Away"

In contrast to all this magnificent scenery, the bus headed towards an ugly power station where lines of grey smoke billowed out from tall metallic chimneys; there was an unhealthy smell of crude oil like diesel permeating all around which gave one the impression they were passing by a refinery. Roland made a comment that if he knew there was going to be a nuclear power station nearby, he would have brought his Second

World War gas mask.

There was a grocer's shop in Middleton which sold potatoes, fresh eggs, butter, bread and little else but this was the convenience store which was frequented by Harold to buy produce for his barbeque on the beach.

The Rigby's arrived at Mat Jollies holiday camp no worse for wear following their picturesque journey along probably one of the worst dirt tracks in Britain. The bus, having passed under a red and white security barrier which looked like the English Electric Aircraft Factory in Warton, stopped directly outside the reception hall where several 'Humbugs' were waiting to assist and to tell them where to go. On arrival, Joe Coyle and his security staff, who were called the 'boys in blue' were all standing in line, at ease and looking very matter of fact in front of a hut which looked like the one at the entrance to the Guards Depot in Purbright. The patrolmen, who looked every inch like real policemen, did a fine job, especially during the night when one or two drunken campers tried to emulate Lester Piggott and jump over the barrier at the main gate.

Harold's first impression of the camp was how wonderful it all was. There were lots of fragrant red roses growing in beds of soil; colourful sweet peas planted in hardwood boxes; geraniums and South African violets trailing down from beautifully arranged hanging baskets which were suspended by metal chains attached to fifteen-foot high green ornamental lamp posts. The wishing well situated in the garden across from the reception and ballroom combined the feature on his first day at Middleton Towers.

Everyone had to be in receipt of two round plastic Jolly Holliday badges, one large and one small, depicting a saucy lady wearing a red polka-dot swimsuit; children collected these and ran competitions to see how many they could glean by the end of the week.

Standing just inside the glass fronted doors leading into the reception stood the entertainments manager, 'Bugger lugs' Bert Symonds, the sports manager, 'Fit bugger' Steven Hall, five Jolly babies, Dorothy Smith, Brenda Redman, Deborah Hall and Sheila Draper; the 'humbugs' consisting of Patrick Waterman, Mike Brindle and Bill 'Fat man' Flowers, an entertainer who was grossly overweight, and every time he jumped into the swimming pool he caused a 'Tsunami', a gigantic tidal wave that reached Grange over Sands.

The resident Welsh Charlie Chaplin, the reverend David Hewell Jenkins was in evidence, sporting a brand-new dog collar and he was the only man everyone knew who could organise a requiem for a dead pigeon. The interdenominational church at Middleton Towers was the only place on site where Pakistanis could meet in private before taking up ballroom dancing lessons which were organised by the two 'Jitter buggers', Samantha and Nicholas Taylor.

There were many porters to assist campers with one's luggage before wheeling it to their chalets which wouldn't have been out of place up a precipice of a Swiss mountain where Hansel and Gretel appeared at different times of the day to report on the weather. However, it was a beautiful summer's day with a hazy blue sky and without a cloud to be seen.

The distinctive sound of Ray Conniff's big band and his twenty-five singers were bellowing out loudly from the camp's loudspeakers; the tunes being "Memories Are made of This", followed by, somewhat appropriately "Smoke gets up your Nose".

Miss Fanny Hargreaves, the children's 'Super Nanny' who was in charge of the Fanny Auxiliary Nursing Yeomanry was waiting to take the ankle-biting kids to the kindergarten prior to them having a late lunch in the dining hall away from their parents.

The Number One's of the fifties continued with "Whose Sorry Now", sung by Connie Francis which came as no surprise to Roland, Harold's father when he realized this was the point of no return and to forget having to check on his small lucrative pork pie and sausage roll manufacturing industry in Preston. And as for Margery, Harold's mother, she couldn't have cared less if her husband fell into the sea to join the crabs that congregated around the base of the Stone Jetty.

Next in the queue to add to the campers' entertainment was the 1950s skiffle group singer, Tommy Steele, with his rendition of "Singing the Blues" which brought upon instant home sickness to some of the camps newly arrived intake.

There was no show without 'Punch' when standing in the wings was Gary Wiseman, the Middleton Tower's 'Punch and Judy Man', and it was during the following week someone made comment that because of the shape and size of his nose, it was very difficult to tell the difference between Mr Punch and Mr Wiseman. It was when his show began he would persuade the audience to clap their hands to the Jewish dancing tune, "*Havah Nagilah*" to stop them from falling asleep, and it is of little importance to tell you that the title of this jolly tune sounds like 'Have a nag you all'.

The reception hall was at the front of a huge hangar type building which also housed the ballroom with its immaculately polished floor and apart from a tiered seating arrangement at the end facing the stage there were chairs placed along the sides. There were various shops situated on either side which focused on the well-being of the campers. In particular, there was a newsagent's shop which sold postcards to send to one's colleagues, friends and relatives, just to wish they were there to enjoy and to participate in this wonderful post-war holiday camp experience. There was a photography studio, a toy shop, a tobacconist kiosk, a sweet shop and a boutique which sold tee-shirts, baseball caps and red plastic sou'westers just in case it rained and to stop Miss Mannequin from getting her hair wet before she goes on stage to collect her 'Tart of the week award'.

And, by the side of the seats there were two flights of stairs which led up to a coffee shop where one could purchase light refreshments in a friendly atmosphere. The stage being the focal point of the ballroom had a Benny Goodman free-standing microphone in the centre which could be adjusted higher or lower, depending on how tall the person was using it. There was a glitzy set of drums in the centre back and twenty-four music stands for Jack Powell and his band; he used to say, never turn your back on the audience and conducted the band looking out onto the dance floor.

The resident pianist and organist, Ray Sands, became the grannies' friend when they sang along to him playing, "A bicycle made for two" and "Oh, you're driving me crazy". It is of special note to tell you that when the grannies were sitting on deck chairs around the swimming pool, they all sang "Oh I do like to be beside the seaside", but unfortunately, this was before some of them were forced to walk Captain Morgan's gangplank.

Above all of this were revolving golden globes suspended from the ceiling accented by slithers of colourful glass which reflected beams of light when it shone in dimmed conditions, and to give everyone on the dance floor the impression they had contracted heat-spots.

And, going around precariously on a unicycle outside was the children's entertainer and resident clown, Paul Mathews, his arms and legs moving in time with the spasmodic rotation of the wheel, and I'm not afraid to say Uncle Paul was as funny as a broken leg.

It was at this point, the American 1950s singer, Rosemary Clooney burst into song with the head-dipping song "This Old House", and it is of little wonder why the camp pharmacy did a roaring trade in selling '*Aspro*' tablets to cure severe headaches and migraine.

Not before time, the Rigby family all went for lunch in the Dining Hall, situated to the rear of a building resembling a concrete ocean liner, complete with funnel. It was aptly named the "S. S. Berengaria" which housed the Astra theatre and coffee shop towering above the stern and overlooking the sports arena. The seating capacity in the theatre held an amazing two-thousand people and there were nine-hundred chalets to accommodate the campers and holiday camp staff. And, most importantly, especially to Harold's father, there was an old farm house next to the camp which served as a pub.

The huge dining hall resembling an aircraft hangar had row upon row with what seemed to be parachute tables which were covered with white cotton table cloths and apart from hundreds of bottles of HP Sauce and Heinz Tomato ketchup, there was nothing to disguise their original usage, namely inside Britain's No 1 Parachute Training Centre in Manchester.

The Rigby's first meal consisting of Oxtail Soup, Bangers and Mash and a Peach Melba to finish was a thankful beginning to the start of their holiday; according to Roland, it tasted like shit, but you could live on it

Harold had somehow managed to find a gook of a friend called, Cyril

Birtwistle, who was from the Wirral in Merseyside. Cyril had brought with him an adenoidal Liverpudlian Scouse accent to make the ex-politician and current radio presenter, Derek Hatton, sound like a member of the Royal Family; the circular rimmed National Health glasses accentuated the roundness of his face which looked like well bashed pizza dough. It was to be some years later when Harold wrote several poems to describe the character in his book who became the editor of the Salvation Army newspaper *"The War Cry"* in Skelmersdale, Lancashire. The poem is called Cyril from the Wirral and begins:

Cyril from the Wirral

"A holiday camp was all I had

Every year when I was a lad

My mum and dad took me there

And it was their intention

For me to relieve some of my tension

I spent most of my time on the beach

Lighting fires out of arm's reach

Roasting potatoes and a bottle of pop

It was better than any 'Chip Shop'

My friend Cyril was really keen

To spot a Japanese submarine

Lurking off the shore late at night

He sent coded messages with '*Pifco*' torchlight

He covered up his ears and waited for the 'boom'

As a torpedo headed for the ballroom

He had this thing that it was a kinda false

To prance around to a last waltz

For him it was a strange fascination

To add to his imagination

It gave me the greatest of pleasure

Watching him dig for unwanted treasure

One day again he was acting the fool

He fell into the paddling pool

There was no way of holding him down
He said he could swim and wouldn't drown
After a week I was at my wits end
I needed to find a girlfriend
It was so sad, he was all too much
We never did keep in touch"

Harold found his red 'Chicago Bulls baseball cap after looking down into the wishing well, he had been hoping to find some coins down in the depths but alas, he had to make do with taking empty bottles back to a shop to retrieve a small deposit.

Chapter Five

The afternoon continued with Harold and Cyril doing an exploration of the camp grounds, taking in every metre of geography into account having selected a signpost telling them where everything was situated.

As they headed north towards the amusement arcade they stumbled across the social cycle, bicycle and go-kart manager, Brian "Screw Loose" Blackburn, who was shouting at one of the campers for unnecessary speeding around the grounds in what looked like a racing-green tin bucket on four wheels and it was two hours later the contraption was brought back to depot in a state of collapse after it had been dragged out from the deep end of the swimming pool.

The amusement arcade which was situated by the side of a road next to the static maritime acropolis, S.S. *"Berengaria"*, became a God send to Harold after he learned to slow the wheels down inside the slot machines, and how to win on the glass-top Grand National horse racing table, where he would wait until a miniature filly with a number six painted on its back raced on towards the finishing line; it was only until then he would quickly press his penny, a large outside diameter copper coin down into the appropriate slot to win with odds at six-to-one on. All of this did much to enhance his knowledge when several years later he became an electrician and learned how to slow down wheels on primitive electricity metres to reduce his bills.

And, to the left of the entrance there was a rifle range with real Winchester repeater guns which were loaded with real.22 ammunition. The man in charge of the target practice was called Tom Watson who after wheeling a small cardboard target back to the firing line from an area stacked with sandbags presented it to a prospective army marksman or a wan-a-be Buffalo Bill.

'Where are the grenades?' Harold would shout after totally obliterating the target beyond recognition and destroying part of the wall behind.

The man in charge of the amusement arcade was called, Lionel Green; his assistant called Donald Redman and the husband of the shapely 'Jolly Baby' Brenda Redman was the arcade's 'monkey see, monkey do', and it was interesting to ask the question why Lionel Green always sat behind a reinforced glass booth to exchange the punters money; he had pennies, halfpennies, three penny bits and sixpences stacked up to the ceiling and could spot one of these lying on the floor at forty paces.

Harold, when he was at home had to work hard for his pocket money, usually by cleaning the windows in their old house in Naze Lane. Veronica, however, pretended to dust and vacuum on Saturday mornings, and she craftily collected her pocket money from both her mother and father without either of them knowing what was going on. After a while, Veronica became a sort of human depository when she gave most of her money back to her father in order for him to buy cigarettes and a pint of beer at his local pub in Freckleton. It was in the spring of 1973, Veronica became married to Bill Crosby, a Californian recruitment officer who worked for the Boeing aircraft industry in Seattle, he spent most of his time in the Crest Hotel in Preston successfully poaching engineers from the British Aircraft Corporation; meanwhile, during this time, Veronica was employed as a hairdresser in Preston's exclusive 'Freda Hair Salon' in a salubrious area called Church Street.

Passing by a children's assault course called 'Happy Valley', ankle-biters would climb up a ladder to use the slide or hang on to a revolving roundabout which NASA could have used to train Air Force fighter pilots, Harold and Cyril made their way down towards the beach. They watched as an unsupervised underling stood on the seat of a swing with the intention of going over the top of the bar, and then to sit on a seesaw before hurtled across to Billy's Oyster Bar by way of the Ladies and Gent's lavatories.

The tide was out, and one could see oceanic debris, flotsam and jetsam, scattered as far as their eyes could see and one had to be aware of the occasional oil slick disguised as a heap of wet sand. Cyril would look for messages inside open-top green bottles which he said pirates had thrown into the sea, and regardless to say, one of the bottles advertised 'Boots the Chemist' engraved on its side. He said his spectacles were in need of repair because the screws had worked loose at the stems; his mother must have used a full roll of Sellotape to stop them falling from his face and on to the ground, however, this didn't explain the reason for his short-sightedness.

Another poem which was written to explain the incredible eccentricity of Cyril Birtwistle was called, "Cyril Rides Again", much to the annoyance of a Merseyside Radio presenter who told Harold to sod off after it was read out to their listeners.

Cyril Rides Again
"A year went by he's back again
Driving everyone insane
Cyril's back again
Trying to find another friend
With his plastic binoculars around his neck
Nobody cares, they say what the eek
He's on his own still out of reach
Lighting fires on the beach
His mum doesn't care whatever the cost
She gives him two bob and tells him to get lost
In the maze of amusements he cannot understand
He finds more pleasure in a few grains of sand
Still trying to find a periscope
Out in the sea he hasn't a hope
In hells chance he's a silly dope
One day he fell into the 'Wishing Well'
And, Cyril thought it was very funny
When inside his jeans he found loads of money
He lost his spectacles and in the end
Was pulled out by another friend
They stayed together for the rest of the week
Back on the beach playing hide and seek"

The holiday camp's beach was never the same after Cyril and Harold had finished with it, and after continually setting fire to planks of discarded oil-based wood which had been canonized and blown away from seventeenth century Spanish 'Man of War' galleons' onto the shores of Morecambe and bay. They roasted potatoes in the smouldering embers of the inferno, the smoke blackening their faces, and later, Harold and Cyril gave one the impression they had both entered into an Al Jolson competition. It was a case of 'McDonalds' eat your heart out when they found a grocer's shop in Middleton where they could spend their spoils to buy provisions, potatoes, butter, tasty Cheddar cheese and bottles of home-made lemonade and ginger beer.

Harold had borrowed his big sister's 'Benkson' transistor radio, and both he and Cyril listened to the dulcet tones of the American crooner, Perry Como, singing "Magic Moments", which was recorded the previous year in 1957.

It was now ten-thirty and time to depart the shores of Middleton, and its breathtaking panoramic stretch of beach, leaving behind an encampment below the sandhills with a fire raging until the early hours of the following morning.

The tide was now in and just a few feet away from the shoreline. The moon was full, and as bright as a button; the occasional shadows from the clouds passing overhead were reflecting on the waves. The cockles, mussels, and clams waiting to see them go after turning up every stone and pebble to find a crab large enough to be thrown into a pan of boiling-hot water.

Harold and Cyril walked back into the camp by way of a steep incline, passing by the Cod Cottage, the fish and chip emporium run by Mr and Mrs Cookson, Reginald and Mary and Billy's Oyster Bar, run by William and his wife (Mrs Bun) Florence Lancaster. The pub, situated along this narrow lane was called, Ye Olde Dog and Bone', appropriately had a bright red telephone box with a button 'A' and button 'B' to press, and to enable one to lose their money in an instant. It was here Harold learned from Cyril how to tap into the complexity of the British telephone company's network system and listen in to people's conversations without paying a penny. This was when Harold realized that Cyril was not a Scouser for nothing and wondered just what else or indeed tricks he had lurking up his sleeve.

Harold and Cyril parted company on amicable terms that evening and arranged to meet outside the dining hall after breakfast the following morning. However, the show was far from over when Harold said to him:

'Did you see the buoy bobbing up and down in the water?'

'I didn't know there was a boy in the water, Harold.'

'Not that kind of boy, you fool; they are large tethered floating balls placed out in the sea where fishing boats can tie-up in an emergency, and to inform ships when they are in shallow or about to enter into deep water.'

'It's a bit like my mum,' Harold disclosed. 'she said if I didn't arrive back to the chalet by five o'clock, I would be in deep water.'

'Oh, no.' Harold said with a look full of dread.

The ballroom was the next port of call where Harold's mother was busy quick-stepping and striding out around the dance floor with someone who, by some strange metamorphosis, didn't look at all like his father; he was tall with black hair, had a thick droopy moustache and looked as if he had just flown in from *Wassackstan*.to join a workforce of a failing cotton industry in Burnley, Lancashire.

It was an untimely deliverance as Jack Powell struck up his band with "We'll meet Again", the last waltz of the evening. Veronica, without her transistor radio, had long since gone to bed in the cuckoo clock village where the colourfully painted chalets wouldn't have been out of place lining the coast at Scarborough. Veronica couldn't tolerate being upstaged by her mother and always believed she did everything for effect and was a downright floor-walking embarrassment. The 'Hoofa-doofas' Samantha and Nicholas Taylor, the camp's resident ballroom dancing couple had already said their goodnights after wearing out the soles of their shoes since ten o'clock that morning.

Harold, meanwhile, black as the 'Ace of Spades' made an exit for the door after his mother asked him to partner her in the last waltz. He made the exit faster than a rabbit being chased by a ferret down a hole; this was definitely not the time or the place to join in with her extreme mobile dexterities.

Mr Rigby came back from the pub to join his wife, Margery in their own chalet around midnight.

'I'm going to enter you in the 'Wobbly knees' competition tomorrow.' she said, looking at a man who had just downed six pints of Lyon's premium real ale, pumped up from a season cask oak barrel, and eaten his way through two packets of salt in a blue bag of 'Smith's' crisps, a complementary bowl of salted peanuts and a bag of chips wrapped up in newspaper to go..

'Don't you mean the 'Knobbly knees' Flash Harry competition, Margery?'

'Yes, Roland.' kicking him directly where it hurts.

'I'm off fishing tomorrow with some of the lads down the pub, and I won't be back until five-thirty, just in time to have my evening meal.'

'And what may I ask am I going to do while you are away?' she asked before climbing into bed with her long-suffering husband.

'Do what you always do, Margery; go ten-pin bowling with Veronica, she can be at one end and you at the other.'

'And, at which end would you like me to be, Roland?'

'The end where all the skittles are arranged before they are knocked down by a bowling ball that weighs a ton.'

'Good night, Roland.'

'Good night, Margery, pleasant dreams.'

The children shared the chalet next door to their mother and father and much to Veronica's displeasure; it was of no surprise to Harold to find the door locked when he returned from his adventures on Treasure Island, however, there was a window open to the side of the door where he clambered in to see his big sister pretending to be fast asleep in one of the two comfortable beds.

'Good night, Veronica.' Harold said, knowing she could hear his words.

'Good night, Al, whoops sorry, Harold,' she replied softly. 'I thought the coal man had just come in through the window.'

'Ah, that was very funny, Veronica.'

'Oh, and where is my transistor radio?' she asked jumping out of bed quickly in a failed attempt to find it.

'Oh no, I've gone and left it on the beach.' he replied, remembering the earpiece was still plugged in and the volume had been turned up.

'Well, you had better go back down there and retrieve it.' she said, with a disgruntled look which could hypnotise and charm a cross-eyed cobra.

To compensate for his forgetfulness, Harold on his way back from the beach called into the 'Cod Cottage' to buy some fish and chips to take back to Veronica, who was now at her wits end in the chalet knocking the stuffing out of her sorry looking teddy bear.

And, feeling even more sorry was Reginald and Mary Cookson, the manager and manageress of the shop who handed over to Harold, the last remnants from their deep fat fryer. Thinking he was a relic from the past, a Victorian chimney sweep, an Oliver Twist, a ragamuffin or indeed a street urchin, they offered him the opportunity to clean himself up using their deluxe bathroom which was situated in the adjoining house.

'Where have you been until this time, Harold?' Veronica asked, looking at a nice clean boy.

'I have just been for a late-night dip in the sea, Veronica, it was lovely and warm; here have some fish and chips, they will keep you quiet for at least five minutes.'

'Good night,' Veronica said, turning on her radio to find the 'Ever Ready' battery defunct and as much life left in it as a dead plastic dodo.

***

And this was how it all was; the difference between today and yesterday when children and teenagers could buy cigarettes, buy hunting knives, powerful air rifles, pistols, catapults and make themselves up to look like adults before they went to the pub. And this was the time where parents couldn't give a damn about leaving their kids alone while they spent hours in the boozer on a Saturday night. There was always a child to blame when a whistling kettle, or a pan of boiling hot water fell from the stove on to the floor, and it became even worse when the housekeeping money ran out and the entire family were subjected to a blazing row.

It is so different, today; children are supervised and identity cards common. We now live in our world where it is an offence to carry knives, guns and dangerous weapons, punishable by years of imprisonment.

Chapter Six

The next morning dawned and it was off to breakfast we go with Ray Conniff and his big band orchestra playing George and Ira Gershwin's "It's wonderful, it's marvellous" bellowing out from the twin loudspeakers, and then Perry Como, again singing "Magic Moments" for the hundredth time since the Rigby family arrived at Middleton Towers the previous day.

The itinerary for the daytime entertainment was as follows: breakfast at eight and bringing up your food time at nine. The knobbly knees competition was at nine forty-five followed by trampoline activities in the ballroom at ten.

The start of the 'Scrubber of the week award', the beauty competition was to begin at two pm around the swimming pool, but alas, there was a struggle to find anyone suitable to participate that afternoon because of inclement weather conditions, and the girls didn't want to get their hair wet just for the sake of wearing a satin sash and winning a vanity set consisting of a silver hair brush, comb and hand mirror presented to one of them at the end of the day. It became apparent and noticeable that the winner in this vulgar competition was always invited by the head of the jury to have dinner with him afterwards.

Roland couldn't get away fast enough and to go into Morecambe fishing with his new-found friends, and for Margery and Veronica to try and shoot up through the roof from a trampoline which had more springs in it than a 'Slumberland' mattress. Meanwhile Cyril and Rosemary, his mother, were both waiting outside the dining room for Harold to arrive, and she would insist on calling her son Herbert-Cyril which was in fact his real name.

'Hi Cyril.' Harold said, fearing the worst for having kept his friend away from his mother the previous evening.

'He is called Herbert-Cyril' it's hyphenated.' she said making it absolutely clear that when he was christened it wasn't entirely a complete and utter waste of time. 'We are from the Wirral; it's by the sea you know.'

'Oh, I didn't know, and what is it that is hyphenated?'

'It is two names that are joined together with a dash.' Rosemary explained eloquently in a well cultured Merseyside twang, accentuated by Scouse diphthongs' which could only have been acquired between Strawberry Fields and Scottie Road.

'That reminds me, Cyril, sorry Herbert-Cyril, and I have to dash because we have a date with a hot dog stall.'

'But you've just eaten your breakfast Harold.' Rosemary said with a worried look which could have turned milk sour.'

'I know, Mrs Birtwhistle, but did you see those chipolata sausages, they were burnt to a frazzle and wouldn't have been out of place inside a dustbin.'

'Here is two bob, two shillings, Herbert-Cyril, go and have a good time.' she said, knowing he would come back with three times as much.'

They both departed her company not before time and it was at the entrance to the crazy golf, Harold asked Cyril.

'Why did your parents call you Herbert-Cyril?'

'It was because they both had an argument as to what names they were going to call me; my mother wanted to name me Herbert, and he, Cyril; that is why I have two Christian names, and don't worry about my mum she is as crazy as this putting green.'

'And where, if I may ask, is your father now, Cyril.'

'Oh, he abandoned us shortly after the christening.'

'You mean to say he buggered off?'

'Yes, and I have to go down to the municipal building in Birkenhead to collect my weekly child allowance of one pound every week.'

'You do very well, Cyril, my weekly pocket money only amounts to a half-a-crown; two shillings and sixpences, and I have to work jolly hard for that. Anyway, you can start by buying me a hot dog with lots of red-hot 'Coleman's' mustard and 'Heinz' tomato sauce.'

The American 1950s singer, Paul Anka, was heard singing "Diana" coming out from the camps tannoy system and the song had absolutely nothing to do with the British Royal Family.

The morning which started off pleasantly warm gave birth to a thunderstorm around midday and this was when campers flocked into the ballroom to hide from the rain. The resident pianist and organist, Ray Sands was pulling out all the stops with a melody of popular tunes beginning with a lively Frank Sinatra number, "I've got you under my skin" followed by "You're nobody until somebody loves you", popularized by Dean Martin. The huge trampoline was dismantled at eleven-thirty and the demonstrations and audience participation ending without any fatalities; it was now time for the 'Glitter and Jitter buggers' Samantha and Nicholas Taylor, to make their appearance. The regular 'Come Dancing' team making a spectacular entrance by them twinkle-toeing onto the dance floor like two sugar plum fairies; and with him holding her hand, she twirled around before they gave everyone their interpretation of Bill Haley's "Rock around the Clock"; it is of small wonder why many years later, the film "Grease", starring Olivia Newton-John, and John Travolta, became an instant success after suffering Nicholas and Samantha Taylor every day during a holiday camp stay.

Suddenly, it was time for the people sitting around the ballroom to join in with the fun and joviality; it was similar to the wartime Freckleton Co-op on a Saturday night.

Margery and Veronica, who, after going through a period of translation, became friendly with Cyril's mother.

'Tell me, Rose,' Margery asked. 'Do they all talk like you in Liverpool?'

'*Yea yea, yea; dei do dei, do dei do,*' Rosemary replied with a sigh. (And translated into some kind of language we can all understand that means, they do don't they); 'and, we live in Birkenhead, if you don't mind; it's by the sea you know, and by the way *luv, da* name is Rosemary.'

'I'm sorry Rosemary but it was Cyril who told me your name was Rose.'

'Oh, don't pay any attention to him; he takes after his father, I hardly see him from one day to the next, and by the way my son is called Herbert-Cyril, and not Cyril.

'You mean, your husband keeps disappearing, Rosemary; that's terrible.'

'No, Margie, I mean Herbert-Cyril.'

'And where is your husband, Rosemary?'

'Oh, he was a 'docker', a Liverpool dock worker, and he buggered-off a long time ago, and I still don't know where the hell he is living. Someone once told me they saw Brendon in an Irish pub in Manchester but then, they could have mistaken him for being the American actor, Schnozzle Durante, you know the one with the bulbous conk, and Margie.' She added. 'Where is your husband?'

'Ah, that would be Roland; he went into Morecambe fishing with a couple of friends he met in the pub last night, and by the way I am called Margery, not Margie.'

'Oh, I do apologise; so *that* was your husband I saw standing at the bar; the one who charms the ladies, couldn't stop eating, smokes 'Capstan Full Strength' cigarettes, and called into the fish and chip shop on his way back to his chalet.'

'Mum, can we go ten pin bowling now, I'm beginning to come on with a headache.' Veronica put in.

The time on the huge square art deco clock above the stage showed precisely one o'clock, and for campers on full and half-board to start a mass exodus, a tedious trek from the ballroom to the dining hall, a non-convenient soup kitchen several miles away. It was for most holiday-makers an either or either, neither or never situation, and for those who wished they could have put the clock back and booked for bed and breakfast only to lower their costs.

The Rigbys had without hesitation concluded and decided after a lengthy discussion the previous day, to eat their evening meals at a second sitting, and they were not wrong because after avoiding the daily cavalry charge, and a competition on a colossal scale to see who could devour the most food in record breaking time, they would be able to sit down and enjoy their soup, SPAM and Corned Beef fritters, mashed potatoes, processed peas and Bisto gravy in peace and quietness.

'Is everything to your liking?' One of the duty humbuggers would ask as she walked from table to table in the dining hall.

'No, it bloody well isn't.' Roland said one evening when he found a strand of blond hair swirling around inside a bowl of oxtail soup.'

'Don't get up from your seat, sir.' Sheila Draper, the fair haired high-kicking 'Jolly Baby' said. 'I will go and get you a replacement.'

'A replacement hair or a replacement bowl of soup?' he said, loud and clear.

'Keep your voice down sir, otherwise they'll all want one.' she replied whisperingly.

It was on another occasion Bill 'Fat Man' Flowers came to the table and asked if we had any complaints? And this was when Roland blew a fuse and said. 'With the exception of the *chicken tikka masala*, and the curried to death *Bombay roast potatoes*, which had been specially cooked for a table situated in a Far East corner of the dining hall, everything is fine, and, have you managed to drown anybody around the pool today?'

'No but there is plenty of time yet, and do lower the tone of your voice sir, because everyone in the dining room will all want some.'

Back to the ballroom, Cyril and Harold made their appearance after they had cleaned out the amusement arcade of most of its small change.

'Are we going to eat soon?' Harold asked his mother.

'Yes, Harold, what would you prefer, a beef burger or a Steak Canadian sandwich; they are quite popular here in the snack bar.' she added.

'And Rosemary, where will you and Cyril, sorry, Herbert-Cyril be dining this lunchtime?'

'Oh, I am thinking of taking him to Billy's Oyster Bar, they have a seafood platter which comes straight from the sea, you know.'

After a certain amount of deliberating, conjugating and determining that shellfish were a product of the sea and not from the sky, Margery, Veronica and Harold made their way up a flight of stairs into the ballroom's self-service dining area.

'Would you like to go into Morecambe this afternoon, they say it's quite pleasant on a Sunday afternoon, and you never know we might see your father fishing on the end of the 'Stone Jetty' or staggering out from a pub. Your auntie Alison once told me a story about the Angling Club in Freckleton, of when they went to Morecambe on Sundays to fish from the end of the jetty; half of them were in the pub while the other half waited for the tinkle of a bell which was clipped on to the thinner part of the rod. And, after several pints of Lyon Ale were sunk, they would return and fill her kitchen sink up with the day's catch before going to the 'Coach and Horses' to argue over who caught the largest fish.'

'I would like to buy a small telescope,' Harold said. 'You know, mum, the ones that can be extended and adjusted to see out to sea.'

'And I would like to buy a teddy bear, mum, because the one that was given to me by my dad fell to pieces last night.' Veronica asked despairingly.

'You can both have whatever you want because if I am proved right in what I'm thinking, I will have your father's guts for garters and personally take him to the cleaners.'

'What are you thinking, mum?' Veronica asked with a puzzled look.

'Just wait, Veronica, just wait.'

'These sandwiches are really good, mum, do they come from Canada?' Harold asked when he inspected the triangular shaped pieces of bread before transforming them into a square.

'No Harold, they are from Barrow-in-Furness, it says so on the plastic container.

'It also says 'Minute Steak' on the box, mum.' Veronica put in. 'That is because, unlike your regular sirloin steaks which take a long time to grill, those thin slivers of beef take less than a few seconds to fry in a pan.' Margery so knowledgeably pointed out with the aid of her index finger.

'It's a funny old world, isn't it?' Harold said, shaking his head in bewilderment.

The intrepid travellers boarded a Morecambe and Heysham borough double-decker bus at two pm to take them into town. Ray Conniff, and his big band orchestra were now playing "On the street where you live" followed by "Dankeschön", a popular German song which was sung during the Second World War when the troops nicked the British Red Cross parcels.

They hadn't been on the road for very long when the heavens decided to open up and put down heavy rain, cascading and flooding parts of the road running along the village of Middleton.

It was, as they suspected, the end of the bathing beauty competition which was to be held around the swimming pool, but alas, there were other activities to be had, namely darts, snooker and table tennis competitions run by the sports manager, Steven Hall, and a voluptuous 'Jolly Baby' called Dorothy Smith who flaunted her shapely legs twice a week when she doubled up as another one of the camps high-kicking Tiller girls.

The bus entered leisurely into Morecambe Promenade and stopped at the terminus across the road from the old railway station and just a few yards away from its Stone Jetty.

Typically, it was still raining, the wind gusting about thirty miles an hour and the tide fully in when they got off the abandoned bus to walk along the jetty which had the appearance of not being finished. Margery, wearing her plastic translucent 'Rainmate' bonnet, led the way in order of size, one behind the other, Harold being the last one to join in with his mother's bounty hunting expedition.

The three musketeers arrived at the end of the jetty to find there wasn't a soul in sight, and as Margery suspected, Roland would have made a beeline for the nearest pub, namely, 'The Two Friendly Fishermen' next to an opening leading into a small fairground to the north of the railway station where the smell from a potted shrimp factory abounds, and which by some strange reason are 'By appointment to Her Majesty the Queen'.

Harold and Veronica were taken into the fairground and unpardonably left to their own devices after being put into a ghost train car by their mother. Meanwhile, the search continued with Margery going into a sleazy seaside pub. Roland was sitting at a beer- stained table facing the low beamed bar in the lounge; there was a young woman sitting with him who Margery had known for years; her name was Jean Turton, a busty barmaid from Freckleton.

'Just what the hell do you think you are playing at, Roland, and what is that tart doing here?'

'Jean is here because her husband has come to Morecambe to fish from the end of the jetty.'

'Well, we didn't see any evidence of this not so long ago.' Margery went on angrily before she removed her sodden 'Rainmate' headdress, and then continuing with her statement, pulled a couple of draw strings to gather it back into shape after splashing the table with water.

'What do you mean, Margery and where are the kids?'

'Oh, they'll be okay; I left them in the fairground.'

'Which fairground Margery, Morecambe has two.'

'It is the one next door Roland; the one that has a rifle range, bows and arrows and catapults; the type of things which can kill a man at forty paces.'

'Come on Margery, let's go and get them before something happens to them because there are a lot of peculiar people hanging around on this beach, if you ask me, especially those who come from Giggleswick, Wigglesworth and Skipton.'

It was at this high point, a wind-swept Tommy Turton, Jean's husband, and what remained of Freckleton's angling club that day, staggered into the pub and said:

'Hello, Roland; fancy seeing you here.'

Veronica was standing alone at the bottom of the helter-skelter having just spiralled her way down a fifty feet tower which had the appearance of a peppermint candy stick; the rubber doormat used for sitting on was lying on the floor next to her feet. Harold had disappeared over the main road towards Morecambe Winter Gardens, the Victoria Pavilion and the venue for the swimming baths, a grand theatre, a restaurant and a ballroom, and to the rear of this incredible landmark building and facing the sea was an open-air arena where colourful deck chairs faced a wide and enclosed stage.

'Where the hell is Harold, Veronica?' Roland desperately shouted at her.

'I think he's gone over to the Pavilion.' Veronica began to explain. 'There is a junior talent competition going on there this afternoon, and I think after seeing the dodgem car man, he wants to be another Elvis Presley.'

Oh, he does, does he, we'll see about that.' Margery was quick to put in.

Suddenly the wind and rain had changed course moving to a northerly direction and was heading towards Grange-over-Sands and the Lake District.

On the approach to the open-air theatre and having missed being knocked down by a miniature fire engine, they could hear the dulcet tones of Harold Rigby singing Tommy Steele's popular 1950s number one hit single "Singing the Blues"; the Mackintosh audience clapping and giving him a standing ovation when he won, and was presented with a balloon, a bat and ball, and a plastic telescope.

Chapter Seven

Meanwhile, it was back to base camp and all was forgiven

Following a shopping spree which lasted all of half-an-hour, the Rigby family returned to Middleton Towers holiday camp no worse for wear after their harrowing ordeal in sunny Morecambe.

The tide began to bow out gracefully leaving a stretch of wet sandy beach where rock pools, colourful pebbles and glistening seaweed could be seen clinging to the fortified sea wall. Veronica was in possession of a brand-new teddy bear, a long playing record of Doris Day's most notable songs, "Whatever Will Be, Will Be" (Que Sera, Sera) and "Let's be Happy", and most importantly a replacement battery for her transistor radio, all of which were purchased by her father from 'Woolworths' which was conveniently situated along the promenade. The store, sadly, no longer exists and made way for an amusement arcade with its flashing lights and irritatingly loud noises; 'place your bets now', and slot machine nudge buttons that penetrate one's brain when one walked by the building.

Veronica held the bear tightly in her arms, and it was quickly named Arthur; she kept the cuddly toy for several years until it became ravaged by the family's first dog, a rather unfriendly pit-bull terrier called, Bruce, that later had to be put down because of him chasing Police Constable Harry Hornby, the village policeman, who had been pedalling his bicycle around the village, but that was until the mutt forced him to dismount and afterwards pay a visit to the local clinic.

Harold had got what he wanted, a telescope which Captain Bligh would have been proud of when he was cast out to sea from his ship "Bounty" before it was scuttled by Fletcher Christian in the South Sea Islands, also, if he had sung "Singing the Blues" like Tommy Steele. Holding the telescope firmly up to his eye, Captain Bligh may have said, "This place never looked better looking back", to quote the American film actor, Lee Marvin.

There was a shop in Regent Road where Harold father had hired his fishing tackle, and this was where he bought Harold a fishing line which came with a hook, line and sinker; this was to prove valuable during the remainder of his stay at Middleton Towers when he laid the extensive line out on top of the sand and waited for the tide to come in. It was a question of what to do with the fish he had a caught during the week, but this was soon remedied when Reginald and Mary Cookson from the 'Cod Cottage' agreed to take the fresh produce in exchange for fish and chips.

It was when the Rigbys were walking along the promenade to catch the next bus back to camp, Harold, said:

'I've got a good joke to tell you.'

'Go on, Harold, let us all hear it.' Margery said, with a view to getting it over and done with as soon as possible.

'How do you hire the donkeys?' he asked.

'We don't know; how do you hire the donkeys.' his mother went on.

'You hire the donkeys by using a screwdriver underneath the saddle.'

'Yes, well that was very funny.' Roland said and before making headway towards the bus.

'And, how do you raise a family in Freckleton?' Margery said with great admiration to those who worked for the English Electric aircraft manufacturing industry at Preston, Samlesbury and Warton, and had earned vast amounts of money to help bomb the shit out of Dresden, Köln and Berlin.

'I haven't a clue.' Veronica concluded.

'It is with great difficulty.' Margery inferred.

'I can remember the tales of the extravagant Christmas parties which were held for the kids during the war years.' Roland said sorrowfully.

The conductor, looking at all the recently acquired presents must have thought it was Christmas and not the second week of July when he appeared on the top deck to dispense his tickets from an apparatus which looked like an old-fashioned mincing machine. And, apart from a helium-filled balloon which had ascended towards the earth's stratosphere outside a suspect souvenir shop which sold bayonets, kukris, flick-knives, Samurai swords and replica pole-axes, all the day's shopping was in brown paper bags and stacked up on a seat opposite to the children.

'I hope you're not thinking about going fishing tomorrow, Roland.'

Margery said without hesitation when she saw a smear of red lipstick on his collar.

'What do you mean by that statement, Margery?' Roland asked with caution.

'Well, for starters, you never know what you might catch.'

The bus moved off quickly, and again the Rigbys were travelling along the top country roads leading to Middleton, disturbing potholes which were filled with muddy water collected from the violent rainstorm that afternoon.

Joe Coyle, the resident security expert was waiting in readiness outside his guardroom to pull up the barrier by pushing down on a weight which was on the end of a red and white pole, and it was not dissimilar to the one called 'Check-Point Charlie' in Berlin. The passengers having shown him their visas, a coveted Jolly Holiday badge to enable them to pass through the Brandenburg Gate, the bus then headed to the camp car park where everyone was pleased to step back onto *terra firma*.

And, standing just in front of his Interdenominational church was the resident Charlie Chaplain, the bible-punching Welshman from Swansea; The Reverend, Mr David Hywel Jenkins. He was trying to enhance his congregation by rounding up a few campers for a service that evening.

Mr Jenkins tightened up his narrow black leather stable belt which surrounded his cassock and said:

'I don't usually have to beg, but please do come to church this evening, otherwise I will fast become a member of the country's unemployed. And, after the service, there is tea and biscuits in the vestry where you can buy one of my second-hand paperback books, and that will be fun, won't it?'

'Tell me, sir,' Roland said. 'Does this Inter-demoralized church bring in a multitude of Western Oriental Gentlemen and their ladies?'

'Shut up, Roland.' Margery suggested, and at the same time looking up to what could only have been described as a biblical sky, where a large opening in a formation of clouds allowed a brilliant ray of light to beam down on to the ground.

'But, of course, everyone is welcome in my church; it was only last week.' the Reverend David Jenkins went on. 'I was privileged to have a whole tribe of Indians in my congregation; they were very civilized, and after their more than generous offertory had taken place, one of them bought my entire collection of 'Mickey Spillane' books; does that answer your question?'

'Yes, I suppose it does.' Roland said, continuing with his unnecessary enquiries. 'And does your generosity extend to '*Camp Coffee*'?' he added.

'Roland, will you please shut up and let the vicar get on with his soul-searching.' Margery said, gratingly, and sounding as though she had just drunk two large measures of '*Listerine*', an antiseptic mouthwash and a toxic nerve agent contained in a bottle. 'And, while we are on the subject of soul-searching, if you think I'm going to remove the lipstick from your collar, you will have to think again.'

'I suppose, under the circumstances '*Camp Coffee*' instead of '*Listerine*' would help remedy your speech impediment, Margery.' he said underneath his breath which had been contaminated with five pints of premium '*Lyon*' real ale.'

'Just watch it, Roland; you have gone too far this time.' she said.

'Far, far, it is not far enough.' Roland replied.

'Listen, Roland,' Margery said. 'am I going to enter you into the 'Man of the Week' award tonight, or not?'

'Don't you mean your regular 'Dick Head' award?' he asked.

'That is only if you wish.' she replied.

'And what if I may ask will I have to do to win the coveted wooden trophy that is only fit for kindling bonfires and keeping Guy Fawkes company.'

'Just be yourself, Roland; you can do that can't you?'

'And, considering we have only been here for just over a day, why is it being held in the ballroom tonight? Roland asked, continuing with his enquiries.

'Oh, for God's sake, Roland, you only have to wear a dark suit, bow tie and a trilby hat, twirl graciously around on the dance floor with a toy pistol, and then after running down to the bottom of the ballroom to give me a fireman's lift, you will only have to say: 'All because the lady loves,

'Milk Tray'.'

'Will you keep your voice down, Margery; we are standing in God's country and on consecrated ground which has been blessed by Matt Jolly himself.'

'After the competition is over and you have won your prize, a plaque to which you can proudly hang on the wall and you have accepted a free 'Jolly Holly' for two in Scarborough, we can all settle down and enjoy the remainder of our holiday.' she said smiling for the first time that day and then continuing to inform him. 'There is a rock band called, Jonnie Lane and the Sapphires who will be entertaining us in the ballroom, but first of all, the resident pianist and organist, Ray Sands, together with the camp's compere, Des Corner, commonly known as 'Pop Corner', the two vocalists, Christopher Charmers, alias Mike Martin and Connie Faye, real name Francis Longbotham from Rottenstall, who will be doing their damndest to stop everyone from falling asleep after eating mounds of steak and kidney pie in the dining hall.'

Harold had never heard of anything as ridiculous as this in his life thus far, and, escaping from any further embarrassment, he and Herbert-Cyril quickly made a swift exit towards the door; some years later he wrote a poem dedicated to his father which goes like this:

Man of the week Award
They all lined up to perform a stunt
To win a prize and become the 'Shirt Front'
Of the week, wearing bow tie and jacket
All who entered looking a packet
Appearing to be smart all dressed in black
Each one labelled with a number on his back
They leapt off the stage holding a rose
And were greeted with loud applause
Racing down the ballroom to grab the wife
Someone said, why don't you get a life
They had to run back to the stage and say
It is all because the lady loves 'Milk Tray'

Spot the idiot, it was all good fun'
And, don't you know
He won a holiday in the snow

Needless to say, Roland won, and at the end of the week he was presented in the Astra Theatre with his wooden shield and a free 'Jolly holly' winter holiday in Scarborough.

It was some years later, Bill Crosby, Veronica's husband and Vietnam veteran, passed a comment to Roland, his future father-in-law as he looked at the amateur piece of woodwork placed high on a wall in their family home in Naze Lane. He said to Roland; 'Do you know sir, that 007 James Bond, is just another regular thick 'Squid Brain' who is licensed to kill?'

'Ah, that is maybe, but he can't make sausage rolls, pork pies and pastry like me, can he?' Roland said smugly after they had come home from the pub.

'Hey man, I don't suppose anyone would *wanna*.' Bill said with a '*Howdy Doody*', Los Angeles accent, and with a look that could blow every tyre on a Californian highway.

'I've heard about the food you lot eat out there; it tastes like ......

'Now, that's quite enough, Roland.' Margery put in before the conversation got out of hand. 'We all know how prejudiced you were towards foreigners; spiders I think you called them down at the pub, and if it wasn't for the American airmen coming here to Warton and Freckleton, we wouldn't have won the war.' she added.

'Bullshit.' Roland said confidently and then continued with his bouts of historical rhetoric by saying: 'The American Air Force, who were here during the war can only be remembered for their contribution towards building a cinema, increasing the population by ten-percent and to install a resident gardener to tend a graveyard after one of their aeroplanes crashed into the village school.'

'And, where were you when the call-up papers were sent out?'

'If you remember, I went down with a bad case of food poisoning.' he said.

'As I can recall,' Margery said and continuing to pile on the pressure for an answer as to why he escaped the draft. 'You didn't have food poisoning for four and a half years though, did you?'

'Well, I was exempt and protected in a reserved occupation, which meant I was in meaningful employment keeping the British families in those days supplied with the essential nourishment they truly deserved.'

'That is rubbish Roland, and you know it; you were in Preston selling provocative nylon stockings with seams up the back, and American '*Camel*' cigarettes to tarts in the pubs of New Hall Lane. I had to put up with drawing a line up the back of my legs with an eyebrow pencil.'

'Ah, but you never went hungry did you Margery, I kept you in sausage rolls, pork and beef pies for years.'

'Roland, will you please stop talking about the war and your bloody sausage rolls.'

'Excuse me, Margery; it was you who started it.'

'Do you know Roland that alcohol is the brain's favourite playground?' Margery said as he adjusted the plaque to bring it more into focus.

'That is interesting, Margery, I always thought the Gaiety Bar next to the Tower Ballroom in Blackpool was your favourite playground, I can remember, it all too well when everyone sang "Kiss my arse, my arse, whatever will be will be" inside what could only be described as a ground-floor cesspit swimming in beer.'

'Well, Roland, if it wasn't for that ground-floor cesspit, you wouldn't have had the privilege of meeting me.'

'No, that's true, more's the pity.'

'Hey, you guys break it up; let's go get some fish and chips, and you never know I might be able to enhance the population of Freckleton by another ten-percent.' Bill sarcastically suggested.

'I think your idea of an American dream, Bill, is fast fading.' Veronica said, looking daggers at a six-foot two, eyes of blue, *couchie, couchie, couchie coo,* who had just threatened to bring some life back to the village.

***

Meanwhile, to continue down memory lane, it is back to 'Jollies' and the ballroom where the resident compere, Des Corner had finished introducing the Rock and Roll band, Jonnie Lane and the Sapphires, and after tuning up their electric guitars, they were ready to make a noise comparable with an English Electric Lightening aircraft or a juke box playing at full volume.

The lead guitarist and singer, Jonnie Lane adjusted the microphone again to a height parallel to his mouth by way of a butterfly screw half-way down its stand. And, behind him was the rhythm guitarist, Mike Smith, and bass guitarist, Jeff Banks; the group's drummer, Spike 'Jacko' Jackson, tapped his drumsticks twice to begin the first song which was popularized by Buddy Holly, and was called "Peggy-Sue".

The floor show had begun in earnest when Margery got up on her own to show off her dancing skills, prancing around the ballroom floor like a demented rabbit. Veronica had seen it all before down at the village club, where a moronic tune called "Wheels" and the "Cha Cha Cha" became a regular occurrence, and a popular source of common embarrassment.

Roland had somehow managed to escape to the 'Ye Olde Dog and Bone' pub after the humiliating experience of winning the prestigious 'Man of the Week' competition. Mr and Mrs Worth, the pub's manager and manageress having heard of Roland's recently acquired title, took steps to ensure he maintained it by offering him a yard of real ale which he had to drink quickly from a glass tube with a bulbous balloon at one end. Needless, to say, Roland came back to his chalet drunk and was immediately attacked by Margery after attempting to gain access to one of the chalets which was occupied by the camp's reception team manageress, the busty, Pauline Evans. It was of no surprise to Margery to find out that Pauline, the notorious leader of the camp's 'Waspie Belt' Club was sharing a bed with the resident magician Tony Hart, whose head and shoes should have been poking out from a chalet three doors down.

It was for Harold, the first time he had become tired of spending his leisurely hours on the beach with his friend Cyril, and after leaving the ballroom he immediately retired to his bed.

Chapter Eight

At breakfast the following morning, hiding behind the cornflakes

It was Monday morning and after the Rigbys had vacated their chalets, they made their way to the camp's dining hall to join the masses to take breakfast, and this time it was Roland's turn to hide behind giant boxes of Kellogg's cornflakes which were placed in the centre of the long dining tables. He had been suffering from acute depression after being ridiculed by some of the revellers in the pub the previous evening, also to being kicked in the nether regions by his wife, Margery, when he attempted to gain access to Pauline Evan's 'Love Shack'. The whole affair was, however, a simple case of gross misunderstanding when Roland lost his bearings and ended up wandering around the staff's living quarters; I suppose the situation could have been more interesting if he had fallen into the swimming pool, or at worse, to have been thrown into the guard house with Joe Coyle and the boys in blue to keep him company.

The highly polished knives, forks and spoons were neatly laid out at each place setting, together with the ceramic 'Jolly Holly' cups and saucers, glass tumblers and jugs which contained fresh orange juice to enhance one's vitamin 'C' intake, ready for the sporting events which were to take place inside the recreation hall that morning. Roland had been known to have said to one of his snooker partners: 'It's no use taking vitamin 'C' when you're dead.'

'Oh no, it's 'Bill Fat' Flowers about to appear at our table.' Roland said with an air of apprehension. 'He's going to ask if we have any complaints, to which I'm going to say yes, and how is it that every time I sit down to eat my meal, someone always comes over to our table and says, have you any complaints, any complaints, and I am bloody well sick and tired of it.'

'He's only doing his job Roland, don't be so grumpy.' Margery replied benevolently when she saw Bill's stomach resting on top of the table next to theirs.

'Good morning campers; have you any complaints, and is everything to your liking?' Uncle Bill asked.

'Yes and No,' Roland said, looking at the zip in his trousers which was about to fly open at any second. 'Yes, everything is fine, and no, I haven't got any complaints this morning.

'Dad, I thought you said you were going to tell Uncle Bill off for interrupting your breakfast?' Veronica desperately wanted to know.

'Well, there is nothing like starting the day on a pleasant note, is there Margery?' Roland said with caution. 'Oh, and, by the way, Veronica,' he added. He's not my uncle; my uncle is eighty and lives in Poulton le Fylde.'

'You should have thought about that last night after you had come back from the pub.' Margery had to put in.

It was when the holiday was over, Roland said to Margery: 'I have never seen a magician run so quickly back to his chalet after being discovered sharing the same bed with Pauline Evans. He was the only man I know who could set fire to a pile of rolled up newspapers after putting them in a pan, and then produce a plastic fruit cake from the inferno; it's of little wonder we and the Astra theatre didn't all go up in smoke.'

'And, so it is better not to cause any aggravation.' Roland said. 'We don't want to upset Bill Flowers, because he, amongst several other 'humbuggers', will be on stage on Friday, presenting the prizes to all those who have won competitions throughout the week, and we don't want to end up spending our free holiday in Timbuktu, do we?'

'Tell me, Roland, what was Pauline Evans wearing when she was caught unawares?' Margery asked.

'It looked like a nurse's uniform, because she had a red cross in the centre of her white hat.'

'Well, I suppose it could have been worse.' Margery suggested. 'She could have been pretending to be a firewoman.'

The auditions for the talent competition were to be held that morning in the Astra theatre and this was when Herbert-Cyril made an appearance to bring back some light entertainment to the campers who by now were literally bored out of their skulls.

It was during that morning, Cyril had taken on the guise of an American folk hero, Davy Crockett, but then several years later, still under the tempestuous smothering from his mother, returned to 'Middleton Towers' holiday camp, turning himself into a pop star who became famous, lasting less than a week. All those years of practicing with a cordless broom handle had nevertheless payed-off.

   Rock on Cyril
Cyril is back in the holiday mode
And to bring you all another episode
Of him spending a few hours
At a holiday camp called 'Middleton Towers'
In his drainpipe trousers and fluorescent socks
Which came out from last year's Christmas box
He is back no longer as a child
Wearing a shirt like Marty Wilde
The kids thought he was off his trolley
In his specs, he looked like Buddy Holly
Cyril practiced his singing in the chalet
He sounded like a high-pitched Frankie Valley
And in the theatre there was a petition
When he won the talent competition
It was hit or miss, the judges reckoned
When a little girl with a hoola-hoop came second
His mum in the audience wasn't his biggest fan
When he sang, "My old Man's a Dustman"
She stood up full of rage
And it was then he tripped and fell off the stage

After taking breakfast, it was time for Harold to check his fishing line which was meticulously laid out on the seashore before the tide came in the previous evening. The fifty-foot extent of line, consisting of three hooks and a lead sinker which looked like a large Polo Mint was pulled up by Harold from the saturated sand to reveal two large plaice and a three-pound haddock; all of the catch he sold to Reginald Cookson, the manager of the 'Cod Cottage' that morning.

The morning continued with Cyril dressing up like Davy Crockett, the last of the Native American Mohican tribe, and King of the Wild Frontier, who, with his mother were on their way to the Astra theatre to audition for the first round of the talent competition. Rosemary was wearing a jacket made from brown chamois leather cloth, of the type used for cleaning windows, and it was possible Doris Day could have worn the same garment it in the film "Annie Get Your Gun".

Harold could remember his father taking him to a cinema in Preston to see the 1955 Walt Disney block-buster adventure movie "Davy Crockett" King of the Wild Frontier, and afterwards, cutting up his mother's fur coat to make a hat similar to the one worn by the American actor Fess Parker.

Davy Crockett

'King of the Northwest Frontier'

"We sat in an orange box paddling our canoe

Davy Crockett in the front seat

Humming his gazzoooooooo!

In the back yard three men in a boat

Decided one day to cut up a fur coat

With mum out the shops and coming
home soon

We changed whole specie from Mink
to Racoon

A cat with nine lives on the wall
did a runner

When a cork from a popgun gave
it a stunner

Mum came back from the shops

And found us all out

She gave us a clout, and a clip
around the ear

We were the 'Kings of the Wild Marton Mere"

This poem has been brought to you by Sadbury's, the makers of the finest quality Milk Chocolate.

Cyril went through to the second round after singing the theme tune to the film and afterwards attempting to shoot the judges with the aid of a replica matchlock pistol should they have placed him low down in the order of merit. His mother, however, was given the ultimate in insulting behaviour when she was told, 'don't call us, and we won't call you' as she attempted to sing Rosemary Clooney's head-dipping song, "This Ole House"; and regardless to say, she sounded like a cat, whose tail had just been stepped upon by an overweight African elephant.

'And, why are you wearing that silly jacket, Mrs Whistle?' another comedienne asked. 'You look as though you have just come out from a shredding machine.'

'The name is Birtwistle, Rosemary Birtwistle, if you don't mind, and this is my son Herbert-Cyril, we are from the Wirral, and it's by the sea you know?'

'Couldn't you have gone to Marks & Spencer like everyone else?' One of the judges remarked.

Rosemary, looking like a shapeless bag of rubbish tied up in the middle, suggested in her eloquent Liverpudlian accent that they should all go and boil their heads and then continued to say:

'Oh, this is too much like hard work.' Margery said before she hastily walked off the stage. 'I'm fed-up with all this stopping and restarting; how come I don't have any problems down at the Birkenhead line-dancing club on Saturday evenings?' she hollered.

Meanwhile, Margery was busy trying to impress, the 'Hoofa Doofa's', Samantha and Nicholas Taylor, who were all dancing and wheeling their way around the dance floor to the then popular "Cha, Cha, Cha"; this being the only dance Margery could do on her own without any help from her partner, namely her husband, Roland.

Veronica, however, was playing it safe when she decided that morning to go ten-pin bowling. She had met a boyfriend called Alan Hayes, who specialized in making dents in the wooden floor panels when it was his turn to send the ball hurtling down the alley at top speed in order to demolish the entire building.

Roland had somehow managed to win the first round of the snooker championships, and it was one disgruntled player who described it as a 'load of balls' when the black ball was finally potted to end the game. This was when the 'Punch and Judy' man; Uncle Gary Wiseman appeared on the scene complaining that someone had nicked his whistle; the voice synthesizer he uses during his half-hourly shows.

'Perhaps you swallowed it?' Roland mentioned to him.

'I'll have to find it because I'm due to do another show in ten minutes time and there are a lot of angry looking kids out there.'

'Oh, no, there isn't.' Roland said when he saw Harold's black face peering in through one of the windows of the Recreational Hall.

'Oh, yes there are.' Gary Wiseman said, thinking he may have to rapidly change his show into audience participation when he saw orange peel being thrown towards the curtain of the 'Punch and Judy' theatre.

The next sporting attraction was the ten-pin bowling competition which had been organised by the sports manager, Steven Hall, and his lovely wife Deborah, your two regular fitness freaks from Middlesbrough. Veronica Rigby, and Alan Hayes; suffice to say won the junior competition by playing against an Indian family from Burnley, whose s*aris* kept getting in the way of their legs every time the ball hit the ground. And when the competition was over they were presented with an onyx trophy which was firmly embedded on a square concrete base, but a problem followed as to how it could be shared by the winning couple. It was Veronica who suggested they take it in turns to hold the coveted piece of ironmongery, which could only be described as fodder for the nearest dustbin; the scenario between them lasted for almost five days until Alan was threatened by Veronica to be bashed around the head with a table tennis bat should he continue with his bouts of avarice

***

The bathing beauty competition which had been postponed the previous day because of bad weather, resumed around the swimming pool after lunch.

The weather in contrast to Sunday was warm and humid; the sun now

73

high above the camp and moving towards the west.

The frolicking began with several campers being chucked in the pool at the deep end by a couple of 'humbuggers', Patrick Waterman and Mike Brindle, under the sole direction of Bill (Fat Man) Flowers, whose re-enactment of Neptune with a green plastic trident onboard a ship that didn't go anywhere, left everyone to believe he was mad and belonged in an institution.

At about two pm that afternoon the knitting needles were put away and the deck chairs raised to a higher level by voyeurs and subscribers to rude monthly magazines called "Health and Efficiency", "Sandy Balls" and "Nudist Colony"; something of the like, by today's standards could easily put you in jail for several years.

The pageant began with the bathing beauties being lined up, one behind the other dressed in colourful swimsuits and high-heeled shoes, and almost invariably some of the shoes were brown to match their faces; Miss Nicaragua, however, had won the competition the previous week and was now back in Bradford weaving carpets and rugs.

Under the direction of two 'Jolly Babies', Deborah Hall and Sheila Draper, all twenty contestants paraded around the swimming pool holding cards in their right hand, stating their name, rank and number written crudely with a black felt-tip pen. One of the entrants was an auburn-haired eighteen year-old rubber scrubber, called Simone Wilcox who, sporting a No2, came from Leicester; she asked Sheila Draper at what time did she get the chance to meet one of the good-looking judges to enable her to win "The Scrubber of the Week Award", the answer to this was made very clear when Auntie Sheila suggested they take coffee together in her chalet. Needless to say, a busty blonde-haired Marilyn Monroe look-alike won the competition and she was precariously walking around the holiday camp grounds for the remainder of the week looking as though she had just fallen off a Morecambe Bay donkey.

'Do you like swimming?' One of the judges asked Simone, who had been nervously standing in front of a table for several minutes before having her imitation boobs photographed.

'Oh, yes, I like women very much.' she replied with a well pronounced lisp.

Meanwhile, Roland was back at the pub, sitting at a summer table underneath a chestnut tree missing all the action which was going on around the swimming pool that afternoon.

'Be careful, Roland.' Eileen Worth said when she circumnavigated the pub to collect the beer glasses. 'The conkers usually begin to fall from the trees about this time of year; we don't want you going home to Freckleton with a headache, do we?'

'I had one of those last night when I returned to the chalet,' he said and feeling ashamed.

'Yes, I know you did, Judith Ward, your chalet maid told me all about it this lunch time; her chalet is next door to Pauline Evans; the chalet you were trying to break into last evening.'

'Bloody Hell, is nothing sacred around here.' Roland said when he looked at his wristwatch which was now reading three o'clock precisely. 'Oh, look at the time, I must be going.'

It was at this point, Harold who was on his way down to the beach saw his father walking very quickly past the red telephone box next to the pub.

'Hi, dad,' Harold shouted out. 'Did you get drunk last night?'

'Put a sock in it, Harold, I've had quite enough of your mum and Veronica today, and if that were not enough, the manageress of the pub had to put her five eggs in as well.'

'Can I have some pocket money, dad, I need to go to the shop and buy some potatoes to put on the fire.'

'What is so attractive about lighting fires on the beach, Harold; sometimes I think you are turning into a pyromaniac?'

'And, just what is a pyromaniac, dad?'

'It is someone who is careless with boxes of matches.'

'I heard a similar word when I was sitting around the pool watching the bathing beauty contest; someone said to the 'Jolly Baby' Pauline Evans that she was a nymphomaniac.' Harold said; what is a nymphomaniac, dad?'

'It is a woman who smokes a lot.' he replied.

Chapter Nine

Time to go home; waking up to reality and back to the land of the living

The square Westclox travel alarm clock rang out loudly at eight o'clock which was placed on the bedside table next to Harold. He had been dreaming all through the night about the strange and wild events which occurred during his first visit to 'Matt Jollies' holiday camp at Middleton Towers in Morecambe.

The day began in earnest when Harold brought Mabel her usual cup of tea while she was still in bed. Her rollers protruding out from underneath a hairnet resembled a well-used Earl Grey tea bag; the foundation cream and makeup which had been removed by soap and water the previous evening left little to be desired as she sat up in bed sipping her early morning moment of luxury.

'You were doing a lot of talking in your sleep last night Harold.' Mabel said with concern. 'Were you having a nightmare?' she asked.

'No, on the contrary, Mabel.' Harold replied, removing his Prince of Wales dressing gown before placing it on a hook at the back of the bedroom door. 'I was dreaming about the first time my mother and father took me to Matt Jollies holiday camp in Morecambe; I sort of got round to one of the better bits, and then I woke up.'

'You mean when you were innocently sitting around the pool watching all those sluts and strumpets parading up and down in front of the judges?'

'Not exactly; no Mabel, I dreamt about buying my first packet of cigarettes at the tobacconist in the ballroom; they were called '*Matinee*'; it was, as I can recall a moving experience when I was caught smoking behind Brian 'Screw loose' Blackburn's bike shed by my mother; she immediately told my father, with the result I was not able to hear Tommy Steele singing, "Singing the Blues" for the umpteenth time through the camp's loudspeakers which in metaphor, became music to my ears.'

'Well, you can thank your father for you not smoking all these years, Harold.' Mabel went on to say.

'What did you say?' Harold said, putting his hand up to one of his ears, giving one the impression he was deaf.

'Now, don't joke with me, Harold, the day has only just begun and you have a lot of washing-up to do this morning.' she said, diluting the conversation to a few moments of silence.

'And when, if I may ask, are you going to take part in all this cleaning up; it's like ground zero in the kitchen.' Harold mentioned as he stood in front of the cheval mirror to check his appearance.

'I'll get up when I'm good and ready, Harold.' she said putting the cup and saucer on the bedside table before turning over and re-adopting the prone unsupported position.

'Now let's see, where did I put that photograph album?' Harold muttered to himself when he began to look in every drawer of the dressing table.

'It's in the sideboard.' he was quickly informed by a muffled voice coming from underneath a fifteen-tog duvet.

'Well, I haven't looked inside the sideboard for several years, Mabel; you never know I may find my old Kodak Brownie 127 Bakelite camera in there as well.'

'That piece of worthless equipment is lying in the bottom drawer of the sideboard, but you will be hard-pressed to find a shop which sells ancient film of the type Agatha Christie may have used to photograph the pyramids in Egypt.' she said, emerging from underneath a floral IKEA headboard which wouldn't have been out of place in a chapel of rest.

'I'll have you know, Mabel, that I saw a 'Kodak Brownie' camera being displayed on 'Bing' for twenty-two pounds, and so it isn't a worthless piece of equipment after all.'

'There's nothing wrong with our 'PENTAX' digital camera, Harold, we can take pictures, bring the camera home, put the SD chip into the lap-top, and then use the printer to produce quality colour glossy photographs; it is far more convenient than taking a film into the SPAR shop for developing, and paying for photographs you take with my eyes closed. Also, I can remember the time the RAF's 'Red Arrows' aerobatic display team came to Warton; I took a picture of a Hawk trainer hurtling down Calder Vale Avenue dispensing red, white and blue smoke into our back garden; this I took with a simple 'Halena', no frills 110 camera. Meanwhile, you, as I can recall, Harold, used a complicated 'Yashica' 36-millimetre FX-7 Super camera, and by the time you had opened the shutter, the planes had flown back to the aerodrome and were parked up on the airfield.'

'Listen, Mabel are you going to get out of bed and cook my breakfast, or are we going to continue talking about cameras all morning?'

'Yes dear.'

'Yes, you are going to stay in bed, or no we are going to talk about cameras all day?'

Harold had found what he was looking for. It was the family's brown and beige hardback photograph album which came complete with a decorative tassel and tissue paper to separate and protect the pictures on each of the twenty-five pages. This historical book which contained priceless works of photographic art began and for the most part with portraits of Harold's family; his mother, father, grandmother and grandfather, his sister and a rogues' gallery, depicting, aunties, uncles and a nephew he was yet to meet.

The pages were being flipped-over quickly now; the rustle of tissue paper sounding reminiscent of an essential utilization found in a bathroom. Eventually, Harold's *flippin'* fingers stopped at a photograph which showed him and his family boarding the train to Morecambe from the platform on Lancaster railway station; rumour has it the guard took the picture and the train arrived in Bare Lane several minutes late.

Following on through the pages and seeing displays of gay drunken abandonment, Harold was taken back to the time when he met a girlfriend in the ballroom of 'Matt Jollies' holiday camp at Middleton Towers. The glossy black and white photograph was taken of her on the beach, wearing a swimsuit and as luck would have it, they met just a couple of days before the end of their holiday. Her name was Jillian Beadmore and came from Bangor in North Wales; she was the daughter of an American car salesman and except for Herbert-Cyril's mother, he was in-love for the first time. However, the correspondence came to an abrupt stop and the relationship ended when a week later he received a letter giving him the elbow, saying she had already got a steady boyfriend and two would be two, too many. And, so that was the end of Harold's idea of having a free holiday in sunny Bangor and for him getting away from regular farmyard smells, the irritating sound of geese, and cockerels' that crow at the break of day.

Harold had an ancient Boots the Chemist diary somewhere in the attic which went back to the year 1958; it was later during the afternoon, he was to climb up the drop-down ladder to try and find the document of historical importance because written in the address and telephone pages were Jillian's name and the estate where she lived in Bangor, North Wales. The whole idea of trying to get in contact with these people after all these years was completely bizarre and out of keeping with his normal behaviour.

The next photograph to attract Harold's attention was a signed photograph of one of the 'Jolly Babies' twenty-seven-year-old Manchester born, Brenda Redman who was provocatively posing for the camera. She, being the tallest of the high-kicking dance team, was wearing a white skirt with a wide open seam split down the side where one of her shapely legs came out into the open, leaving nothing to the imagination, and together with two cones of flesh protruding out from the top of her tight-fitting blouse and a pair of high-heeled shoes, this was all that was needed to complete the sexy outfit.

For several years Harold had wondered who had taken that particular photograph, but this conundrum was solved when he removed it from its hinges and looked on the back; the photograph had been developed and printed at the photographic studio at Middleton Towers, and on the reverse, and unbeknown to my mother, Auntie Brenda Redman had written her name, address and telephone number to allow my father to get in touch with her.

Is this the way it was at 'Matt Jollies' Middleton Towers Holiday Camp in 1958? I would say, yes, this was the way it all was; everyone having it off with everyone else, letting their hair down, and having a wonderful time, extra marital bliss relationships in full view of lone campers, who preferred to use a huge powerful naval telescope firmly fixed to the ground to observe the strange goings on in the sand hills of Middleton Towers. This was how Herbert-Cyril spent most of his time, getting rid of all of his pennies, being left with sore eyes, partially blind and ending up with only two halfpennies to rub together; and as for Harold, he couldn't have cared less, to put his money into a slot with nothing coming out; pressing button 'B' in a Telephone box was more adventurous and in keeping with his extra mural activities; listening-in to private conversations after tapping someone's phone inside the Admiralty buildings of Whitehall in London.

The next photograph to bring tears to his eyes was a picture of another eleven year-old girlfriend, Margaret Hogarth from Freckleton, whose anonymity had been kept a closely guarded secret for years, less, Mabel found her husband out to be an insufferably wild Casanova, and running the risk of being cut-off from the finer things in life, 'The Coach and Horses' pub, was just one before naming but a few others.

A picture of Herbert-Cyril Birtwhistle donned one of the pages. He was wearing his khaki shorts, a multi-coloured snake belt, a grey woollen 'V' neck pullover and long grey socks, one up and one down which spiralled around his ankle; a pair of binoculars were slung around his neck with the aid of a black plastic strap which looked similar to a length of 'Bassett's' liquorice, and noticeably, his round National Health spectacles placed askew over the bridge of his nose. He became the next point of contact when in, the same diary, Rosemary's name and address appeared, understandably underneath the letter 'B'.

Suddenly the silence within the reference library was broken when Mabel appeared at the bottom of the stairs and said:

'I knew this is what you would be doing, Harold.'

'I'm just looking through the family photograph album, something of which you and I have not done for years, Mabel, and by the way I found our old cameras, the Kodak Brownie 127 together with your bright yellow Halena Vision 110 MINI PIX, and my old Yashica FX-7 Super, stashed in one of the drawers in the sideboard, not that they would be any use to anyone; the Harris Museum of Antiquities in Preston may be interested, perhaps? Maybe, I could take a photograph of you cooking my breakfast with our PENTAX digital camera, I could have the photograph printed before my sausages, eggs and bacon arrives on a plate.'

'I can see it's going to be another one of those days.' Mabel said, holding a cistern flush handle firmly in her hand.'

'I will try and get in touch with Les Barnes on the mobile to fix the toilet, but you know Mabel, it is Saturday and he goes into Blackpool early to watch the 'Tangerines' play football.'

'I don't care if he's going down to Wimbledon to watch Andy Murray playing tennis, I just want the toilet mended once and for all.' she said, angrily.

'Yes, dear, anything else, buy a bottle of champagne; hang some balloons, set off a few party crackers when he has finally finished destroying our bathroom.'

'It wasn't my fault, Harold, that when we inherited your father's house in Naze Lane, Les Barnes tried to block up a hole in the bathroom ceiling, and how the hell was I to know it was a dysfunctional chimney which was packed full of soot.'

'Oh, I can remember it as if it were only yesterday, Mabel, there was soot everywhere, and it took us years to recover from what started off to be a simple job to stop a few drops of rainwater from falling into our lovely pink bath.'

'I was only trying to be helpful, dear, while you were at work and besides he is cheap and quick.'

'Mabel, how is this breakfast coming along, or will I have to go down into the village and pay Raman Chaterjie a visit; the proprietor of the 'Bombay Mix' Indian takeaway, he is one of Bollywood's better exports.'

'Don't be so silly, Harold; that is tonight's culinary delight, *Chicken Madras*, *Pilau rice*, *poppadoms*; *onion* and *mango chutney* and that should keep us going, won't it?'

'I'll say, which is the reason why we should get the toilet fixed as soon as possible.' he said, transfixing his eyes on another photograph of his mother, Margery doing a fancy quickstep around the ballroom with, Benjamin Mallk, an Imran Khan lookalike, the Indian cricketer who became famous for a while.'

'He was a good dancer.' Mabel said looking back at the time Harold and she were introduced to each other on the dance floor of the now famous Middleton Towers holiday camp in Morecambe.

'Yes, it sure beat the hell out of snake charming when he was introduced to Veronica after he and my mother had strutted their stuff around the highly polished floor, dancing to the "Military Two-step"; I can recall, it was like reviewing the Bengal Lancers; there were several occasions when he nearly knocked himself out when he gave her a compulsory salute.'

'And where was your dad when all of this was going on?' Mabel asked after all these years of wonder.

'Oh, as you know he wasn't into dancing, Mabel.' he replied, giving his father some sense of machismo, albeit some years too late. 'He had gone fishing that day in Morecambe and it became reminiscent of the first time we went to Middleton Towers and my mother found him drinking in a pub with Jean Turton, the wife of the ex-labour-councillor Tommy Turton.'

'Well I never.' she said, sounding not so surprised. 'It was only yesterday I saw them both outside the library in Freckleton; she always looked like butter couldn't melt in her mouth, and as for Tommy, he is archaic and always knocking it back in The Coach and Horses.' Mabel continued to add.

The Coach & Horses

Bring me a Flagon of thy finest Ale Wench

For my thirst I must indeed quench

Bring me tobacco and a Clay Pipe

Then bring me a platter of your Honeycomb Tripe

For to light up my Pipe

Bring me a long Taper

Then bring me a copy of today's Pickwick Paper

For the Mush in the corner some cheese and a Flagon

Before we all board the next Stage Coach Wagon

'Wasn't she the daughter of David Ball and his wife Jessie, the "Bonnie and Clyde" desperados from Freckleton who were on the run from the police after stealing motorcars from London, and transporting them to the North of England in the 1920s and 1930s?' Mabel just happened to mention.

'Yes, they were the family; they had the cheek of 'Old Nick' those two.' Harold remarked

'An artist's impression was printed in every newspaper in the country, and wanted posters were also pasted on most public conveniences in the West End of London, apparently. It was in the 'Daily Mail' at that time when someone wrote an article about him.' The article appeared in the London Daily Mail on Tuesday August 25th 1931, and this was what was written:

RIGHT NEXT DOOR TO SCOTLAND YARD

The Expert Mechanic and a Treasure of a Maid

A "Wanted" MAN

London

Recently the proprietor of a garage in Whitehall which is overlooked by the windows of Scotland Yard, advertised for a motor mechanic and a maid.

The advertisement brought replies from a husband and wife who having provided references were engaged
The man proved himself to be a very good mechanic, while the woman was all that could be desired as a maid in the garage proprietor's flat.

The new mechanic frequently commented
upon the nearness of Scotland Yard, declaring
no thieves would dare visit them.

And Then—

Then came the blow.
The maid who had proved to be such a
treasure disappeared. So too, did the expert
mechanic.
And, so too, did the contents of the till,
an almost new motor car, many gallons of
petrol and oil, and some rags.
The facts were reported to the next door
neighbours--Scotland Yard--and the C.I.D
got busy.
The missing couple, complete with car were
traced to Lancashire and then lost again. And
now the Yard has discovered that the affable
motor mechanic who was always ready to
perform any service for the detectives was a
man whom they have been anxious to trace
for the last eight years in connection with
motor thefts.

'Well I never.' Mabel said, shaking her head with disbelief.
'Well you never, what?' Harold asked.
'Well, I never did believe all those old fancy motor cars came from
around here.'

Chapter Ten

Sunday morning in Calder Vale Avenue, and what could be finer than Sweet Carolina

Caroline Cartwright is a curvaceous blonde-haired woman in her early forties and lives but just a few yards away from the Rigby's in Calder Vale Avenue. She must spend most of her leisurely hours accentuating her figure by looking at herself in a tall bevelled mirror which is an integral part of a wardrobe that has double-sliding doors. She fills most of her days by assessing people's furniture and possessions prior to it being transported overseas, or to another town or village boasting similar traits of insularity. It is much to the displeasure of Harold, late on Sunday mornings when a 'Mr Whoopee' ice cream van appears to obscure his line of vision when, after she returns from the Catholic Church of the Holy Family on Lytham Road; the sun always seems to shine into her ground floor bedroom when she disrobes out of her Sunday best clothes to reveal two mounds of undulating flesh before she disappeared into her back garden to improve on her sun-tanned body.

Harold's excuse to Mabel, for using his powerful German *Zeiss* 8x10 prismatic binoculars to peer into Caroline's bedroom was that he was using them to observe BAE Systems prototype aircraft which frequently flew past their houses; the binoculars which he had kept since his train-spotting days on Wesham railway station were used to spot trains which were very few and far between having only one line and ran only every half an hour. A regular business commuter who travelled from Kirkham to Blackpool every day of the week became disgruntled when he missed getting off a British Rail steam train at Wesham and ended up being stranded in Preston, and to make matters worse it was in the middle of winter; the snow was deep, hampering his return journey somewhere along the line; it was a good story at the time, but not a classic anecdote.

Mabel was totally confused at Harold using a pair of binoculars on a Sunday and she asked:

'I have often wondered, Harold, as to why you use a pair of binoculars on a Sunday; BAE Systems don't fly aeroplanes at the weekends.'

Ah, that's where you are wrong, Mabel, the flying club get to together on Sunday afternoons.'

'I don't see any of those Cessna what's their names flying around, Harold, but, it is only midday and Caroline Cartwright has only just walked back from church having cleansed herself of all of her sins for at least another week; someone once told me, Harold, the more one puts into that collection box, the nearer you are to God, and a seat on the Fylde Borough Council.'

'Bullshit, Mabel, and you know it.'

'Now, now, Harold, no need to blaspheme on Sundays, you don't know who's listening?'

'Well, I hope it isn't her husband, Mabel, because Jeffrey is due home from Saudi Arabia next week.' Harold said, muttering underneath his breath.

'What did you say, dear?' she asked.

'Nothing, Mabel.' he warily replied

'It's time we got ready to go to the pub, Harold, you know what the regulars are like around here, and if we give 'Ponkies', 'The Coach and Horses' a miss for Sunday Lunch; they make it a Day of Assumption when, if they can't think of anything positive to say, they just make it up.'

'I know Mabel, but unless we pack our bags and decide to live in Outer Mongolia, I'm afraid we are well and truly stuck with it.'

It was when they were walking along a stretch of road opposite to Freckleton's Co-operative CO-OP Late Shop, where the prices are comparable to Selfridges and Harrods in London, Harold said to Mabel:

'Did you know Margaret Thatcher, along with a few other University students, invented Mr Whippy' ice cream?'

'Yes, Harold, you've told me hundreds of times and she has a great deal to answer for, namely Douglas Hurd's outrageous hair-do which is shown on television's 'Spitting Image'; someone only has to put a Cadbury's chocolate flake on the top of his head and he would look like a ninety-nine ice cream cornet. Also, Harold, she is stopping you from using your binoculars; I suppose, if push came to shove, you could always use your grandfather's old World War One periscope you keep hidden away inside the garage; rumour has it, he used it before going over the top in the Battle of the Somme during the Great War in 1916.'

'What was great about The First World War, Mabel when well over a million British soldiers lost their lives over a fall-out between, Queen Victoria's grandson, Kaiser, Wilhelm and King Edward the seventh's eldest son, King George the fifth, it was all a to do with a row over Prussia taking control of the Balkans; do you think we will ever get down to the pub, Mabel; the roast beef, creamed mashed potatoes, vegetables and Yorkshire pudding will be going cold as we speak.'

'I must admit you're very knowledgeable, Harold; I'm very impressed.'

'Yes, those volumes of Caxton Encyclopaedia were a good purchase, Mabel; the guy who I bought them from was a bit strapped for cash, and so I thought twenty-pounds was a small price to pay for the wealth of information contained within them all.'

'Okay then, Jeremy Paxo, where does a loofah come from; the banana shaped implement you use to scrub your back in the bath.' Mabel asked, in an attempt to destroy his secondary educational skills.

'Oh, that's easy, Mabel, it is a type of course sponge which comes from the Great Barrier Reef in Australia; you could buy them in Woolworths in Lytham but that was until they went bust. And, the intellectual television 'University Challenge' host is called Jeremy Paxman, and not Paxo.

'Yes, I know, but I seem to have stuffing permanently on the brain, and, incidentally, who went bust, Harold, Woolworths or the loofahs? Also, Mr Know-it-all, a loofah is a tropical plant commonly used for carrying water as well as scrubbing your back. Have you noticed, apart from the colourful flower arrangements firmly embedded in the hanging baskets, nothing hardly ever changes around here.' she said looking at a decorative ornate village clock which showed the time as being twelve fifty-two precisely.

'Yes, I had noticed.' he replied before synchronising his watch to the clock behind the cenotaph.

The Village Clock
Tick Tock Tick Tock

That's the sound of the Village Clock
Tick Tock Hickory Dock
Round and round goes the Village Clock
Tock Tick in the Bar
Tick Tock have a Jar
Tick Tock in the Pub
Tock Tick in the Club
Find the key that fits the lock
The key that winds the Village Clock
Tick Tock Tick Tock
The Mice are all run down by three o'clock
Tick Tock Tick Tock

'Can you remember the clock which was on the promenade in Morecambe; it was called an autominer and did everything but tell the right time.' Mabel said gazing at the village timepiece which wouldn't have been out of place standing graciously on top of their wedding anniversary cake.

'Yes, I can remember it all too well, Mabel, especially the time when you and I went to Morecambe on a British Rail have-it-away day, and we missed the bloody train back to Lancaster, and you missed your connection from Preston to Southport because of the clock being one hour fast.

Meanwhile, the short distance to the pub continued.....

'You two are late.' Philip Bassett announced, from where he was sitting alone outside the pub on one of those bench seats where splinters play havoc with one's backside. 'Did you have another party last evening? There are a number of people in the lounge wondering why they weren't included in your forty-fourth wedding anniversary celebrations last Friday evening; they seem to think you owe them a drink.'

'I owe them nothing, Philip Bassett, and if you are playing spokesperson for those people who just wanted a free drink and a plate of *hotpot*, then I would suggest you go and pick on someone else.'

'Well done, Harold, he needed that and I couldn't have dealt with him better myself.' Mabel said, keeping her praise down to the bare minimum.

'Oh, don't mention it, Mabel.' he said after ignoring Philip's blatant sarcasm. 'As you know, he is a gossip who picks things up, and then, puts it down all over the village; you never know what outrageous stories he will come out with next, and if wit was shit he'd be constipated. He's the only man I know who carries a digital camera around attached to his belt for the sole purpose of making a scoop when he sells the photographs to the Lancashire Evening Post in Preston for vast sums of money. It was a few years ago he sold one of his impressive pictures which he had taken from outside the airfield perimeter fence of a Russian Aeroflot Antinov transport plane which flew into Warton; it just so happened it was the largest cargo aeroplane in the world, larger than the American Air Force Galaxy.

'What did he get for it?' Mabel whispered, so not to let everyone know the amount of his ill-gotten gains.

'It was a mild ticking-off from MI5 and a kick up the arse from BAE Systems security chiefs; apparently.'

They both walked stealthily up to the bar and were greeted by Mr and Mrs Carter, an inseparable couple who tend a small holding in nearby Kirkham.

'Good morning, Harold, Mabel, nice to see you, to see you, nice.' Joe Carter said to them both and sounding like Bruce Forsythe when he bends down and tries to emulate a Mr Universe in the television game series, The Generation Game. 'Jennifer and I were wondering as to whether you would make it to the pub this week because of your wedding anniversary revelling on Friday.' he diplomatically added.

'I suppose you would like us to buy you both a drink, a little aperitif, some Champagne or a cognac perhaps; do you know, Joe, we could have brought you and Jennifer a doggy bag full of leftovers from our party on Friday evening, the '*Heinz*' cucumber sandwich spread and watercress tea rolls are delicious and would go down nice with your small bottles of '*Perrier*' water.'

'There would be no need for that. Harold, we have just had our lunch and yours will be going cold.' Joe had to say.

'Do you know Mabel,' Harold said after receiving a sudden burst of inspiration. 'These spiders are all the same, those who come into our village expecting to be treated the same as everyone else; they should pay a visitor's tax when they approach the traffic lights.'

'And would this new ruling, benefit Kirkham Town Hall when you visit the 'Derby Arms' at Trailles.' she asked.

'Well, that's different because, as you well know, when I became a qualified electrician in the late sixties, I did a lot of contracting work in Salwick and so I would be exempt.'

'What a load of 'Tommy-rot'.' Mabel said, shaking her head from side-to-side like a Bollywood dancer. 'I've heard some stories in my time, but this takes the biscuit.' she added.

Mick Jordan, the temporary relief manager of The Coach & Horses reached up to a shelf above the bar to obtain a glass in the shape of a barrel, and then using an old-fashioned pump, proceeded to dispense the pub's one real ale, a dark liquid called Boddingtons beer which flowed upwards and towards a measuring line engraved on its side displaying an imperial measure called a pint. The other draught beers on the Pub's extensive list of beverages include, Fosters, Carling, Carlsberg, Stella Artois, Worthington, Tetley and Strongbow cider; a wide selection of white, red, rosé and sparkling are available, together with a huge variety of crisps and nibbles.

The 'Coach & Horses' pub in Freckleton has a large beer garden, and a car park at the front of the building where, in the early nineteenth century, stagecoach wagons parked up on their way to Blackpool. The pub boasts five TVs, two of which have large screens just in case you miss what is being shown on the other three, and rumour has it Colonel T.E Lawrence, Lawrence of Arabia, once visited the pub and paid two regulars to beat him up outside in exchange for two bags of chips and a steak pie.

'And, for your lady wife, Harold, what would she be drinking today, her usual gin and tonic, ice and a slice?' Elaine Jordan, the wife of Michael put in before taking their order for Sunday lunch.

Another celebrity, who was standing at the bar, was Sergeant Dave

Pennington from the local constabulary.

'Got rid of all your headaches then?' he asked in a way a typical policeman would.

'And have you collided with any members of the Tour de France lately because bicycles seem to be the favourite pastime around here.'

'Now, now, Harold, just because your son and I had a little misunderstanding on Friday evening.'

'As I explained on Friday evening, sergeant, it was entirely my fault.' Mabel said sorrowfully. 'George could still have been banged up if it wasn't for me leaving my bike in the village.' she added.

'Anyway, it's all water under the bridge now.' Dave said offering to pay for the round of drinks which were still waiting to be presented on to the rucked bar towel. 'Oh, and by the way, the Scottish smoked salmon sandwiches and the Anniversary cake was wonderful.' he disclosed knowing two representatives from the Carter family were listening.

'And, that's what they needed.' Harold said after Joe and Jennifer Carter banged their *Perrier* water bottles down on top of the bar in front of him before turning around to quickly walk out through the main door.

Jean Turton, the ex-barmaid, was purposely standing in a state of monogamy, alone by the door munching her way through a packet of pork scratching waiting for her husband to fall out of bed so that she could claim on his life insurance; his Saturday night revelling in The Coach & Horses brought back memories to Harold when Tommy Turton, her husband, was found to be a little worse for wear in Morecambe.

'Which table will you be seated at, Mr Rigby?' Mick Jordan asked, pointing in the direction of two vacant seats in the far corner next to the vault.

'A table which is far away as possible from spongers, ankle-biters, muck spreaders and sheep dippers, how does that sound, Steven?'

'Well, in that case we have a table outside which may suit your immediate requirements but in the long term, I would suggest you sit in front of the dartboard, it could be less dangerous sitting there.' Steve suggested. 'And don't worry about your food going cold, our full extensive food menu, as you know, is served until six pm.'

'At what time are George and Abigail going to arrive, Mabel?'

'Oh, about tea time.' she replied enthusiastically. 'George is going to show us some photographs and a DVD of when the family were in Cyprus, and that will be fun, won't it?'

'Yes, that's if I can see properly after eating a huge meal, sinking several pints and trying to watch so many screens all at the same time.'

Chapter Eleven

Afternoon tea at No 23 Calder Vale Avenue

Tea and cakes were the order of the day at No 23 Calder Vale Avenue and at four pm this was where light refreshments were served and for the Rigby family to participate in an afternoon of shear indulgence, consisting of chicken and stuffing triangular sandwiches, home-made individual jam tarts, marmalade muffins, apricot and almond flapjacks, and a well-rounded citrus tart with double cream taking centre stage on the table; all of which was washed down with flutes of 'Blushing Strawberry Fizz' and 'Earl Grey Tea'.

It was three forty-five precisely when George, Abigail, their three siblings, Patsy, Lillian and Warren, and Bobby the Yorkshire terrier arrived outside the bungalow in a recently washed Land Rover, and it was with the aid of a little soap and water, George was able to transform a dusty off-road vehicle into a clean desirable motorcar; the significant transformation was amazing.

Everyone, as usual were pleased to see each other including the two dogs. Prince, the Rigby's cow-eyed Golden Labrador proceeded to jump in the back of the car as soon as the door was opened with the intention of moving in with Bobby. The two dogs began with a kiss and a sniff around their backsides, and this was when Harold and Mabel knew they had two queer dogs on their hands when they cosily snuggled up on the back seat and refused to move.

'It is best not to inform Arthur Wigglesworth who lives at No 19.' Harold seriously mentioned to Mabel. 'He might think it's his lucky day when he takes his miniature poodle out for a walk which is around four in the afternoon.'

'Don't worry Harold.' she said concernedly. 'Their secret is safe with me.' she added

'Will everyone go inside the house now please?' Harold shouted, gesticulating with his forearm where the door to the bungalow was situated when he saw Arthur closing the gate to his driveway.'

'Is there a curfew on or something, or have you been given advanced pre-warning of a Soviet attack on Warton Aerodrome?' George enquiringly asked, knowing his father had drunk a few pints of Boddingtons that afternoon and was a little hot-headed and somewhat worse for wear.

'It may be of interest for you to learn, George, that Arthur Wigglesworth used to work as a cinema projectionist in Blackpool, but that was until he was caught sitting on his own in the stalls watching dirty movies; a crude black and white film called "Pinocchio" which had been produced inside a studio on Central Drive, was just one of a series of pornographic block-busters at that time, and Pinocchio, as you know was a film about a wooden puppet who came alive and, every time he told a lie, his nose grew longer.'

'I don't suppose "Snow White" was complaining.' George replied bursting out into fits of laughter.'

'What are you laughing at George?' Abigail asked, as she tried to move the two dogs from the back seat before going into the house.

The spasmodic spurts of merriment continued with Harold's grandchildren joining in, not knowing what the subject matter was that had promulgated the laughter.

Arthur minced passed in front of the Rigby's low garden wall and he was holding on to a lead attached to his poodle called 'Poo Poo', which looked as though she had just come out from a Vidal Sassoon hair salon and was heading for the dog show at Crufts.

It was young Warren who asked, who was taking who for a walk; Poo Poo or Arthur Wigglesworth after the man and his dog had disappeared out of ear-shot distance into Beechnut Drive.

The family eventually settled down in their favourite chairs; a seating arrangement which had been worked out over several years of occupancy in Calder Vale Avenue.

A plate stacked high with chicken sandwiches was brought into the lounge by Harold, who had taken on the role of the congenial host for the afternoon tea party; the *'Paxo'* stuffing, and the fresh extra strong *'Coleman's'* mustard, he declared, was specially prepared by him, and were both bi-products from packets of seeds which were as hot as a stokers shovel.

'There is a jar of mild Belgravia prawn and onion dip on the table which has a Mogulite label on its side depicting the Taj Mahal; it is by appointment to Her Majesty The Queen and has been specially imported to Freckleton from a Square somewhere in the Southern hemisphere with a river running through it.' Harold said as if things weren't hot enough.

'Don't pay any attention to what he is saying.' Mabel said when she began adding to the story. 'The curry sauce came from the 'Bombay Mix' takeaway; Raman Chaterjie and Beau Jaffrey will tell him anything to get rid of their gone-past their sell by date products.' she went on.

Some of the freshly baked cakes began to filter through into the lounge from the kitchen following a quick exodus of sandwiches which instantaneously vanished from hand into mouth.

Mabel, the hostess, offered an assortment of cakes with great reverence, knowing she had baked them herself to her mother's original recipes; the almond flapjacks being her favourite confection because of her Liverpool, Scottish background.

'Would you all like to try one of my homemade muffins?' she asked, and then waited for a positive response, or a modicum of praise.

Lillian, the youngest of the three children made a point of mentioning that the 'Blushing Strawberry Fizz' was particularly good and refreshing as it is made with strawberries, sparkling white wine and soda. It is interesting to note that the ingredients used to make it was published in a 'Dairy Diary' in 2003, and the volume and gravity is enough to blow one's head off, if its drunk to access.

'Do you think I could have another glass of 'Bucks Fizz', grandma?' Patsy asked circling the inside of the flute with her finger. 'It sure beats the hell out of drinking bottles of cool '*Desperado*' all evening because the *Tequila* doesn't half make your mouth dry; I think it's something to do with the pieces of lime the bar tender shove down their necks.'

'Which neck Patsy; yours, or the neck on the top of the *Desperado* bottle?' George said when he looked at another 'dead soldier', an empty *demi-sec* magnum making its way back into the kitchen.

'I think I'll have another can of Guinness from inside the fridge; it's supposed to be good for you.' Warren said, getting up from a manoeuvrable green Montgomery tapestry pouffe at the side of the fireplace.'

'It's best to drink Guinness from outside a fridge and not inside. Warren.' his granddad tried to warn him. 'You'll catch your death of cold and die from hypothermia.'

'Well, how come, granddad, that when the 'White Star' passenger liner, the "Titanic" sank in nineteen-twelve, most of the Irishmen had smiles on their faces when their bodies were recovered from the Atlantic Ocean?'

'That was because they were drinking Guinness in the Steerage Class and not in one of the salubrious first-class smoking salons which ran along the port side.'

'And, how the hell do you know all of this, Warren?' his father curiously asked.

'From James Cameron's epic film, dad; Leonardo de Caprio was never the same again after making that film.'

'I don't suppose he would be, Warren; he died from hypothermia.' George suddenly remembered.

'Well according to my son-in-law, Doctor James S.R Wilson, there is a sudden comfort in dying from hypothermia.' Mabel had to put in.

'Listen, are we having our afternoon tea inside a funeral parlour or are we standing at the stern of the 'Titanic' waiting for it to go down into the depths of the Atlantic Ocean.' George said concernedly.

'Would you like to see some of our photographs?' George said to Harold and Mabel, as he searched through an untidy pile of pictures trying to find something suitable to impress his father. 'Some of them were taken years ago when I was a smart cookie, a rookie at Lympstone in Devon, undergoing my Commando Training; this black and white one, in particular, shows me receiving my green beret having completed the All Arms Commando Course.'

'You know, I could have been a Royal Marine Commando, but unfortunately I missed being called up for National Service.' Harold said tongue in cheek, hoping his grandchildren would believe every word of his story.

'Get out of it, Harold.' Mabel said with her arms folded, and at the same time looking up towards the ceiling to find something more appealing to focus on. 'You are like your father Harold, full of hot air; and rumour has it that when war broke out in nineteen thirty-nine, he told everyone he was in a reserved occupation and would be exempt from mobilization, but I wouldn't call making sausage rolls and pork pies a reserved occupation, would you?'

'Well, rationing went on until nineteen fifty-two and Veronica and I didn't starve when we were kids; that's if you could *thoil* eating 'SPAM' and mash potatoes every night.' Harold replied.

'Here we go again, you only think about yourself, Harold; it is a wonder there was any sausage meat to make his pork pies and sausage rolls during those early days.' she went on.

'Ah, but you see Mabel, in addition to an air-raid shelter in the back garden your father-in-law had an allotment where he grew carrots and potatoes and so he was able to make delicious potato pies as well. There was a story abound that he made the best meat and potato pies in Preston, and the queues stretched from his baker's shop in New Hall Lane, and all the way down to Manchester Road. There was a competition in the Lancashire Evening Post for the first person to find more than two pieces of meat inside one of his pies; his answer to this was that his customers could buy two meat and potato pies instead of just the one.'

'This one of me was taken when I was twenty and was posted to 42 Commando at Bickleigh Barracks near Plymouth, Devon.' George insisted on showing his father. I had a period of peaceful relaxation there but then I was further posted to Northern Ireland on a wide range of operational tasks.

'And this one was when I became a Sergeant during the new millennium when I witnessed 42 Commando being deployed on Operation 'Telic 1' for the invasion of Iraq in two-thousand and three where we launched a helicopter assault on the Al-Faw Peninsula to support 40 Commando; this is me climbing into a helicopter.'

'Oh, and this one.....'

'Dad, when are we going to show grandma and granddad the photographs you took of us all sitting on the rocks in Cyprus?' Patsy asked when she began to get bored with having to see the same old photographs for the umpteenth time.

'Just a minute, Patsy because this is when I was a Colour Sergeant serving with 'Mike' Company of 42 Commando during Operation 'Volcano' in Afghanistan in two-thousand and seven; I was for my sins, part of a Close Combat Company, engaging the enemy daily. And, this one shows our Close Combat troop contacting the enemy during Operation 'Sond Chara' in Afghanistan in two-thousand and eight.'

'So, you had telephones, then, dad.' Warren burst in.

'You know Warren, for a person, who wishes to follow on in his father's footsteps, I think you had better buck your ideas up.'

'Well, if you mean renovating rickety-old ironing boards, wardrobes, tables and chairs which have been camouflaged and re-painted several times over the years, then no, I won't buck my ideas up. And, as for all that combat training and going into battle guns blazing; does that include calculating and adding up the Battalion's ration commutations in a Quartermaster's department store?' Warren went on barracking and before he burst into song with: "There was gravy, gravy, enough to sink a navy, in the Quartermaster's store; my eyes are dim, I cannot see, I haven't brought my specs with me, I have not brought my specs with me".

'Okay, Warren, I think we've had enough of Frank Sinatra; and you mum, would you like to see this photograph of Abigail and me standing on the shore of Lake Windermere before we were married.'

'Oh yes please.' Mabel said before Abigail disappeared up the stairs to go to the bathroom. 'We heard all about the disastrous visit to Windermere and Bowness, and how you were caught with your pants down on Fantasy Island.'

'Who told you that?' George asked disapprovingly.

'It was none other than your good lady wife who was responsible.' Mabel replied.

'I think I will go out on to the patio to have a smoke.' Warren said bringing out a crumpled-up packet of 'Benson & Hedges' from a trouser pocket.

'Be careful, not to set fire to yourself, Warren, because it is my intention to get you all back to Portsmouth in one piece tomorrow.'

'And by the way, dad, apart from the driver of a 'Chieftain' tank, I have never heard of anyone going into battle sitting down.' Warren said, retaliating to his father's internal combustion warning.

'When do the choc-ices come around?' Lillian asked, looking out through the window and out into the street.

'Just as soon as 'Mr Whippy' has moved out of sight into Rydal Water Avenue and Harold has put his binoculars away for the weekend.' Mabel said correctively.

Since George Rigby, Warrant Officer Class II, retired from 42 Commando Royal Marines in May 2013, it has taken over from 45 Commando as the lead Commando task group. They are now deployed as part of the COUGAR 13 Response Force Task Group exercising in Albania and the Middle East.

Chapter Twelve

It was seven-thirty and the evening continued with George, Abigail and their three children, Patsy, Lillian and Warren saying goodbye to Mabel and Harold before returning to the 'The County Hotel' in Lytham to spend their last night prior to them returning to the South of England the following day.

'Thanks granddad, grandma, for the tea,' Patsy said with an air of appreciation having drunk several glasses of 'Blushing Strawberry Fizz' during the afternoon and this didn't include the Rosé wine she devoured at lunchtime to accompany her roast beef dinner.

'We are hoping to see you at Christmas.' George said to his mother and father before asking if Bobby and Prince were still in the garden.

'I shouldn't have thought so.' a voice bellowed out from across the road. 'I saw them both heading towards the village, and if you don't watch it Harold, we may be stepping into a few more 'Poo Poo's' around here.' Jeffrey Cartwright said when he was paying the taxi driver an exorbitant Sunday tariff following a long and tedious journey from London's Heathrow Airport.

'I thought you weren't coming home until next week, Jeffrey.' Harold said puzzlingly, and was glad to have put his binoculars away; out of sight and out of mind.

'But, it is next week, Harold, and my missus will be stirring the 'Bisto' into the gravy as we speak, and I have arrived back just in time to receive our new wall-to-wall storage cupboards which are being delivered from IKEA tomorrow; the ones we have in the bedroom are not user-friendly because one night I was confronted with my own reflection in one of the six-feet long mirrors, and for a fleeting moment I thought Caroline and I had company.

'Thanks for a wonderful afternoon, grandma, and granddad.' Warren seriously said. 'And I'm sorry about kicking Arnold, your garden gnome into the fish pond, I was only trying to recover my Benson & Hedges cigarettes when they fell into the water; the gnomes' fishing rod is a little bent but then, he's not the only one around here in Calder Vale Avenue who isn't perpendicular .' he added.

'Do you mean Arthur Wigglesworth, or Poo Poo, the dog?' Harold asked after picking up a decorative "Itsy bitsy, teeny weenie", yellow polka-dot bow tie accessory from the pavement which had been attached to either the dog or its owner.

At that precise moment, Prince and Bobby returned home no worse for wear by not having to suffer irritable extendable leads which are normally used for hanging-out washing out to dry in yards or back gardens.

'Where the hell have you been?' Harold said to the two dogs, as if he was going to get a response from them in a prominent Lancastrian, Freckletonian accent which could have originated and been perfected in an Oxford University laboratory.

Bobby jumped into the back of the Land Rover to take up his favourite position inside his basket on one of the back seats.

'Thanks, grandma, for a fun afternoon, the tea and cakes were wonderful.' Lillian said, giving her a kiss on the cheek before adding. 'I just wish we had time to show you the DVD that dad took of us all when we were stationed in Cyprus; he does go on, doesn't he when everyone has to listen to him talking about the day he came under fire in Iraq, and his endless feats of macho dare-devil activities, including one occasion when he did a free fall parachute jump from four and a-half thousand feet and inadvertently dropped into a Sainsbury's car park in Plymouth.'

'Thanks, mum, dad, it's been a wonderful weekend, and we hope to see you on the run-up towards Christmas.' Abigail said with tears in her eyes as if she didn't want to go back to Portsmouth where everything and everyone seemed so unfriendly.

'Give my regards to the flag ship, The Mary Rose.' Harold said to George before he opened the door to get into the driver's seat. 'And don't go dropping into any Sainsbury's car parks because if you haven't bought yourself a Mars bar or a packet of chewing gum to enable you to stay on their premises all day, you will be presented with a hefty fine.' he added.

Everyone, except George and the dog waved through the windows as the off-road vehicle moved the short distance before turning left into Beechnut Drive.

'Well, that was fun, wasn't it Mabel; and it won't be long before we take a trip down memory lane again when our son-in-law, Dr James S.R Wilson arrives with all his entourage, and I can carry on from where I left off talking to Susan about Middleton Towers holiday camp.'

'Yes, Harold, you can even show her some of the photographs in our family album; she will enjoy seeing those, especially the one of Margaret Hogarth, your ex-girlfriend who is still mucking-out the stables on Smith's Farm.'

'Bloody Hell; is there nothing sacred around here?'

'You should know by now, Harold, that it would only be a matter of time before I noticed the similarity between the sixteen year-old Margaret Hogarth and a sixty-seven year-old Shire Horse.'

'And, you should be more sympathetic towards her.' Harold emphatically said; 'she suffers from depression and chases her cat around the house when she runs out of Prozac.'

'She can be suffering from galloping foot rot for all I care; just remove that full-frontal image from our photograph album, and quite honestly, Harold, I can't tell the difference between her and the brewery's Dray which was used to deliver the barrels of beer to 'The Coach & Horses' all those years ago.'

'There is no need to get too excited, Mabel, because when we were young, Margaret used to take on the role of the Virgin Mary every year in the junior school nativity play.'

'What's changed, Harold?'

'Perhaps, she is still waiting for Mister Right to come along.' he replied, hoping his words were enough to convince Mabel she was still looking for a man who was capable to cope with her outrageous behaviour.

'You mean Richard Wright from the Gas Board?' she asked.

'Well yes; he'll do for starters.' Harold suggested.

'It was Alison Hornby who told me yesterday that the library in Freckleton is about to close next year by Lancashire County Council, and will be transformed into either a community centre, a Turkish kebab house or another Indian Take-away.' Mabel said. 'But, she is not quite sure as the information she received was proffered to her by Irene Clayton, and it wasn't very clear which ethnic group was about to move in.'

'Anyway, I don't suppose having another lot penetrating the heavily fortified citadel of Freckleton via a set of traffic lights which are permanently on red to outside prospectors will make any difference; the village smells more like Calcutta every minute.' Harold liberally replied.

'Have you been to Calcutta, Harold?'

'No, dear; I've never been to Bradford either, but I've heard all about it; the city has ten Indian restaurants per capita of population, and furthermore, I have driven down Friar Gate Hill in Preston on a number of occasions on my way home, and by the time I had reached the University of Central Lancashire, I was hallucinating because of inhaling the aromatic aroma of curried-to-death *chicken tikka masala* and oily fish and chips.'

'But, Indian restaurants and take-away places don't serve fish and chips, Harold.'

'Give them time; just give them time.' he replied.

'You never complain when you visit the 'Bombay Mix' on Saturday evenings when Mr Chaterjie gives you free Bombay potatoes, poppadoms and out of date jars of prawn and onion chutney which tastes like wallpaper adhesive.'

'Well, he and Jaffrey are different; they are both throwbacks from the Indian Raj, and, furthermore, the new Mayor of London, Mr Sadiq Khan could turn out to be the chief promulgator of a twenty-first century Pakistani Mutiny, when some of them are forced to have their names changed by deed-poll and their Masonic status taken away from them.'

'You do talk rubbish Harold; Sadiq Khan is a British-born politician and comes from Tooting in South London.'

'Who the hell told you that? he comes from the Himalayas, and you mark my words, Mabel, if Jeremy Corbin wins the next General Election, the Indian delegates will have to say goodbye to their weekly visits to the Royal National Hotel in London where they have to go through a ritual of standing on one leg blind-folded knowing someone or something was coming up behind you.'

'Do you know, Harold, I think you are prejudiced towards anyone who wasn't born outside of Freckleton.'

'Me, no, I just think that if it wasn't for the Indians, Britain wouldn't have had its Empire.' Harold was quick to put in. 'And did I mention to you Mabel, I once visited an Indian Restaurant in Blackpool, and it was there I swallowed a bone from a Hot Madras curry. The proprietor asked me if I wanted to see a doctor, to which I replied, yes; it turned out he was his brother and had a pay-as-you-go surgery in Bispham.'

'Tell me, Harold, what is the difference between Pappadoms, Poppadoms and Puppadoms?'

'How the hell should I know, Mabel.' he said, checking the time on their new anniversary clock before getting ready to go to the BAE Sports and Social Club.

'Well, Poppadoms, Poppadoms and Puppadoms are explosive pieces of cardboard which disintegrate in an instant once they have been broken into two pieces; their outside diameters are measured in order of size; Pappadoms being the largest, and Puppadoms being the smallest.'

'Is that before, or after they have been cooked and puffed-up in a deep fat fryer?'

'They are similar to the prawn crackers which we sometimes order in the Cantonese take-away, aren't they Harold; the crisper ones have a habit of exploding in front of your very eyes.' Mabel said, comparing the crackers to home-made terrorist devices.

"Rule Britannia, marmalade and jam
Five Chinese fire crackers up your arsehole
Bang! Bang! Bang! Bang! Bang"

'I hope you are not going to be like this in the Lightning Club, Harold; I don't think I can stand anymore of your nonsense this evening.'

'What does a Pakistani do when he visits the Scottish Highland Games in Braemar?' Harold jokingly asked.

'I don't know, Harold, I think I will pass on this one.'

'He tosses the Kaiber.'

'You think you are so sharp, Harold; one day you will cut yourself, and according to our Christian faith, they are all our brothers and sisters.'

'Well, Mabel, our white Caucasian brothers and sisters live in America but, as for that other lot who spend most of their time pushing discarded chicken leg bones through their noses and wielding bows and arrows, assegai spears and wooden clubs, I wouldn't class them as my brothers.'

'You've been watching too many episodes of "The Flintstones" recently.' Mabel said with a big grin on her face.

'They are all the same, the Chinese, Indians, Japanese; they are not dissimilar to the Masai Warriors of Northern Kenya, the head-hunting tribes in the Amazonian jungle and the flesh-eating cannibals of Easter Island in the Pacific; you cannot trust any of them. You know, Sam Fenton, our local gardener's merchant in Freckleton, he once told me a story that he and his missus once went for a short break to London and on their first night they visited a Japanese restaurant in Soho and had to leave their shoes outside in exchange for a pair of hygienically approved flip-flops, and to make matters worse, after they had eaten their meal, Sam and Daphne discovered that their shoes had disappeared and had to return to their hotel bare-foot; the restaurant was called "Lucky Lou's" or something like that. Samuel said the coach excursion from Freckleton to London was during an extremely hot spell in the summer of nineteen seventy-six, and he went on to tell me that when he sat down on his allocated seat, which was covered in brown vinyl, he jumped up and hit his head on an overhead light switch, and not to add insult to injury, the sun continued to shine through a near-side window without a shade.'

'Yes, well, that was very interesting, Harold; do you think we can go and get ready for this evening's programme of entertainment?'

'He had to go and visit the health centre when he returned from London.' Harold mentioned in more dispatches to his loving wife as she attempted to step on to the first rung at the bottom of the stairs.

'And, why, if I may ask did he have to go and visit the doctor?' Mabel asked turning round.

'It was because he had a huge red ring around his backside and was suffering from mild concussion and sore feet.'

'And, how the hell did you know that?' she questioned.

'It was when he showed me his injuries in the pub.'

'I can see it's going to be one of those nights, Harold.'

It was when Harold was in the bathroom he asked Mabel if she had a paper tissue because he had just cut himself shaving.

And, it was on their way out of the house, she said to him: 'Come on Barney Rubble, we have a date with the 'Bed Rock' Sports & Social Club, who are seeing-off one of your favourite asinine managerial adversaries, Bill King, but firstly, you must promise not to embarrass me by coming out with any of your stupid poems, namely the one you told to a principle BAE aircraft engineer two weeks last Saturday.'

'You mean the one which is called, "One and One makes bloody Three" and goes:

'One and One makes Three'
In my life I've figured out
How One and One make Two
It must be engineering to
Bring this final clue
With all the lies, the answers lay
Inside a firm called 'Al-Marconi'
With genetic cloud all around
It's called Weinstocks macaroni
And for them that drink from
Poison Chalice
Will have a life of hidden
          Malice
They go where Angels fear to tread
Underground amongst the dead
When Broadswords wield from
          History
That's when One and One make-a
          Bloody Three; 'Faith, Hope, but no damned Charity'

***

The Lightning Club later that evening

Mabel, having exchanged a driving wheel for a comfortable seat in the House of Commons, recalled a conversation which she heard when she and Harold were standing in front of the bar the previous week; it was between a local window cleaner, Bert Cookson and a hardware store manager, Bob Snape which went:

'What do you want to drink, Bert?

'I'd like a Bitter Shandy, Bob'

'A Bitter Shandy, Bert?

'Yes, a Bitter Shandy, Bob'

'And, are you having a drink as well Bob?

'Yes, a Lemonade Shandy, Bert'

'A Lemonade Shandy, Bob?

'Yes, a Lemonade Shandy'

'Would that be a pint or a half, Bert?

'I think I'll just have a half, Bob'

'And, are you having a half, Bob?

'Yes, I think it's only wise, Bert'

'Would you like a packet of Crisps, Bert?

'Yes, I'd love a bag of Crisps, Bob'

'And, what flavour of Crisps would you like, Bert?

'What flavours have they behind the bar, Bob?

'I'll ask the Barman what he's got, Bert'

'Do you want any Crisps, Bob?

'Yes, I'm going to have a bag of salt and vinegar, Bert'

'Bloomin eck, just look at bloomin time, Bob'

'It's five to bloomin seven, Bert'

'And, just look at the bloomin queue behind us, Bert'

'Bowlers need a bloomin seat'

'It's time we both went bloomin home, Bob'

'It's Coronation Street ta neet'

Sitting alone in a corner of the bar area was the dapper, Squadron Leader Sabu Singh, an aircraft projects engineer who enlisted in the Indian Air Force in 1986 and became an F-16 jet fighter pilot based in Mumbai.

Harold, having purchased a round of drinks at the bar, consisting of a pint beer for himself and an orange squash for Mabel, burst into song with a catchy nineteen-sixties tune called "A dedicated follower of Fashion" which was popularized by a band named "The Kinks".

"They seek him here, they seek him there
His clothes are loud but never square
Everywhere he goes, he's got to buy the best
Because he's a dedicated follower of fashion"

'Shut up, and behave yourself Harold, Sabu Singh was a respected pilot in the Indian Air Force and now he works for the *dooin's* next door, one of the largest toy manufacturing industries in the world.'

'See what I mean, Mabel, they have no morals, no standards, no backbones only the ones which protrude out from their noses, and furthermore; he was flying for the wrong side; Sing, sing or else show me your ring.' he went on.

'After the next round of drinks, Harold, can we go home?

'Yes, of course, Mabel, but not until Bill King has bought me a large Scotch and Soda, and you another Orange Squash "Sing sing a song, make it simple to last the whole night long"

Chapter Thirteen

The beginning of a colourful week and its Morecambe and Lunesdale here we come.....

'I've got a good idea, Mabel, why don't we have a day trip to Morecambe tomorrow, calling in at the village of Ribchester by the River Ribble, and then revisiting Lancaster Castle; it will bring back such happy memories of when we first met.'

'What a good idea, Harold, perhaps you would like to take your binoculars and you can sit around the pool and gloat at the contestants who are participating in Morecambe's bathing beauty competition, and then, afterwards we can watch some of the Pendle witches being tossed over the balustrades of Lancaster Castle, and that will be fun won't it?'

'I just thought it may have been a good suggestion, taking you away from Freckleton's Women's Institute where, playing endless games of whist, and consuming cup after cup of insipid 'Maxwell House' granulated coffee, are high on your list of things to do, especially on Monday mornings.'

'Yes, you are right as usual, Harold; maybe I can take some photographs of you standing in front of a dungeon before the gaoler locks you up and throws away the keys.'

It was when Mabel and Harold were about to hit the sack following a long and tiresome day, he told her a story about the time he and his friend John Ashworth were in the Boy Scouts in Freckleton, and it was during the memorable icy winter of 1962, they experienced a weird and bizarre series of events linked to the Pendle witches deep in the heart of the dense Forest of Bowland.

'I'm going to tell you a story, Mabel, and it's not for the faint hearted.' Harold said when she yawned and looked forward to having a good night's sleep.

'You sound like the late Max Bygraves, Harold; you're not going to leave me to shack up with Margaret Hogarth are you? Or worse still you have been secretly having a love affair with Arthur Wigglesworth behind my back.'

'No, seriously.' he replied, gazing out through the bedroom window to observe a sinister full moon with intermittent grey clouds obscuring its brightness. 'And, what I am about to tell you, Mabel, will be enough to make your hair curl.'

'My hair is already rolled up in curlers so this, I'm sure, won't make any difference to the way it will look in the morning, but please do go on; I just can't wait for the alarm clock to go off and hear the finale.'

'It was when I was a lad and in the Boy Scouts, my friend, John Ashworth and I ventured five miles eastward outside the periphery of Preston towards the mountainous regions of the Trough of Bowland and the Ribble Valley. It was during a weekend, and as I can recall it was snowing very heavily when we departed from the Plough, the geographically well placed pub in Freckleton to take us to the bus station in Preston. I can also remember standing at the top of Marsh Lane in the village, staring out at the most wonderful scenery; snow covered fells in the far distance and to me it was like another world. In those days neither my parents nor I had never even been to Blackpool and I thought the Tower looked similar to a vinegar bottle for one of the town's huge fish and chip shops. And standing in the centre of a bridge overlooking the River Ribble in Preston, one could see Parlick Pike, a huge mountain of earth pointing up, one thousand four hundred and seventeen feet towards the sky along the Pennine Way, and it is situated on the outskirts of the old picturesque village of Longridge along a straight Roman road. In addition to all this lovely scenery, there is Ribble Valley, Beacon Fell, Pendle Hill, Newton and Winter Hill, famous for their peaks and troughs, some of which extend into Yorkshire and as far as the Borough of Greater Manchester; the broadcasting and television masts predominantly dominating its high ridged sky-line.

'Go on, Harold, I'm beginning to fall asleep and the suspense is killing me.'

'Well, Mabel, John and I began our adventure which was to take us to the Ribble Valley and beyond. We had two Bergen rucksacks which contained a Bivouac tent, ground sheet, mess tins and the necessary blankets to keep us warm; a primus stove which was later filled with petrol became the most important part of our equipment. We also used an old army prismatic compass which we had hoped to find our way back on a bearing from a place which is now famous for nothing in particular. In those days, no one cared about where you were going just as long as you returned home on Sunday evenings in time for school on the Monday.

'I would have cared, Harold, but then, you didn't tell me where you were going.'

'Anyway, to continue, it was during the first day we both went on a short bus ride to Longridge, it was so cold and we both wore Anoraks and bobble hats, trying to emulate the Mount Everest climbers, Sir Edmund Hillary and Sherpa Tensing.

'Come on Harold, get on with it, I'm going to catch my death of cold if you carry on for much longer.'

'To continue with the story, when we arrived at Longridge we braved the several hundred feet to climb to the top of Parlick Pike. It was when we began the descent a mist came down from the heavens to surround and envelope at least three-quarters of the fell below. Ironically, we could see the summit, but it was like trying to penetrate through layers upon layers of snow-white cotton wool.'

'Is this the end, because I feel, there is more you are going to impress me with.' Mabel asked looking at the time.

'No, and yes, there's more. The mist cleared, and we were able to continue with our descent with the aim of putting our feet back onto *terra firma*. We trekked along a narrow country pathway towards Ribchester, a village containing an antiquated Roman Villa which we learned later, had been occupied from seventy-nine AD until the Romans buggered off back to Rome in the early fifth century. We ended up beside a small group of cottages in a cul-de-sac leading up to a labyrinth of dark entrances below a line of evergreen trees. Having negotiated Grey Squirrels Lane, an overgrown stretch of road, and then having to stoop down to follow a nature walk of some several hundred yards we came to a rotunda, a circular copse inside a forest; there was an air of unpleasantness all around which was tangible giving one the impression that one shouldn't be there. However, having been invited into one of the cottages by a woman who we thought, was a respected local lady and a pillar of the community, we were to realize later that this was not the case and a far distance away from the truth. She was commonly known as Elizabeth Wall, a local artist, a reader of tea leaves and other things and furthermore, was in charge of a witches coven organising weird stuff around the district; we, nevertheless pitched our tent in the copse hoping we could settle down and enjoy a good night's sleep without any further interruption.'

'You mean, like me, Harold, having to stay awake until six o'clock in the morning, waiting for you to finish this story?'

'Listen, there's more. She gave us both a 'stoneware' soup plate full of broth which consisted of the biggest mushrooms you have ever seen, and she said they would give us energy when we were out in the cold.'

'Samuel Fenton grows mushrooms like that, Harold, he says if you put garlic and Soya Sauce in the centre where the stalk has been, it keeps the witches and ghouls away.'

'Ah, this is where you are wrong, Mabel, Elizabeth Wall gave us black magic mushrooms that swirled around in a garlic soup which could only be described as frogspawn disguised as Vermicelli. John and I began to hallucinate in the middle of the night and became delirious, especially when we witnessed a log fire burning in the centre of the copse with a black cauldron hanging from a chain inside a triangle supported by three wooden poles. There were four witches and several female wood nymphs dancing naked around the fire; it was like watching the Bolshoi Ballet, and I can recall quite vividly, Elizabeth Wall smelling of urine; her breath reeking of puke and alcohol. And sitting by the side of her was Louise, "Hubble, bubble, toil and trouble" Hubbard who was stirring the pot with a large wooden spoon. To add more frogs, toads and fat into the cauldron was Alice Duckworth, the smallest of the group, who was wearing a black pointed hat and had long filthy toe nails which curled round like a wild boar's tusk. Then there was Janice Ferguson, alias Doris Crapper, a descendant and throw-back from the Scottish contributory militia, who fought against the Parliamentarian 'New Model Army' in the

Battle of Preston English during the English Civil War. She had a nose, the shape of a bent banana, and of the type which pre-dated the Roman Emperor, Julius Caesar. Ferguson, who had more lines on her forehead than Preston railway station, and for reasons of health and insanity, only ventured out at night, and with the aid of a broomstick she was able to fly over the chimney tops of Clitheroe on Halloween Night, and then somehow manage to circumnavigate the British Aircraft Corporation airfield at Salmesbury just in time for her to crap on a parked up Canberra Bomber or pissed-up revellers who were successfully purporting to be devils and witches coming out from the 'Nabs Head' and the 'New Hall Tavern' pubs.

'You were that close, were you Harold?'

'Yes, and we were forced to strip out of our pyjamas and join in with all the *dooin's* and frolicking which was happening around the fire.'

'Wasn't it cold, Harold?'

'Of course it was cold Mabel; it was in the middle of bloody winter.'

'It's a wonder you had time to pull up your pyjama trousers, Harold.' she uttered before attempting to duff up one of the duck down pillows to make a lasting impression in the centre.

'Oh, that was another thing, Mabel, our pyjama bottoms went into the pot and the next day we found them hanging down from a clothes line, ready to wear inside the copse; the 'Burton's' coat hanger came in quite handy later when I drip-dried my white nylon shirt.'

'Do you know, Harold if I didn't know you any better, I would say you should have taken more water with it after visiting the pub in Longridge, but then I'm inclined not to believe you because you were both too young to drink alcohol.'

'Honestly, Mabel, I know it is a story which borders on the realms of fantasy, but believe me it's true. We actually carved our names on one of the trees inside the forest and I bet you they are still there.'

'Okay then, show me tomorrow, but in the meantime, good night Harold.'

'Did you know that witches have the ability to stop clocks, watches and magically turn the arrow of a prismatic compass so that it always points in the direction of Lancaster Castle?'

'Harold,'

'Yes dear?'

'Go to sleep; Good night.'

'Good night, dear.'

'Oh, and please pray tell me, Harold before I begin to experience a series of unpleasant nightmares; did you see this representative from Wall's Ice Cream when you both struck camp and trekked back by her house?'

'No, Mabel but there was a rather vicious Doberman Pincer in the front garden and a donkey roaming around at the back.'

'And what did you deduce from that, Harold?'

'That she was heavily into security and had a business along the promenade in Blackpool?'

'And, what became of John Ashworth because he could verify your story.' she emphasised.

'Oh, he was last seen panning for gold in Queensland Australia.' he carefully replied, knowing John, until his retirement, worked as a conductor on the tramway in Blackpool.

Harold was finding sleep difficult to achieve that night, and so he got up from his bed and made himself a cup of '*Ovaltine*'; this was when he penned a poem called: "Computerised Witch".

Computerised Witch

There is a Witch who lives in a House

And every night she plays with her mouse

When you hear a very loud scream

You know she's logged on to the Internet screen

She plays with a stick

It's her bundle of Joy

It's just another Ann Summers Toy

She scours the Net for someone to stitch

Or to find another Computerised Witch

Lancaster Castle is a medieval castle in Lancaster in the English county of Lancashire. Its early history is unclear, but may have been founded in the 11th century on the side of a Roman fort overlooking a crossing of the River Lune. In 1164, the Honour of Lancaster, including the castle, came under royal control. In 1322 and 1389 the Scots invaded England, progressing as far as Lancaster and damaging the castle. It was not to see military action again until the English Civil War. The castle was first used as a prison in 1196 although this aspect became more important during the English Civil War.

The castle buildings are owned by the British sovereign as Duke of Lancaster, which leases part of the structure to Lancashire County Council who operate a Crown Court in part of the building. Until 2011, the majority of the buildings were leased to the Ministry of Justice as Her Majesty's Prison Lancaster. The Castle was returned to the Duchy's ownership by the Ministry of Justice in 2011.

In 79 AD, a Roman fort was built on a hill commanding a crossing over the River Lune.

Little is known about Lancaster between the end of the Roman occupation of England in the early 5th century and the Norman Conquest in the late 11th century. The layout of the town was influenced by the Roman fort and the associated civilian settlement; the main road through the town was the route that led east from the fort. After the Norman Conquest in the second half of the 11th century, Lancaster was part of the Earldom of Northumbria; it was claimed by the kings of England and Scotland. In 1092, William II established a permanent border with Scotland further to the north by capturing Carlisle. Lancaster castle still has a bin from the Roman times on site. It is a strategic location. The castle is the oldest standing building in Lancaster and one of the most important. The history of the structure is uncertain. This is partially due to its former use as a prison, which has prevented extensive archaeological investigation.

As there are no contemporary documents recording the foundation of the castle, it is uncertain when and by whom it was started, but it is supposed that Roger de Poitou, the Norman lord in control of the

Honour of Lancaster, was responsible. If it was Roger who began construction, the structure would have been built of timber, probably incorporating the earthworks of the Roman fort into its defences. The form of the original castle is unknown. There is no trace of a motte, a mote, so it may have been a ring work, a circular defended enclosure.

Roger de Poitou fled England in 1102 after participating in a failed rebellion against the new king Henry I. As a result, the king confiscated the Honour of Lancaster, which included the castle. The Honour changed hands several times. Henry granted it to Stephen of Blois, his nephew and later king. When the Anarchy erupted in 1139, a civil war between Stephen and Empress Matilda for the English throne, the area was in turmoil. Stephen secured his northern frontier by allowing David I of Scotland to occupy the Honour in 1141.

It is possible that David refortified the castle at this time. Due to a lack of investigation, there is little evidence to suggest additions to Lancaster in the mid-12th century. However, the uncertain construction date of the keep means that the King of Scotland could have been responsible for building it. The war came to an end in 1153. It was agreed that after Stephen died, he would be succeeded by Henry Plantagenet (later King Henry II), Matilda's son. Part of the agreement was that the King of Scotland would relinquish the Honour of Lancaster, which would be held by William, Stephen's son. After William's death in 1164, the Honour of Lancaster again came under royal control when Henry II gained possession of the Honour.

On the death of Henry II, the Honour passed to his son, Richard the Lionheart, who gave it to his brother, Prince John, in the hope of securing his loyalty. One of the functions castles served was as a prison; the first record of the castle being used in this way was in 1196, although the role became much more important after the English Civil War. Since the 12th century, the monarch appointed a sheriff to maintain the peace in Lancashire, a role usually filled by the duke and based at the castle. In the late 12th and early 13th century, many timber castles founded during the Norman Conquest were rebuilt in stone. Lancaster was one such castle. Building in stone was expensive and time-consuming. For example, the late 12th century stone keep at Perveril Castle in Derbyshire cost around £200, although something on a much larger scale, such as the vast Château Gaillard cost an estimated £15,000 to £20,000 and took several years to complete. For many castles, the expenditure is unknown. However, work on royal castles was often documented in Pipe Rolls, which began in 1155. The Rolls show that John spent over £630 on digging a ditch outside the south and west walls, and for the construction of "the King's lodgings". This probably referred to what is known as Adrian's Tower. His successor, Henry II also spent large sums on Lancaster; £200 in 1243 and £250 in 1254 for work on the gatehouse and creating a stone curtain wall.

For the next 150 years, there is no record of building work, although accounts are incomplete. The Well Tower is thought to date from the early 14th century. If there was no work on the castle, this may indicate that it was not important enough to warrant expenditure beyond upkeep, as Lancaster was not near a border. Though the region was generally peaceful, the Scots invaded in 1322 and 1389, reaching Lancaster and damaging the castle. The holdings of the Duchy of Lancaster extended beyond the county, and Lancaster was not especially important. However, when Henry Duke of Lancaster ascended the throne as King Henry IV in 1399, he almost immediately began adding the monumental gatehouse. A further devastation of the town, as inflicted in 1389 would have been an embarrassment for the new king; his expensive programme of building at the castle helped protect against this. The gatehouse Henry replaced was probably a simple structure, no more than a passage between two towers, but once complete, it rivalled the keep as the strongest part of the castle. Records show that between 1402 and 1422, the year Henry IV died, over £2,500 was spent in building work. While most of this sum would have been spent on the gatehouse, some may have been used to make alterations to the top storey of the keep. Since then, the castle has remained in the ownership of the Crown.

After the Scottish invasion of 1389, Lancaster saw no further military action until the English Civil War. A survey in 1578 led to repairs to the keep costing £235. With the threat of a Spanish invasion, the castle was strengthened in 1585. After Elizabeth I was excommunicated in 1570, she retaliated by declaring Roman Catholic priests guilty of high treason. Any discovered in Lancashire were taken to Lancaster Castle for trial. During the period 1584-1646 fifteen Catholics were executed in Lancaster for their faith. The notorious Pendle witches trial took place at Lancaster Castle in 1612.

At the outbreak of the Civil War Lancaster was lightly garrisoned. A small Parliamentarian force captured the castle in February 1643, established a garrison and set about building earthworks around the approaches to the town. In response, the Royalists dispatched an army to retake Lancaster. The outer defences fell in March; a siege of the castle lasted just two days as Parliamentarian reinforcements were heading to Lancaster from Preston. The Royalists unsuccessfully tried to recapture Lancaster in April and again in June; the town and castle remained under Parliament's control until the end of the war. Orders were given that "all the walls about (Lancaster Castle) should be thrown down". The instruction was not followed, and in August 1648 the town withstood a siege from the Royalist Duke of Hamilton who led an army south from Scotland. King Charles I was executed in January 1649 and shortly after Parliament again ordered the slighting of the castle, apart from the buildings necessary for administration and use as a county gaol. The monarchy was restored in 1660 and Charles II visited Lancaster on 12 August and released all the prisoners held in the castle. Lancashire's High Sheriff and Justices of the Peace petitioned the king to repair the castle. The buildings were surveyed and repair work estimated at £1,957. After the slighting of the castle, including the demolition of the Well Tower, it was militarily redundant.

In 1554, martyr, George Marsh, was held at the castle before standing trial at Chester Cathedral. Some Quakers, including in 1660 George Fox, were held at the castle for being politically dangerous. County gaols, such as this one, were intended to hold prisoners for short periods immediately before trial. The castle also served as a debtors' prison. In the 18th century it became more common for county gaols to hold longer-term prisoners; as a result they began to suffer from overcrowding.

Prison reformer John Howard (1726-1790) visited Lancaster in 1776 and noted the conditions in the prison. His efforts to instigate reform led to prisoners in gaols throughout the country being separated by gender and category of their crime. Improvements were also made to sanitation; in the 18th century more people died from gaol fever than by hanging. In the last two decades of the century, around £30,000 was spent rebuilding Lancaster's county gaol. Architect Thomas Harrison was commissioned to complete the work. Under his auspices, the Gaoler's House was built in 1788 in a Gothic style. Separate prisons were built for men and women.

The Shire Hall and Crown Court were complete by 1798. Harrison had to divide his time, between Lancaster and designing and building Chester Castle's Shire Hall and Courts; work at Lancaster slowed, partly because of dwindling funds due to war with France, and Harrison was released from the work as the Justices of the Peace felt it was taking too long. The artist Robert Freebairn was paid £500 to paint twelve watercolours of the work in 1800 to be presented to the Duke of Lancaster, King George III. In 1802 the castle received more funding and Joseph Gandy was commissioned to complete the interiors of the Shire Hall and Crown Court.

Those sentenced to death before 1800 at the castle were usually taken to Lancaster Moor, near where the Ashton Memorial now stands, to be hanged. After the Georgian remodelling of the castle, it was decided it would be more convenient to perform executions nearer the castle. The spot chosen became known as Hanging Corner. Lancaster has a reputation as the court that sentenced more people to death than any other in England. This is partly because until 1835 Lancaster Castle was the only Assize Court in the entire county and covered rapidly growing industrial centres including Manchester and Liverpool. Between 1782 and 1865, around 265 people were hanged at Lancaster; the executions were frequently attended by thousands of people crowded into the churchyard. The Capital Punishment Amendment Act 1868 ended public executions, requiring that criminals be put to death in private, after which 6 executions were performed inside the castle, at first from the Chapel steps then later in a purpose-built execution shed, on the inside of the wall of Hanging Corner. This shed remained until the mid-20th Century, allegedly still containing the Gallows. The last execution (of Thomas Rawcliffe, wife-murderer) at Lancaster took place in 1910. The prison closed in 1916 due to a national decrease in the number of prisoners, although for part of the First World War it held German civilians and prisoners of war.

Between 1931 and 1937 the castle was used by the county council to train police officers. Lancaster was once again designated for use as a prison from 1954 onwards when the council leased the castle to the Home Office. The last Assizes were held at Lancaster in 1972. As the court and prison were so close, and contained within the castle walls, Lancaster was used for high-security trials.

The castle formally opened as a prison in 1955, becoming a Category C prison for male inmates, and a crown court. In July 2010 the Ministry of Justice announced it was intending to close it, stating it was outdated and costly. The prison closure was confirmed for March 2011.

The crown court continues to be located at the castle. Closure of the prison will eventually allow the castle to be opened to visitors and tourists as a permanent attraction. In the meantime, while access to the keep, towers, battlements and dungeons is currently denied to visitors, the castle operates limited guided tours seven days a week. The Castle Courtyard opened to the public 7 days a week in May 2013 and now has a café called NICE @ The Castle and regular events now take place every month.

To commemorate the 400th anniversary of the trials of the Pendle witches, a new long-distance walking route called the Lancashire Witches Walk has been created. Ten *tercet* way markers, designed by Stephen Raw, each described with a verse of a poem by the Scottish Contemporary Poet Lauriat of the United Kingdom, Carol Ann Duffy have been installed along the route, with the tenth located at the castle, to mark the end-point. She was preceded by Andrew Motion, the controversial Poet Laureate who wrote about the sun, the moon, the stars, the sky and other things of way-out proportions. It was in later years, a modern contemporary poet penned a poem of somewhat notoriety and criticism by the media and the public, only to be rejected by the '*Sunday Times*' newspaper; the poem was called "Words in Motion" by Bernard Doolittle, a controversial poet from Shepherds Bush, in the East End of London and began:

"Words in Motion"
It is time you sat down to go into reverse
And write a few lines which fall into verse
It is time you forgot the sun, the moon and the stars
in the sky
Before the lead in your pencil decides to run dry
It is time you remembered there are readers
out there
Who can't understand your writings and fall
into despair
It is time you called a fork'n knife a knife
And a spade, a *bloomin'* spade
Some may say you've got it made
It is time you began your writings in the sand
And keep to a language we can all understand
It is time, Andrew to put your quill away
To come back some day in another way
When the tide comes into Morecambe Bay
Your words will have been forgotten and all washed away

The keep is the oldest part of Lancaster castle. It is uncertain when the keep was built, although it probably dates back to the 12th century when it was the residence for the lord of the castle – the owner or his representative. In the event of an assault, the keep formed the last line of defence. It is 20 metres (66 ft) high with four storeys; each floor divided into two rooms. The outer wall is 3 metres (9.8 ft) thick; along the exterior are buttresses at each corner and in the middle of each wall. Like most Norman keeps, Lancaster's would have been entered at the floor level. Construction in stone would have been costly and a time-consuming exercise, taking around five years and costing £1.000. The medieval hall stood south-west of the keep and was dismantled in 1796 during the remodelling of the castle. The late 18th- early 19th-century Shire Hall next to the keep is a large ten-side room.

In the south-west corner of the castle is a cylindrical tower names Adrian's Tower from the popular legend that it was built by the Roman Emperor Hadrian. The tower was, however, built in the early 13th century, probably during the reign of King John. Although the exterior was refaced in the 18th century, medieval stonework is visible in the interior.

The main entrance is through a 20 m (66 ft) high gatehouse build at the start of the 15th century. It was instigated by King Henry IV, although legend attributes the work to John of Gaunt, Duke of Lancaster from 1362 to his death in 1399. Two semi-octagonal towers flank a passageway protected by a portcullis. Battlements project over the gatehouse, and would have allowed defenders to rain missiles on attackers immediately below. Above the gate is a niche which would originally have contained a statue of a saint, flanked by a coat of arms of the kings of England. Because of the legend, a statue of John of Gaunt was placed in the empty niche in the 19th century. Three storeys high, the apartment on the ground floor would probably have been used by the Constable of the castle; the two floors above had three rooms each. After the English Civil War, most of the gatehouse rooms were filled with debtors. The sophistication of the gatehouse prompted John Champness who wrote *Lancaster Castle: A Brief History*, to remark "it is perhaps the finest of its date and type in England".

During the Roman era in the 4th century, the fort was surrounded by the "*Wery Wall*" which is believed to translate as the 'green wall'. The wall, described as being a 3m thick 'indestructible mass', with a defensive ditch, now only remains visible on the east slope of Castle Hill. In his book '*The Historic Lands of England*', Sir Bernard Burke suggests the wall may have been visible in more places 100 years prior to his writing in

1849. However, it is unclear where the wall would have been. The remaining *"Wery Wall"* measures 4m x 3m x 3m and consists of only rubble due to the facing stones having been reused elsewhere.

***

The first use of the name *Morecambe* in modern times was by Whitaker in his History of Manchester in 1771, when he refers to the *estuary* of Morecambe. It next appears four years later in '*Antiquities of Furness*' where the bay is described as 'the Bay of Morecambe'.

Chapter Fourteen

"What a difference a day makes, twenty-four little hours, brought the sun and the flowers, where there used to be rain. What a difference a day makes, there's a rainbow before me....." Harold sang before he sat down to indulge in a full-Monty English breakfast to die for, consisting of coffee, his usual pile of *'Kellogg's'* cornflakes, a hearty plate of eggs, bacon, fried bread, Italian peeled tomatoes, *'Bury'* black pudding, *'Wall's'* pork and beef sausages and *'Heinz'* baked beans; the feast being followed by another rendition by Harold singing: "Rule Britannia" the traditional tea, toast and *'Robertson's'* marmalade and jam, five Chinese crackers up you arsehole, bang!, bang!, bang!, bang!, bang!, song which doesn't usually go down very well at breakfast time, especially when Mabel tells him to keep his patriotic tones to himself.

'And, how is Dennis Wheatley this morning, you seem to be in good spirits, Harold?'

'Ah, is that a pun, and yes, it makes one feel good to be alive, Mabel.' he said bashing the top of his brown be-speckled boiled egg with an EPNS teaspoon.

'Well, I didn't have a good night's sleep, Harold because I was dreaming about those witches and 'Pam's People', the wood nymphs you were telling me about in the early hours of this morning.'

'Don't you mean 'Peter Pan' Mabel? He could be another one of those living at number nineteen. And I wouldn't worry about Elizabeth Wall and her "Come Dancing" team, because all but one came to a sticky end when they went on a Premier Coach trip from Preston to Cleethorpes. It was supposed to be a mystery tour, but that was before the bus turned over somewhere between Halifax and Bradford and ended up in a canal.'

'Oh, how awful.' Mabel said, feeling sorry for some of the dubious passengers, whose obituaries were printed that night in the Leeds and Lancashire Evening Post.

'I would say good riddance to bad rubbish.' Harold said when he thought differently about changing his religion to the Roman Catholic Church.

'You know,' Mabel put in 'the French trouble-maker, Joan of Arc? She was convicted of heresy in March 1431, and was burned at the stake by the English in the French City of Rouen to the north of Paris.' she said with an expression of deep academic thoughtfulness which she acquired by having attended a Secondary Modern School near Southport, Lancashire, where the emphasis was to teach its pupils elocution, and to turn them into plastic Scousers. She was continually saying to Harold, that speaking is a skill which one learns from a very early age; the impressionable, albeit obvious words of wisdom falling instantaneously on deaf ears when he retaliated in sending up his Lancastrian mother tongue. 'These here eggs, these here here, are fresh from farm *tha* knows.'

'Do you realize that when I attended Saint Hilda's primary school, I played the part of Dorothy in the "Wizard of Oz"?' Mabel took great pleasure in telling him.

'And, do you know when I attended Kirkham's Academy of fine Arts, I had the pleasure one Christmas to be underneath a blanket playing the arse-end of a camel; it was supposed to be a dormitory, a double-humper, and I can also recall a girl called Sheila being at the front. The headmaster was scratching his head for weeks wondering why the camel continued to walk backwards onto the stage.' Harold so eloquently and so graphically explained. Oh, yes, you are so knowledgeable Mabel, and, I too can remember Joan of Arc very well. She was the one with the short hair, dressed like a man, carried a flick-knife around inside her back pocket, chain-smoked *'Gallouse'* cigarettes and introduced cannabis to Saint Quentin in Northern France; she was also a forerunner of the National Front.'

'Do you know, Harold, you are doing remarkably well to remember that far back; people usually have trouble remembering anniversary cards.' she said reminding him of his forgetfulness. 'And, by the way, the camel was supposed to be a dromedary and not a dormitory; also, it has only got one hump and not two.'

'Well, it must have been my lucky day, and I'm so sorry I forgot to buy you an anniversary card Mabel, it just by-passed my brain and I forgot.'

'You forgot, you forgot, well you can jolly-well make up for your misgivings today by buying me an eighteen-carat lucky charm bracelet from the proceeds of your horse racing winnings which you won on Saturday afternoon; you forgot to tell me about that as well, didn't you, Harold.'

'Well, I was going to keep it as a surprise, Mabel.'

'Just what were you going to keep as a surprise, Harold; the money, or to tell me, once I had discovered it underneath your pillow, that it was there purely and simply to bribe a tooth fairy to supply you with a new set of false teeth to replace the ones you are about to lose.'

'Well, if push comes to shove, I can always use my temporary ones.' Harold said saddened by the fact he had been ripped off by his son-in-law to practice and enhance his dental skills. 'You're not seriously thinking of doing a round trip to get to Morecambe this morning, are you Mabel, because I've just heard the weather forecast on the local radio, and it doesn't sound too great.' he said trying to persuade her not to be so frugal with the orange juice, but then, to go easy on the other kind of juice namely, the high-octane.

'But, of course, Harold, I want to see where this place is you were telling me about last night; somewhere between Longridge and Ribchester you said, and it's not going to snow is it because I will just have to take your mother's mink fur coat out from the attic, you know the one minus a sleeve and a belt to match.'

'I will never in this life be able to live this one down, will I Mabel? I couldn't have let the side down by not wearing a Davy Crocket outfit.'

'It is as wonder you are still alive, having cut-up your mother's fur coat to make a hat which looked like a dead racoon.' she said with great delight.

'The weather will just be a few showers, that's all, my dear, especially in the North of England, and as you know, Mabel, it always rains in Morecambe no matter what time of the year you visit. Can you remember,' continuing to chunter on, 'when we visited Morecambe Bay all those years ago when the Hispaniola, a replica of a Spanish Galleon was moored next to the promenade? It was featured in the television series, "The Buccaneers" starring the late, Robert Shaw; he was good, he was, especially when he hollered from the poop-deck, 'A hoi there mi hearties, where's mi Buccaneers? This was when several of my mates and I would shout in front of the telly, 'They are on your bucking head.'

'Now, now, Harold, we don't want any of your so-called Freckletonian humour to disgrace our kitchen table.'

'Television was good in those days, wasn't it Mabel? I used to come home from school and watch, "I Love Lucy" starring the late, Lucile Ball and her long-suffering husband Desi Arnez; according to my brother-in-law, Bing Crosby, who is still, just about alive, tells me the television series is still doing the rounds in between watching, "Mr Ed" and "Just Dennis". Billy once told me on the phone he stayed in a business hotel in New Jersey and was advised not to turn the television off because it would interfere with the hotel's network system. The problems continued when he began to bray in the middle of the night caused by the continual sound of a horse galloping through his bedroom.'

'Well, he should have been more careful which stable he slept in, after all, he is from California.' she inconsiderately replied.

"My yesterdays were blue, dear; today I'm as bright as you dear; my lonely nights are through dear, since you said you were mine. Since that moment of bliss, that thrilling kiss it's heaven with you, when you find romance on the menu....." Harold continued to sing softly before opening a window to allow healthy farmyard inhalants to penetrate and circulate around the room; the breathtaking smell of recently dug manure, reminding him of ploughman's lunches and the days he used to muck-out at Smith's Equestrian Centre in Freckleton.

"Romance on the menu", 'I should be so lucky.' Mabel said brushing up the greasy breadcrumbs which were scattered on her much-cherished Sicilian white cotton tablecloth she bought during a visit to Catania, and then, by using a '*Haze*' lavender air-freshener, she attempted to decontaminate the room of its impurities which were not dissimilar to Ziklon 'B' camping gaz. 'Do you mean along with the '*Wall's*' pork and beef sausages, and the '*Bury*' black pudding?' she added, refusing to believe a village could be capable of creating such a smell which wouldn't be out of place situated next to the Chemical and Biological Warfare

Centre at Porton Down in Wiltshire.

'Yes, if you want, Mabel.' Harold replied giving her the impression he was only interested in which race horse was going to win the three-thirty at Haydock Park.

'Give me a sign God because I'm just about to hit him with a dustpan and brush.' she said looking down at Prince, the dog, who was also shaking his head because of him having to experience the weekly intake of highly inflammable toxic nerve-agents before being taken for his early morning walk to the village green.

'I thought I saw a flash of streak lightening in the distance, Mabel; it could be the sign you are looking for?'

'You needn't worry, Harold we are still going to Lancaster and Morecambe, via the Ribblesdale Valley in Yorkshire, and that is final; and by the way the flash you saw was either the seven-thirty business flight from Warton to Munich or Caroline Cartwright getting out from her bed.'

'I've got a good joke for you Mabel.' he said without hesitation.

'Come on let's hear it, because you are going to tell my anyway.' she replied.

'Okay, here goes.' Harold said with great enthusiasm. 'What do you call a sexy biscuit?'

'Go on, Harold, surprise me.'

'Randy Crawford.' was his reply.

'Do you know Harold; I wouldn't give up your daytime job if I were you.'

'But, I haven't got a daytime job anymore, Mabel.'

'That's what you think; you can start by washing up all these dishes and making a fresh pot of tea.'

'Bloody hell, what have I done to deserve all of this?'

***

The Trough of Bowland, Lancashire

It was Harold's turn to drive the shiny-black Ford Môndial 1.8 litre motorcar through the vast expanse of nothingness which belongs predominantly to the Duke of Westminster, the County Palatine, and the Duchy of Lancaster. His private number plates HAR 151X which meant a great deal to him and sod-all to anyone else, were displayed gracefully along with a GB sticker just in case they got lost in what seemed to be tundra of overgrowth, trees and forests, and unlike his first visit to these wide open spaces he once thought of as being at the foot of the Himalayas, the climate was far more friendly, and as opposed to the harsh wintery conditions of 1962, the sun was actually shining casting shadows underneath the hedge rows by the side of the road as they headed towards the quaint picturesque villages of Longridge and Chipping after calling in at the 16th century stately home called Samlebury Hall.

'I've made some chicken and stuffing sandwiches and a flask of coffee just in case we become thirsty and peckish.' Mabel said as they listened to 'Radio Preston' on their mobile quadraphonic sound system which has a graphic equalizer as the one installed at The Royal Albert Hall in London when they record all the hoots and toots during "The last night at the Proms". 'I have also brought our Rob Roy tartan travelling blanket to sit on should we decide to have lunch by the river, and that will be fun won't it?' she added.

'Yes, Mabel, we could have a paddle in one of the streams, tickle some trout, and have them on our sandwiches with *'Hot Coleman's Mustard'*; it will make a change from chicken and stuffing, and tell me, when is the carcass from the 'bird in the bag' you purchased from Morrison's last Friday going to end its days inside a dustbin.'

'That's the trouble with you Harold; you are so ungrateful and not satisfied unless you find something to moan about.'

'I know a good joke, Mabel; do you want to hear it?'

'Go on Harold, if it makes you feel any better.'

'Do you know how to get in touch with the Scottish parliamentarian, Alex Salmon?'

'I don't know Harold; how do you get in touch with Salmon?'

'I don't know either, but I'm sure tickling trout is easier.'

'I'm sure the Scottish Nationalist Party would love to hear that.' she said, hoping Harold would heed her warning before he ended up with a set of bagpipes dangling from the seat of his trousers.

'And, tell me, Mabel, how you get in touch with Nicola Sturgeon?'

'That's two jokes, Harold, and is today going to be the start of an 'I hate Scotland week'?'

'No, no, Mabel; the Scots can't help the way they are; it was only last week I was saying to a guy in the 'Coach and Horses', no wonder Hadrian, the Roman Emperor installed a new governor to build a wall extending along the Cheviot Hills from the north of Carlisle to Wallsend, near to Berwick-upon-Tweed in Northumbria; it was to stop them circulating Scottish five-pound notes south of the border, and also to protect barbaric Glaswegians against English prospectors and Geordie transvestites who strayed over the wall.'

'You do talk a load of garbage, Harold, and just how *do* you get through to Sturgeon?'

'It is with great difficulty.' he replied.

'Quite honestly, Harold, you do take the biscuit.'

'So long as they are not those dried-up round things in a tartan box which taste like lard, and those finger shaped biscuits that look like a Neolithic stone pillar at Stonehenge.'

'Tell me Harold, are we getting any closer to Longridge because I would like you to stop and then we could have a pot of tea and some Chorley cake in one of those quaint little tea shops you keep on telling me about.'

'We have just driven through it and what you can see on the left is the precipitous Parlick Pike, the Trough's most prominent feature John and I climbed all those years ago.'

'It is so precipitous, Harold, I can't see the damned thing.'

'Well, poke your head out through the window and then look upwards towards the sky.'

'I've seen bigger slag heaps between Wigan and Warrington.' Mabel disclosed, as the car moved forward into happier territory.

'I can remember when we went on a Shearing's Coach Holiday to Bad Aachen in the Federal Republic of Western Germany, Mabel, and you said the Eifel Mountains, near to the Belgium border, looked similar to sleeping policemen; at least in Britain, we still have our traditional red telephone and letter boxes by the side of the road and not those ugly Second World War tank traps which look like huge pieces of concrete *'Toblerone'*. Remember the time when we went on an excursion to the *'Kuckucksuhrdorf '*, the cuckoo clock village of *Monchau*, near to the four borders, incorporating, Germany, Holland, Belgium and Pakistan; all of which were selling *Bratwurst, Bockwurst, Pommes frites, potato sticks, chips;* whatever you want to call them, also *Pork Cutlet, Sauerkraut* and *Kartoffeln Salat*, at four different prices and units of Mickey Mouse currency; the Pakistani, as I can recall was doing exceptionally well, selling brandy snaps, ginger men biscuits and brown plastic imitation clocks which came complete with the irritating sound of a cuckoo that drove us mad every fifteen minutes. I can also remember the one we bought from him, it was placed on the wall next to the front door at number twenty-three, and every time someone came into the house, the cuckoo fell onto the floor; poor Gretchen, who looked like a member of the Hitler Youth, reminiscent to the "Sound of Music" was sitting on a swing, going up and down on a spring when she fell off and suffered badly with a sore head.'

'Yes, Harold, I do realize the clock was quite expensive and cost a few Deutschmarks and it wasn't a good purchase, especially when Prince finally plucked up the courage to step on it to end its days inside a rubbish sack.'

'You know, Mabel, I used to work for BAE Systems, I didn't bloody well own it; these Pakistanis can fall to a bottomless pit and still come up smelling of roses.'

'Oh, and by the way, Indians and Pakistanis don't eat pork, it's against their religion.' Mabel said, having just read, albeit somewhat belatedly, the much talked about Hindu sex manual, the "Karma Sutra".

'Ah, but when we visited France last year, Mabel, how can you explain that when we went into a Turkish kebab house in Trouville, they had pork merrily going around on a rotisserie for fun; they are supposed to be a Muslim race of people, aren't they?'

'I don't suppose it was much fun for the pig, Harold.'

'No, I don't suppose it was Mabel, especially on the top of two scoops of *Calvados* brandy ice cream and a *pain au raison*; a circular cake which look like a glazed Catherine wheel with sultanas, custard and royal icing in the middle.'

'Well, I was hungry Harold; the Continental breakfast we had in the so-called, welcoming *'Bienvenue Hotel'* in Deauville, left a lot to be desired because I don't call a thimble-full of orange juice, a rubber *croissant*, and a *baguette* similar to an unexploded Scapa Flow Bay torpedo, conducive to trudging around a casino holding a bucket-full of twenty cent pieces and a Mars Bar stuck in my mouth.'

'You could have had a couple of boiled eggs, my dear.'

'I used to work for 'Lewis's department store in Liverpool, I didn't own it, Harold.'

'We will shortly be going past Grey Squirrels Lane, Mabel, and I don't think it would be a good idea to call in for a cup of tea, or to indulge in a magic mushroom sandwich.' Harold said sarcastically, pointing out just exactly where the lane was on his GPS system which could well have alleviated a problem some fifty-four years previously had they been in existence; which reminded him about the poem called 'Poles Apart'.

Poles Apart
An explorer arrived at a pole one day
And found his compass going around
the other way
He had a discussion with a friend
And said they had been dropped off
at the wrong end
He then made a quick decision
to end the entire expedition

Harold put his foot down firmly on the accelerator pedal to enable the throttle to be opened up and to allow the car to move forward at a much greater speed.

'I want to go and have a look at this place, Harold, and because I have heard so much about it, curiosity is killing the cat.'

'There was a black cat that just crossed the road.' he said.

'Well, it is a wonder it's still alive, the speed you are driving.'

The car entered Grey Squirrels Lane drudgingly; the sound of the tyres crunching on the top of a gravel surface until it came to halt outside of a cottage bearing the house number and name, No 3 "Spinning Wheel Hollow" which used to belong to the mad woman herself; the notorious Elizabeth Wall. Harold, who was standing by the side of Mabel, knocked on the door to be greeted by an elderly woman who introduced herself as Bridgette Hubbard, a sister of the witch, Louise Hubbard and the beneficiary to Elizabeth Walls estate.

Having clocked a cauldron and a broomstick in the front garden, Mabel decided not to take up Hubbard's offer of going inside to enjoy a fresh pot of tea and a slice of her seed cake.

'Show me where you both carved your names on the evergreen tree, Harold.' she curiously asked.

It was when they reached the dark and dense forest, Harold pointed out to Mabel the initials which had been firmly embedded in the trunk of the tree.

'Those have just been recently carved into the wood, Harold; like today for instance.'

'There is something strange going on around here, Mabel; let's get the hell out of here.' he said as they both hot-footed back to their ever-faithful means of ignition.

Chapter Fifteen

The Ribble Valley; a short distance by car towards Ribchester, in the County Palatine and the Duchy of Lancaster, the Forest of Bowland and beyond

'I know of another good joke, Mabel.' Harold said, steering the car steadily to Frank Sinatra's catchy tune "It's Witchcraft" which was being broadcast softly on Radio Preston as they headed towards the ancient Roman archaeological site in Ribchester.'

'I was told that Angela Rippon had 'G' Plan furniture.' he continued to say. 'I wondered why she walked funny.'

'That sounds like a Morecambe and Wise joke.' Mabel said, knowing he was going to tell her another repetitive joke which was not dissimilar to the first one.'

'Ernie Wise asked Eric Morecambe what is the make of the '*Rollerflex*' camera he had around his neck? To which he replied:

'It's a '*Yamaha*' *moto*.'

'A '*Yamaha moto*'; that's a motorbike.' Ernie said.

'Oh, I've often wondered why the strap keeps breaking.' Eric replied.

'Now, let's get one thing straight, Harold.' Mabel pointed out in all seriousness. 'I didn't come all this way just to hear your silly jokes and to see a pile of rolling stones; I can watch all of this stuff either on television or from our bedroom window in Calder Vale Avenue when Bernadette Cartmell decides to pull her finger out and employs someone reputable to finish building her garage, and I would much rather sit by the river, Harold and have a picnic lunch.'

'You've no culture, Mabel; that's your trouble, and perhaps we can hook the ducks out of the water with a long pole and then look underneath to see if there is a number to win a prize.'

'Maybe, if we had visited Ribchester a couple of months earlier, Harold, we could have joined in with the festive celebrations during the village Club Day, and perhaps afterwards we could have had a paddle in the fort's Roman bath building or taken the opportunity to offload our chicken and stuffing sandwiches inside the marquee at the village tea party.' Mabel said, insisting on putting in the last word.

'There is a pub nearby, it is called the 'Swing Gate' Arms and it's situated in a small village called, Calderstone. The pub, incidentally, is run by one of Preston's local dignitaries, Councillor Tommy Shuttleworth and his wife Elizabeth, a retired school teacher from Leyland. Apparently, the pub has been leased to the family since 'The English Civil War' and by all accounts the building has a notorious history of having witches peering in through the windows and hanging about in the car park.'

'Harold.'

'Yes dear.'

'Shut up, and can we continue with our journey without talking about witches, ghouls, nymphomaniacs, pyromaniacs and cats?'

'I just thought you would be nearer to that overdue cup of tea, Mabel.'

'I think I can wait.' she replied looking at her watch which was reading eleven-thirty precisely.

'Well, here we are at last in the parish of Ribchester.' Harold interrupted. 'And if I'm not mistaken there goes that black cat again, and, unless it has lost its way, I have reason to suspect it might be following us.' he added, hoping the ongoing curiosity would eventually get rid of it once and for all.

'It is possible the cat may have hitched a ride after getting latched on to one of the side door handles of the car, Harold, and Miss Bridgette Hubbard is going to wait until it gets dark, so she can fly around here on her broomstick trying to find it.'

'Are you taking the piss, Mabel, or are you just being your normal self?'

'There you go again, Harold; can't take a joke.'

Harold and Mabel passed by St. Wilfrid's Church which stands by the River Ribble on what was the centre of the Roman fort built by the twentieth Legion. The church is believed to have been founded by St. Wilfrid in the 8th century. Adjoining the church of St. Wilfred's and its tower are the excavated remains of the granaries which belonged to the Roman fort, and near to the church is the refurbished Roman Museum. The museum houses many of the finds from the Roman fort; the most famous find, the Ribchester Helmet. A short distance east of the village is the White Bull pub, a Grade II listed building with its well-known portico supported by two Roman pillars. And behind the pub, are the remains of the Roman baths. And, two miles upstream of Ribchester lies Ribchester Bridge which was rebuilt in the 1770s, after severe flood damaged it; it is interesting to note, however, that the ancient temples in Karnak and Luxor in Egypt were refurbished by the French during the Napoleonic restoration period in 1798. However, it was Percy Atkinson of Accrington who carried out the brickwork on Ribchester Bridge. And, coincidentally, the television personality, engineer, steeple jack and demolition expert, the late Frederick Dibnah MBE, was quoted in saying that it was a "Bridge too Far" when on a Field Day his steamroller plunged side-ways into the River Ribble, caused by a wealthy Anglo-Lancastrian builders merchant, Henry Alty, who removed a pile of stones from the road to enhance his brick collection in Ormskirk.

Ode to the 'Steeple Jack' Fred Dibnah 1938-2004
A rare breed of person
Who can climb up a slope
With an extended ladder and a tight rope
He can abseil down mountains
Without a sound
Then raises a chimney down to the ground
He sets fire to volcanoes and one only knows
They go up in smoke you cannot revoke
In his hat which is kind of flat
He turns around and says: 'did you like that'

There are three public houses in the village; the White Bull, the Black Bull and the Ribchester Arms, as well as a sports and social club and was the working men's club associated with the cotton mills. To satisfy the fifteen-hundred or so people, there is a local Spar shop, which occupies the site once occupied by the Co-Operative store and a tea room.

'I would dearly like to stop and have a cup of tea, Harold,' Mabel said, 'because I'm about to begin spitting feathers because it's so dry in the car.'

'There is a cream tea room on Church Street, it isn't far from here, Mabel; you can have your long-awaited cup of tea there, if it will make you feel any better?'

'You mean the small Spar shop across the road with a Christmas tree depicted on the sign above the door.'

'Oh, no, it has changed hands again, and one can't win a bloody coconut around here.' he said, shaking his head in total disbelief.

'Well, we'll just have to sit down by the river and hook one or two of those ducks from out of the water, won't we Harold? 'And,' she added, 'how do you know it has changed hands again, Harold if the last time you were stomping around these parts was in the early sixties?' Mabel inquisitively asked.

'I visited Ribchester when I was at school; it was part of our history lessons.' he replied, knowing the story was totally untrue. Harold had failed to reveal that when he and his friend Roy met two girls on the dance floor at a Rivington Barn hoedown, they were both stood-up because of them turning up in a British racing-green Reliant three-wheel jalopy at their homes on Preston Road and Water Street in Ribchester.

'I suppose, you'll be telling me next, Harold, that those initials which are carved into the tree were put there by the Roman Emperor, Hadrian himself, and like you Harold, the Romans and Freckletonians' certainly knew how to put it about.'

'It's funny you should say that, Mabel because in September 1993, the television "*Time Team*" carried out a three-day geo-physical excavation of the Roman fort in Ribchester, only to find a Japanese *Pot Noodle*, three discarded *Mars Bar* wrappers and an empty bottle of *Lucozade*.'

'Well, they must have been ravenous after doing all that unearthing and digging.' she said in all seriousness.

'Who was ravenous, the Romans or Sir Tony Robinson and his "*Time Team*".' Harold asked wittily when he compared Robinson to Baldrick in the long-suffering television series "Black Adder".

'I wonder why there are so many Italian businesses in Britain.' she curiously asked.

'The reason why Great Britain has so many Italian restaurants, ice cream parlours and coffee shops, Mabel, is because of the straggling legionnaires who were at the tail end of the Roman army returning to their homeland; they thought they were still in Portofino and Milano eating choc-ices and '*Ninety-Nine*' chocolate ice cream cornets by the hundreds and thousands; the rear echelon using Blackpool as a rest and recuperation resort before transforming themselves into pyromaniacs, setting fire to towns and villages in England which they had painstakingly constructed in the first place.'

'Do you know, Harold, you are so knowledgeable, I didn't know Blackpool and Spar shops were in existence all those years ago.'

'Oh, yes, that's why they have so many Italian football supporters in the town; the restaurants spend more time watching Blackpool Football Club 'The Tangerines', than cooking macaroni and spaghetti.'

'It is a good thing, the Indians and Pakistanis are not in evidence around these parts as well, Harold, because Ribchester would have another Field Day.' she said, looking into the Spar shop from the car to see who was in charge.

'Well, with all the trees and the brown coloured bracken, it would be nigh impossible to see them.' he replied.

'Who said, "I can't see the forest for the trees, and I can't see the water for the wells" Mabel asked trying to throw some light on to a much-darkened subject.

'It sounds like one of those unfortunate persons who stand outside the restaurant at BAE Systems in Warton holding on to a collecting box which is suspended by a string around his neck.' he said, sympathetically.

'You know, Harold, it is a great pity and a discredit to our so-called caring society, that the management couldn't write the Society for the Blind a generous cheque, instead of them having to stand outside in the cold.'

'I agree Mabel, "No one's as blind as those who cannot see", and the management at BAE Systems cannot see one inch in front of their faces and that is a truism, also a fact, but alas, principles wouldn't have given us a substantial pension.'

'At least we are in agreement with something, Harold, and it is thanks to the poet, philosopher and play write, George Bernard Shaw, that we are blessed with a whole new meaning to life.' she went on.

'Tell me Mabel, are you going a bit funny, or what; it is thanks to the Chief Executive of BAE Systems that we both enjoy a good lifestyle in our retirement.'

'Here we go again, no morals, no ethics and a series of double standards.' she said.

It was when Harold was parking the car in front of the White Bull pub in Church Street, a woman poked her head inside the vehicle and asked Harold if he was lost. The woman, who had distinctive features, striking red hair and a prominent duelling scar down one side of her face, was called Patricia Duckworth, the girl he once knew from way back in the sixties. And, standing a few paces behind her was Annie Pickering, her friend and partner who at the hoedown had a bent for short haircuts and dancing alone around her handbag. After convincing Patricia Duckworth that they weren't lost and Harold made it quite clear that he needed to find a public convenience rather quickly, she said the pub had been closed for some time and pointed in the direction of the nearby hostelry, the Black Bull, silhouetted at night by the dark and menacing skyline of Pendle Hill in the far distance.

'Come on let's get the hell out of here,' Harold said with the aim of putting his foot down firmly on the floor to enable the accelerator pedal to open up the throttle once more to induce a maximum speed greater than was achieved by Sir Donald Campbell's 'Bluebird'.

Which is Which?
To which of these two whiches are
Whiches with which
You compare all the which-ways
And decide which is which
You choose which one
Whichever you glean
You'll find all the answers in a 'Witch' Magazine

'What is this I can see on the left-hand side of the road?' Mabel asked, knowing exactly what the building was.

'My, it's an Indian restaurant; well I never.' Harold replied, taking his eyes off the road for a second to glance up and see a glitzy sign pulsating rapidly above the facia calling it the 'Taj Mahal'; the radiation resembling a slot-machine arcade on Battersea funfair. 'I told you, they get everywhere, and I bet if we were to visit Sherwood Forrest in Nottingham, they would be hanging around there as well, possibly underneath "Ye Old Oak Tree" waiting for a tourist to come along and buy a plastic cuckoo clock.'

Harold continued to drive along the top roads towards Lancaster and Morecambe and this was when he rendered a few lines to Mabel, which is called "Robin Hood" and begins:

'Robin Hood'
Robin Hood took off his boot
He had some trouble with his foot
Under an 'Oak Tree' it was a disaster
When he tried to put on a corn plaster

'Well, that was very interesting, Harold; quite refreshing, and talking about refreshments, how about this one?' she added.

I was standing underneath an evergreen tree
Still waiting for that cup of tea
I will put this into some kind of common language
When are we going to eat that bloody sandwich?

'That was very good Mabel, you could impress the Women's Institute in Freckleton by taking poetry up as a hobby; you are the only woman I know who can make a bunch of dirty carrots sound like poetry.'

And what about these chicken and stuffing sandwiches, Harold?'

'What about them?'

'I can see us sitting and having our lunch on the promenade in

Morecambe.' she said looking back at a woman who was busy scratching her head as if she had company.

'Well, that's not such a bad thing; we have done that before Mabel.'

'I wonder if those ham, cheese and '*Branson*' pickle sandwiches we threw into a litter bin several years ago are still there, Harold, and they, like us, are probably still waiting for the tide to come in.' she said, clocking a speedometer which was reading one hundred and twenty-five miles an hour.

***

Morecambe bay the same afternoon

'Nice, here, isn't it, Harold?' Mabel said, as they sat together on a seat facing the sea and discovering the Lake District once again; its mountainous terrain dominating the skyline in the far distance. She dispensed the 'Maxwell House' instant coffee with great reverence from a flask into two plastic cups, one smaller than the other before asking, who was the man she could see doing a silly dance on the promenade facing the sea? And was he mad? she went on.

'That my dearest, was one of Britain's finest comedians, you know the two jokes about Angela Rippon and the '*Rollerflex*' camera?' he said, unintentionally repeating himself from earlier that morning.

'Harold, please don't wind me up.'

'Is that what you call a pun?' Harold said before taking a triangular-shaped sandwich from out of a plastic '*Tupperware*' box; the '*Coleman's*' mustard looking like the two double yellow lines in the road.

'I am going to get "The Band and Drums of the Royal Marines" to beat the retreat when we open the box of sandwiches,' Mabel suggested, 'or maybe phone George to drop into Morecambe by parachute, but on the other hand, I don't think Sainsbury's are ready to turn another one of their car parks into another drop-zone.

Near to the sea in Morecambe Bay is a statue dedicated to the late Eric Morecambe, the television comedian, and near to the promenade is the Morecambe and Heysham War Memorial which commemorates the men of the town who lost their lives in the two world wars and the Korean

War.

Most importantly, according to some, is Morecambe F.C. (known as 'the Shrimps'), the leading local football club, and on 20 May 2007 won the Conference National playoffs to earn promotion to the Football League for the first time in their history. It was during the 2009-10 season the team moved from its Christie Park ground to a brand new home, the Globe Arena. The old ground was demolished to make way for another Sainsbury's supermarket.

Morecambe once boasted two fairgrounds: a small one to the north of the railway station, which closed down in the 1980s and a larger one to the south of the station, which ultimately became 'Frontierland' and closed in 1999. The only remaining landmark on the site is the Polo Tower, left standing only because of the contract for the phone mast on top.

'And, I wonder if Terry Yuki, the ex-Japanese kamikaze pilot, entertainer and Jerry Lewis look-alike comedian, is still stomping around these parts since the closure of Middleton Towers Holiday Camp?' Mabel asked when she spotted a 'Sushi Sue' restaurant by the side of a road where Harold had parked the car on top of two double yellow lines.

'I shouldn't imagine so, my dear, he would be well into his nineties by now; rumour has it he fell over on the deck of a Japanese aircraft carrier in December 1941 after drinking several glasses of Saki, rice wine and was unable to crash his aeroplane into an active volcano in Hawaii.' Harold replied, feeling genuinely sorry for the short-sighted aviator who would insist in falling off the 'Astra' theatre stage during his act on cabaret night. 'And, another part of his Jerry Lewis impressions was to sharpen pencils with a Samurai sword when he took part in the bathing beauty competition; I can remember his eyesight was so bad he fell into the swimming pool after cutting his finger.'

'Do you mean he was gay?' Mabel asked.

'No he was one of the judges, and the final straw was when a tasty American head-dipper from Texas won the pageant wearing Stars and Stripes, her swimwear outfit; I suppose it could have been worse if one of those innocent looking day-trippers from Bradford believed a 'Matt Jolly'

Holiday at Middleton Towers would bring a glimmer of light back to their dark and dismal lives should one of them have won the competition; and for the winner of this most prestigious social event, which was on a par with the Cannes Film Festival, it would be back to wearing a turban in the cotton mill the following day.

'But, Indian women don't wear turbans, Harold; Beryl Patel doesn't.' Mabel emphatically disclosed.

'Who is talking about Indian women, and especially Beryl Patel, who is only interested in winning at cards on Monday mornings; in those days all the women in the North of England, and that little place to the east of Skipton wore pinafores and turbans and they weren't happy unless they had a mop and a bucket to keep them company.'

'Do you know, Harold, you are really beginning to get up my nose.'

'Well, if I do, Mabel, I shall certainly need a brush.'

Chapter Sixteen

Calling in at Lancaster Castle on the way home was the last bewitching point for nine of the accused Pendle witches who were tried at the Lancaster Assizes between 18-19th August 1612 and, subsequently hanged on Gallows Hill in Lancaster during the same month.

'Well here we are again, happy as can be, all good fun and jolly good company.' Harold said in a semi-melodious tone of voice.

'Oh, look Harold, the castle now has a café where we could have something to eat and drink in the coffee shop; I would much prefer to get my lips around an ice cream cornet, and I bet it's Italian.'

'Don't be silly Mabel; everything around here either belongs to Lancaster Borough Council, the Duke of Westminster or Her Royal Highness Queen Elizabeth II.'

'I thought Giovanni Zaveroni is a Latin name, Harold; it just goes to show how wrong folks can be.'

'This part of the castle, in particular, my dear, is the hanging shed which epitomizes its dark medieval past; criminals who were found guilty at the Assizes went to their deaths through one door and came out of the other inside a metal box; the judges obviously thought that wooden coffins were far too good for them, and as for the witches, it would be more difficult for them to escape after taking the fall.'

'How awful, Harold, it was absolutely barbaric in those days, wasn't it?'

'Now, don't you go feeling sorry for those witches, Mabel, some of them would stitch you up and put you into a cauldron just as soon as look at you; I'm afraid evil flourished here, and Lancaster Gaol was known as here today and gone tomorrow.' he added.

The trials of the Pendle witches in 1612 are among the most famous witch trials in English history, and some of the best recorded in the 17th century. The twelve accused lived in the area surrounding Pendle Hill in Lancashire and were charged for the murders of ten people by the use of witchcraft. All but two were tried at Lancaster Assizes on 18-19th August 1612 along with the Samlesbury witches and others in a series of trials which have become known as the Lancashire witch trials. One of the witches, Jennet Preston, from Gisburn, which was then in Yorkshire, was tried at York assizes on 27th July 1612. She was found guilty and sentenced to death by hanging; her execution took place on 29th July 1612 on the Knavesmire, the present site of the York Racecourse; I suppose it could have been worse should she have taken the fall into a Sainsbury's car park.

Of the eleven who went to trial - nine women and two men - ten were found guilty and executed by hanging, one was found not guilty.

Two of the accused witches were Anne (Chatterbox) Whittle from the Chattox family, and her daughter Anne Redferne, who was regarded by witnesses to be a witch "more dangerous than her Mother", and, unlike her Mother, refused to admit her guilt to the end.

Six of the Pendle witches came from one of two families, each one at the time headed by two women in her eighties, Elizabeth Southerns from the Demdike family and Anne Whittle (Chattox) from the Chattox family. Southerns believed she was the leader of the entire network, but unfortunately, she died in prison before her fate was established, and some would say, unlike the eleven witches who went to the gallows, Elizabeth Southerns wasn't fit to burn. Both women were vying for overall supremacy from making a living from healing, begging, extortion and carrying out illegal abortions; many of the allegations resulted from accusations made against each other during a Malkin Tower meeting held on Good Friday 10th April 1612.

The accused witches lived in the area around Pendle in Lancashire, a county which at the end of the 16th century, was ranked by the authorities as a wild and lawless region, an area fabled for its theft, violence and sexual laxity; where the church was honoured without much understanding of its doctrines by the common people. At that time the people of Pendle remained largely faithful to their Roman Catholic beliefs and for those who refused or denounced the English Church and to take communion was a criminal offence at that time, sometimes punishable by the death penalty.

The Pendle witches were tried in a group which also included the Samlesbury lot, Jane Southworth, Jennet Brierley, Alice Grey and Ellen

Brierley, the charges against whom included child murder and cannibalism; all accept for Elizabeth Southerns who died awaiting her trial, and Alice Grey; the clerk to the court naming her in the overall list of those found not guilty. Margaret Pearson, the so-called Padiham witch, who was facing her third trial for witchcraft, this time for killing a horse, and Isobel Robey from Windle, Lancashire, accused of using witchcraft to cause sickness and little is known about their fate except that a barbecue was raging in someone's back garden.

Among the accused, was the notorious witch, Alice Nutter, who was considered to be comparatively wealthy and the widow of a tenant yeoman farmer. She made no statement either before or during her trial, except to enter her plea of not guilty to the charge of murder. Alice Nutter was found guilty on the 19th August 1612.

Nine of the accused found guilty at their trial at Lancaster Assizes on the 18-19th August 1612, were convicted of being witches and condemned to death by hanging on Gallows Hill in Lancaster on 20th August 1612; they were: Elizabeth Device, who was charged along with Alice Nutter and Demdike for the murders of three men, James Robinson, John Robinson and Henry Mitton.

James Device, however, pleaded not guilty to the murders by witchcraft of Anne Townley and John Duckworth; he was found guilty and hanged on Gallows Hill on the same date. Alizon Device, was accused of causing harm by witchcraft and Katherine Hewitt, was accused of killing a child, Anne Foulds, and Jane Bulcock was accused along with her son, John Bulcock, of the murder of Jennet Deane; only one of the accused, Alice Grey was found not guilty; what a bunch.

It was recorded by Thomas Potts, the clerk of the court, that Elizabeth Device, better known as squinting Lizzie, was an odious witch who suffered from a facial deformity resulting in her left eye being set lower than her right. Warts, polyps and unsightly blemishes were also common among witches, who constantly handled frogs and toads prior to them being tossed live into a cooking pot, the contents of which was called a brew; "Hubble Bubble toil and Trouble" a hook-nosed witch chanted as she stirred a wooden ladle around inside a soot covered cauldron which would have been used to cook rabbit, and manufacture disgusting pharmaceuticals, similar to Proctor & Gamble '*Carbolic*' soap, '*E45*' skin cream and '*Vicks*' vapour rub. It is of interest to note that today, there are so-called pretend witches who use mobile phones and the Internet to practice their devil work and it is not uncommon for them to stick pins into a person's profile with a view to inflicting injury to a person by contaminating the airwaves; their long scratchy fingernails, manicured in one of Preston's more prestigious poodle parlours, '*Nails of Fishergate*' and is the main cause for complaint when the witch finds it difficult to browse and search the Web by using a touch pad; it is to do many things she does with her mouse, stick or a disposable tablet pen after it has been chewed to death several times by a set of green luminous teeth which glow in the dark.

The modern-day witches come in different guises, usually dressed as traffic wardens, who, in the past, were seen hanging around the hardware section in Woolworths where their illicit spoils could be exchanged for a broomstick, an all-night candle, or symbolically worse, a Ken Dodd multi-coloured feather duster with the words "Happiness" engraved on the handle.

They have the ability to make you late for work by stopping clocks, watches and buggering-up cisterns in the lavatory and then, to add insult to injury, it is when a pink '*Andrex*' toilet roll falls from its holder, rapidly unravelling itself as it careers down the stairs into the kitchen followed by a rabid '*Deluxe*' dog.

The modern day Witch continues to pile on the pressure at the workplace by using effortless manipulation, ceaseless charm, power dressing and having the ability to impress their bosses by means of persuasion; this, combined with sitting cross-legged on his desk with a view to having a late breakfast is what the average male worker on the shop floor really wants to know, especially when he hears little Miss Warwick is receiving a salary far greater than he for filing her nails, powdering her nose and going out from her work station every five minutes to have a smoke.

The modern day Witches are full of carefree abandonment and can be detected on Friday evenings, cackling loudly inside a 'Wetherspoons' public free house wearing red and white striped hazard warning cones which had been stolen earlier from the A6 dual carriageway, twixt the villages of Barton Grange and Garstang, or the M6 motorway between the towns of Wigan and Warrington.

The modern day witches go to grammar schools and universities to learn how to make stink bombs, chemical and biological weapons, dehydrated *'Fruit and Fibre'* breakfast cereals which expand and blow up in one's stomach, and *'Mr Whippy'* ice cream that looks like *'Gillette'* shaving foam.

'I would really like to have an ice cream sundae instead of a ninety-nine cornet,' Mabel said with great reluctance when she saw 'Corky', the castles black cat, sitting underneath a parasol licking the last slithers of a Cadbury's chocolate flake which had fallen on to the ground.

'And, I will have a *'Walls'* hotdog sausage inside a bun with onions, mustard, hot chilli peppers and tomato ketchup, all running down the sides.' Harold replied excitedly when he heard the dulcet tones of Giovanni Lunetti, a Zaveroni cook singing "Figaro" with a difference:

"Figaro, Figaro"
I am the Pizza guy, who fixes your pizza pie
With mushrooms, anchovies and olives to go
All brought back from Poland's Warsaw
This you will not recognise
And it is of no great surprise
To find your lasagne and pasta
Has just flown in from sunny Catania
The Mozzarella is a special kind of a cheese
It comes from somewhere between Berwick on Tweed
And Stockton-on-Tees
'Walls' Hot dogs and a cold salad
These ain't, at all, so bad
When I hear you have to go
Figaro, Figaro"

148

'Do you know, Mabel, the castle's black cat looks extremely like the one who has been following us ever since we arrived on the outskirts of Longridge; weird isn't it?'

'Not as weird as the name tag which is on its tartan collar.' Mabel said, feeling traumatically nervous.

'Why, what does it say?'

'I'm sorry to tell you this, Harold, but it shows the name of the cat and the address.....

'Which are?'

Mabel gulped for a second before saying that the cat was called Elizabeth and the address is No 3 Spinning Wheel Hollow, Grey Squirrels Lane in Chipping.

'Bloody Hell, what is going on here; all of a sudden, I seem to have lost my appetite.' Harold said with a look that could have killed the cat.

'Me too,' Mabel replied with a terrified expression on her face which could only have been described as totally bizarre. 'Come on, Harold, let's get the hell out of here and go home, I've had enough of black cats, castles, forts, Roman villas and Viking grave yards to last me a lifetime.'

'I agree.' Harold replied, exiting stage left and a few paces in front of Mabel and hot-footing rapidly away from the coffee shop.

It was around four-thirty pm, a panoramic view of Pendle Hill in the far distance could be seen from the grounds of Lancaster castle, the prominent feature, Parlick Pike and Longridge fell dominating the eastern edge; the mist was now gradually congregating around their base to form a sinister haze.

'Where did Elizabeth, the cat disappear to?' Harold asked as they both made their way back to their car which was parked in nearby Takeaway Street.

'Oh, she is probably on the battlements of the castle, gazing over towards Pendle Hill looking for one of her girlfriends. From what I have heard over the weekend, Harold, it could be one of her boyfriends.'

'Some of us have to sleep at night, Mabel.'

'Well, in that case why don't you have a brew instead of your usual mug of '*Ovaltine*'?'

'What is that, I can see flying towards the A6, it looks like a witch on a broomstick.' Harold inquisitively asked.

'Don't be so silly, Harold, it is a weather balloon from nearby Barton.'

'Can you remember, my dear, when we called in at Samlesbury Hall and had the pleasure of strolling around in the main room where antique furniture was being prepared for auctioning.' Harold said, fiddling around in his back trouser pocket to find an envelope which contained a letter. 'I curiously opened up a secret drawer in one of those bureaus in Samlebury and found this.'

'It couldn't have been all that secret if you found it.' Mabel replied with a sigh.

'Just listen to this, it is a poem called "Lonely Hearts" contained in a white satin envelope addressed to a Lady Geraldine Harkness in July 1914 by a Lieutenant Percival Owen, and reads:

My dear Lady
"When the ugly face of Sadness
Turned into madness
When we couldn't speak and others couldn't spout
And unlike the tide, you always came in
But never came out
You ran away for some kind of reason
As I walked through the gardens
In the last Summer Season'
Afraid of the chase because of straight lace
You pretended to be true and found someone new
And in the grounds of the Palace
You met King George, Queen Mary and Princess Alice
They didn't know you were so cold and very callous?
I wondered about you from the very start
You were just another Miss Lonely Heart"

Written by:

Lieutenant Percival Owen
1st Battalion the Royal Welsh Fusiliers
6th July 1914

'Oh, you have suddenly turned yourself into a tea leaf, have you Harold?'

'What do you mean, Mabel, a tea leaf?'

'You know exactly what I mean, you are a thief; the letter doesn't belong to you, Harold and I would suggest you return it to its rightful owner.'

'I think you would find that nigh impossible, Mabel, because Lady Geraldine Harkness has long since departed this life; she was one of the last suffragettes in London, and was banged up for wearing a pair of men's 'Y' fronts, and padlocking herself to the railings of Buckingham Palace because of being refused a ticket to the annual garden party, and as for Lieutenant Percival Owen; he died in a Hospital in Aldershot after being medically evacuated from Belgium during the first couple of weeks of the First World War.'

'Don't tell me, Harold, you have got a telegram inside your pocket as well?'

'It's funny you should say that, Mabel.'

'Harold!'

Chapter Seventeen

Meanwhile, it was back to No 23 Calder Vale Avenue, where the search for Military and Family history was to be sought by Harold through the Internet.

Aldershot began its 1914 summer without a hint of foreboding of what was to come. There was the usual period of rigorous annual training under the sharp and stern supervision of Earl Douglas Haig. A very minor but human feature of this was between the Officers' Training Corps of Oxford and Cambridge Universities near the Basingstoke Canal. A begrimed and perspiring undergraduate in charge of the scouts of the Oxford corps was seen being bawled, put by a huge sergeant-major. This undergraduate was Edward Prince of Wales, who was to become king and after that the Duke of Windsor.

The effectiveness of the 1914 summer training of the troops was, it was said, soon to be thoroughly tested in the usual manoeuvres. Meanwhile Haig and others were studying a new mobilization scheme without any belief that this was so close to being put into operation. Brigadier-General John Chatteris in his memoirs recalled too that at this time 'some important polo matches were pending'. On the 1st August 1914 Germany declared war against Russia, and two days later against France. The German army invaded Belgium, and on the 4th August, Great Britain declared war. In the words of Foreign Secretary, Sir Edward Grey 'the lamps were going out all over Europe'. But at the War Office and at Aldershot Command Headquarters they burned all night as plans long made for the eventuality of war were prepared for action. On the following day Haig hurried to London for the Council of War called by Prime Minister Herbert Asquith. And Aldershot received its detailed mobilisation orders.

The first war-wounded had been brought to the Cambridge and Connaught Hospitals at Aldershot towards the end of August 1914. The Empress Eugénie was preparing to turn her home at nearby Farnborough into a convalescent home for wounded officers; one of the officers admitted to Cambridge hospital, Aldershot in May 1915, was Lieutenant

Percival Hywel Owen who, after training to be a pioneer officer in Aldershot, was seconded to the 4th Battalion the Royal Welsh Fusiliers, and subsequently died of multiple wounds to his body. The gross mismanagement of field tactics became evident during hard fighting at Festubert, Givenchy, Neuve Chapelle, and Richebourg when hundreds of men scurried over the trenches before being mowed down by two of the enemy Gatling guns placed on each flank to create an inescapable sustained bloody crossfire; this meaningless onslaught being similar to cattle herded to slaughter in the stockyards of Chicago. Then from his grand headquarters, Haig made big strategic decisions, involving the lives of hundreds of thousands of soldiers, without consultation with the ordinary fighting officers and men who shared an epidemic of hatred which was running through the lines at the scene of battle.

At the end of September 1915, the 4th Battalion Royal Welsh Fusiliers, which had already been in France for nearly a year, joined the Division as pioneer battalion. This fine Territorial battalion had its headquarters at Wrexham and was recruited chiefly in Denbigh and Flintshire. After hurried training at Northampton, it embarked for service in France on November 5th 1914, with strength of 29 officers and 850 other ranks; Lieutenant Percival Owen being amongst those who put themselves in the firing line.

Lieutenant Percival Hywel Owen B.A., M.C., born in 1890, the son of David Haydon Owen, a preparatory school headmaster in Haverfordwest, South Wales was just one of the officers who were completely disillusioned and thoroughly spent. However, at Sandhurst he resolved to excel at everything and ended his period first in order of merit. Earlier, Owen followed in the wake of his father at the age of fourteen by attending St. David's College, Pembrokeshire, and then continued with his academic career when at eighteen he was enrolled at Brasenose College, Oxford. During his tenure at college he frequently visited his Welsh relatives in South America, where, on the ponderosas in Central Patagonia his passion for polo was later realized at the Royal Military Academy Sandhurst.

The once dashingly handsome, superbly tailored and groomed British

Army officer with generally manly good looks was the epitome of a lady's man, especially at *the dansants*, the venue at the best hotels and tearooms where making teatime was an occasion. At four and at the end of each waltz, polka and foxtrot, the young officers and ladies resumed their consumption of tea and fancy cakes. The air was fragrant with the aroma of Egyptian cigarettes, so fashionable at the time, also with the exotically scented sachets and cachous of the young ladies pursuing the ultimate in glamour. Sometimes while they danced the couples would sing the chorus of the contemporary pop tunes being played, such as:

'Mabel dear, listen here,
I'm afraid to go home in the dark.'

It was all apparently decent and harmless. Nevertheless, *the dansants* received lots of criticism from serious older folk who saw them as first steps towards a maiden's downfall.

In the months leading up to the declaration of war, Horatio Kitchener, Earl of Khartoum was quoted as saying the war wouldn't last long and would be exciting; the excitement continued for four years with the loss of thousands of men on both sides, most of the British army contingent were volunteers and possessed a patriotism like no other towards their 'King, Queen and Country'.

In the summer of 1914, the now twenty-seven year-old Lady Geraldine Harkness was not the type of woman that one would like to introduce to one's mother. She exuded coldness and her facial expressions continually changed to suit her genetic mood swings which were enough to frighten children, especially when she peered into a "Silver Cross" perambulator to inspect its contents for any signs of ethnic irregularity; 'Mother Nature' had definitely played a nasty and irreversible trick on this woman. However, Geraldine Harkness, the daughter of Lord and Lady James Harkness, part owners of the Dutch East India Shipping Co. in London, had money, lots of it, most of which was inherited from her grandmother, Baroness Christine Van Volkenburg, the wife of Lord William Henry Harkness. A miniscule amount of Geraldine's wealth was realized when it was used as bail money during a temporary overnight stay in an H M prison in London. Incidentally, Geraldine was extremely loud and had a mouth similar in size to the Avon Mouth Gorge in Bristol which allowed sound to travel through it with great deliverance. It was Queen Mary, who once said when she stood on the balcony of Buckingham Palace, "Can these females not be shut up on some island?" she asked and before stating "It's a funny old world, isn't it?' and one 'Tommy', was noted as saying "These suffragettes are a pain in the backside, and some of us have to work for a living".

Lieutenant Percival Owen was introduced to Lady Geraldine by his friend Captain Richard Woodhouse, who, in 1913, served in the same regiment; both officers concerning themselves with public duties in London, and little did they know that when they changed the guard at Buckingham Palace, Lady Geraldine paid homage to Princess Alice.

Lady Harkness who demanded equality and equal rights for women manacled herself to the railings of the palace by means of a padlock and chain, and had B&Q, the Do-it-yourself store in Wandsworth, been in existence at the time, they would have depleted most of their garden accessories and sold them to the suffragette movement in London.

Captain Richard Woodhouse survived the war having been promoted to Major in the field of battle. He was, however, wounded and brought back to Aldershot where he spent several months in Connaught Hospital, and then afterwards, recovering in a convalescent home for officers in nearby Camberley.

The sad life of Percy Owen, the Welshman with an uncanny resemblance to General Sir Redvers Buller, V.C., G.C.B., the officer he so admired, is remembered with great admiration. He was posthumously awarded the Military Cross for his heroism in a corner of some foreign field when he and his platoon came under fire from enemy gunfire.

'Give me the strength to carry on.' Lieutenant Owen said to one of the nurses wearing a symbolic red cross emblazoned on the front of her white tunic. He died before an English Catholic priest had the chance to read out his last rights in front of the Lord Jesus, whose portrait was portrayed on a wall opposite to his bed.

Lady Geraldine Harkness died a spinster in Clitheroe, Lancashire at the age of eighty-seven in 1974; the cause of death being a reaction towards chains, an excessive intake of alcohol and excessive smoke inhalation which constantly billowed out from a 'Falcon' air-cooled pipe.

***

'Tell me, Harold, why did the War Office send the telegram to Lady Geraldine Harkness when it was supposed to have been sent to his mother and father in South Wales.'

'Ah, that was because, there were two telegrams; look at the address, Mabel: No 3 Bellingham House, Belgravia, London W1.'

'It was very clever of you, Harold, to have figured that one out; you should have been a detective.' she said looking at a skimpy bit of paper with the usual words, "It is with regret that we have to inform you" printed in Imperial bold letters.

'My father once told me I should stick to being an electrician, changing light bulbs and re-wiring houses, and not to have designs in joining the Lancashire Constabulary.'

'Maybe, that's just as well, Harold, because they retire at fifty-four, and how would you have spent your time; probably in the pub, which is where you got the idea from in the first place.'

'Ah, but you see Mabel, after retirement, they put you into boring *'Quango'* jobs such as, checking fruit machines, hanging around in hotel lobbies, and participating in undercover surveillance, that sort of thing.'

'Well, you would know all about that, wouldn't you?'

'Oh, give me a break, Mabel, and allow me some credit for what I'm trying to achieve.'

'And, just what is it, you are trying to achieve?'

'How I am to get rid of this bloody poem, and then send it to its present-day owner.' Harold said, as he continued to search the Web for an address.

'In a stamped addressed envelope like everyone does, Harold.'

'Unless you have forgotten Mabel, we have an E-mail facility at our disposal.'

'I am trying desperately to work out, Harold, how you are going to send "Knights in White Satin" inside an envelope through the E-mail system; maybe, our desktop has a secret drawer where you can deposit your letters systematically, and then, as if by magic, they come out at the other end no worse for wear for the experience.'

'It looks like we are flogging a dead horse here, my love, because apart from Colonel Richard Woodhouse's grandson and his family, there doesn't seem to be anyone who would be remotely interested in the poem.'

An anecdote written by William Shakespeare was then quoted by Harold, and it began: "The web of our life is of a mingled yarn, good and ill Together."

'Was he on the Internet, as well, Harold?' she replied, hoping that could be the end of the silly conversation.

'No, Mabel, but I do seem to have his fax number somewhere.'

'I wonder how Lady Harkness's bureau ended up here in Lancashire.' Mabel asked with a grimacing look.

'It was probably bought and shipped up here by one of those house clearance outfits, you know, the one's that come round and buy some of your stuff for two and two-pence halfpenny, and then sell it for a fortune at a Christies and Sotheby's auction room; in this particular case it is to be Samlesbury Hall.'

'You know, Harold, you do talk a load of rubbish, there could be a simple explanation to all of this.'

'You mean Lady Geraldine Harkness had an affinity towards Lancashire where she decided to end her days away from the 'Press' notoriety and her association with the suffragettes, Mrs Emily Pankhurst and her terrorist daughter, Sylvia.'

'Yes, Harold, I mean just that.'

'What a bloody nerve.' Harold said seriously.

'Why don't we go back to Samlesbury Hall tomorrow,' Mabel said positively. 'You could put the envelope back inside the bureau without anyone knowing it had been pinched.' she added, before her suggestions fell on stony ground.

'And why don't we have a picnic on the lawn; we could take some chicken and stuffing sandwiches, a flask of coffee and some Chorley cake to re-enact today all over again, and that will be fun, wouldn't it?' Harold suggested.

'I was only trying to be helpful.' she murmured.

'Have you seen what is sitting by our fishpond, Mabel?' he said looking out from one of the dormer windows.'

'Don't tell me; it's Arthur Wigglesworth from Number Nineteen, to keep Arnold company.'

'No, no, Mabel, shush.....'

'Well, I never, it's the lucky black cat.'

'Yes, Mabel, and it should join its mates inside "Wong's Lucky Kitchen"; the Chinese take-away opposite the village cenotaph; I believe the food tastes good from there.'

'What tastes good, Harold, the *'Cantonese stir fry'*, or the cat which you say, has only one more life to live.'

'And before you get too excited, Mabel, the cat lives at Number fourteen and it is called Fred.'

'Now, what are we going to do with the poem, Harold? Send it to Pam Ayres, or put it back from where it came from in the first place.'

'Somehow, I don't think it will be a good idea to return to Samlesbury tomorrow in order to put the envelope back into the secret compartment in the bureau knowing someone in the future will eventually find it.' Harold said. 'And equally, by sending it to a relative of Colonel Dick Woodhouse, would, I think be disastrous because it will tarnish the memory of Lieutenant Percival Owen if it were to fall into the wrong hands.' he went on.

'Yes, your right, as usual, Harold, but, I only wish you could keep your hands in your pockets when walking around sale rooms.'

'I see we are getting low on prawn and onion chutney.' Harold mentioned looking at the clock to see what hour it was in Rajasthan. What will be your poison for this evening, Mabel, the *Chicken Tikka Masala* or the extremely hot *Beef and Onion Tinderloo*; the stuff that cleans you out faster than an 'Orange' Pay-as-you-go mobile phone.'

'I think I would much prefer you to keep your big mouth shut, if that is possible, Harold.'

'No seriously.....'

'I am being serious, Harold, you are in grave danger of being sent to Coventry for the non-foreseeable future.'

'Where's Coventry, Mabel? Is it somewhere near to Bombay and the Taj Mahal?'

'I think I will just have a fish and chip take-away, it's going to be easier.' she said shaking her head in disbelief.

'And, would that be with *Nan Bread*, *Poppadoms* and *Mango Chutney*?'

'Harold.....'

'You can't take a joke, can you Mabel?'

'And I suppose, you will want to go to the Lightning Club after you have eaten, won't you Harold?'

'No, we will go to the club before we have our meal.' he wantingly put in.

'Well, in that case, I shall just have to phone Alison Hornby to see if she wants to go into Lytham to have a meal at the County Hotel.'

'You will have great difficulty, Mabel, because she and her husband flew off to Tenerife this morning.' he hastily replied.

'Tell me Harold, how did you know that?'

'It was when we were driving down Naze Lane this morning, I saw them getting into a taxi to take them to Manchester Airport.'

'That was very perceptive of you, but.....'

'But, but what Mabel.'

'But how did you know they were going to Tenerife?' she asked trying to throw some more light on to the subject matter.

'It was Martin Hornby who told me in the club last evening.'

'That's funny, Alison told me at the Bridge Club, they were going to fly out to Luxor to join a Nile cruise, but I seemed to have forgotten what date she said they were going.

'Well, they are close to each other.'

'Who are close to each other, Harold? Are they, Mr and Mrs Hornby, King Felipe the Sixth of Spain or Tutankhamen?'

'I tell you what, Mabel, why don't we go into Lytham together and we can visit that new Chinese Restaurant in the High Street; it is called "The Wooden Gong", and then afterwards we could have a look in Thompson's, the travel agent's window to find a suitable holiday before the summer ends.'

'Do you know, Harold that is the best suggestion I've heard from you all day.'

Chapter Eighteen

The evening continues.....

'Here we are, Mabel; it's "The Wooden Gong", Harold said with an interesting look when he noticed a large shiny brass Oriental gong standing behind the window depicting dragons and Chinamen engraved in the centre. 'We haven't gone in through the door yet, Mabel, and already the restaurant has broken the Trades Description Act by displaying something that is supposed to be made from wood; it is only hoped the chop-sticks are not made from brass because they may cause problems to our dentures, much to the delight of my son-in-law, Doctor James S.R. Wilson, to whom we may have prematurely to visit before the weekend.'

'Will you please stop moaning, Harold, and get yourself in there because I'm bloody well starving.' she said pushing his rear end up a flight of stairs leading up from the pavement.

They were both greeted by May Ling, a Chinese hostess, who was standing just inside the door wearing an embroidered red silk dress with a three feet long split up the side of one leg.

'And before you start, you can put your eyes back in their sockets.' Mabel said when she clocked 'Harold the Faithful' looking down at her shapely legs which were accentuated by the tightness of the dress.'

'My name is May Ling, and if there is anything I can do for you, just give me a shout, alright?' she said in her noticeable and impeccable Blackpool accent which sounded like it had derived from 'Base Noodle' the Oriental Shop on Central Drive.

'I don't suppose the Chinaman who is sitting in front of the till is complaining so long as she keeps on pulling them in.' Harold said, continuing with his drooling and ongoing observations.

'Pulling what in Harold?'

'The customers of course.' he replied.

'Well, so long as you are not thinking about that wonder bra she is just about managing to support; it could have Hong Kong, short and long-term consequences stamped all over it, especially for you, Harold because your eyes are like two ping-pong balls working independently on a spring.

'Yes, it is rather uplifting to say the least.'

'The dress was probably bought in Hong Kong as well; they like that type of thing.' Mabel said looking at her drab outfit in comparison.

'It came from Marks & Spencer in Saigon.' The Hostess with the moistest said, putting them in the picture. 'And, for all you Freckletonians living around the world, Saigon is in Vietnam.' she added with a smile which was as false as her lingerie.

'You know, these boat people get everywhere, Mabel.'

'And, do you know, Harold, I cannot take you anywhere these days without you coming out with crass remarks; it is a good thing there aren't any Indians in here because I would have a war on my hands.'

'Don't look now, Mabel, but look who's just come in through the front door with her husband.'

'How am I supposed to know who has come in through the front door if I'm not allowed to look?' Mabel replied, donning a pair of reading glasses to peruse the extensive range of dishes on offer; the complicated set menus being enough to confuse Carol Vorderman whose brain had been extracted by the BBC, and put on a pole somewhere in the British Museum.

'It's Beryl Patel, your Monday morning bridge partner and Robert, her husband.'

'Oh, no, this is all I need.'

'You don't fancy a kebab instead, do you Mabel?'

'No, no, we are here sitting down next to a cosy artificial log fire in amicable surroundings, and where tropical fish, unlike some of us, are about to finish their second course.'

'Hi, you guys.' Beryl Patel said with a sense of enthusiasm, knowing that their bill would be greatly reduced at the end of the meal. 'Can we join you? I missed your company this morning at the Women's Institute, and tell me, what did you get up to today, Mabel?'

'Oh, not a great deal.' she replied, not wanting to go through the whole gamut all over again. 'And apart from being followed by a cat which had lost its way in Longridge, and then being enticed into a cottage by a

Pendle Witch somewhere between Chipping and Ribchester, and then being presented with a car parking ticket in Morecambe, everything was just fine.'

'You will have your little joke, won't you Mabel.' Beryl said with an ease of Indian confidence.

'I'm not joking, Beryl, it was a bloody nightmare from start to finish, and it is by no means finished, is it Harold?'

'Well, if you mean.....'

'Yes, I do mean that blooming poem you so carefully removed from the bureau.' Mabel said not so surprisingly.

'What are you both talking about, Mabel? Beryl asked puzzlingly.

'Oh, it's nothing for you to bother your head about.'

'And before you start looking for *Poppadoms* and *Mango Chutney* in here, they are not on the menu, only *Prawn Crackers* and *Hot Chilli Sauce;* the type which explode in front of your very eyes.'

'I am aware of Chinese restaurants, Harold; I visit them frequently when I go to Peking on business.'

'This is not a Chinese restaurant, Richard, it's Vietnamese.' Harold said, correcting him. 'Did you not see Polpot, the Vietnamese despot, sitting behind his cash register as soon as you both walked into the restaurant?'

'Shut up, Harold, you are beginning to bore the pants off Richard.'

'You should be so lucky.'

'Listen, if I have any more of this, I'm going home.' Mabel said kicking him with a pointed shoe underneath the table.

'Tell me Beryl, do all Indian women walk around showing off their midriffs, and have twenty-two carat gold drawing pins protruding out from their noses?' Harold asked inquisitively. 'It must be very painful when you sneeze or use a handkerchief.' he added.

'Yes, of course, it is considered as mystic.' Beryl replied.

'I bet it's not as mystic as it was on Pendle Hill this afternoon.' he said.

'And do you know, Harold, that underneath this Sari, I wear a skimpy Bollywood belly-dancing outfit, and when Richard comes home from his office, he flings glitter up into the air, and then there's the finale when both of us sit on a magic carpet; one behind the other, and fly out through the window to circumnavigate Calcutta before skipping back to Freckleton just in time to watch "East Enders".'

'It sounds a bit like the "Sound of Music" with a rather discoloured Julie Andrews running down a mountain wearing a cow bell around her neck.' Harold diplomatically put in. 'You could join forces with May Ling on the door, Beryl, she looks as if she is in to that kind of stuff.'

'Harold.....'

'But, Julie Andrews doesn't look remotely like, Beryl.' Richard said gyrating on a circular chair which he said should have been positioned in the centre of the table in order to rotate and celebrate the arrival of the food.

'Ah, but there's time yet for Julie, if the Indian Mr Sadiq Khan gets his way and becomes the new Mayor of London; he will have a foothold in all the theatre and stage plays in Leicester Square, and that will be fun, won't it? And if his Jewish rival contender, Zack Goldsmith gets his way, Julie might be up there on the bill boards keeping Steven Spielberg company.'

'Tell me, Richard, is there something wrong with your backside?' Mabel asked enquiringly. 'Have you got beans in your jeans?'

'It's that magic carpet of his, he's suffering from jetslag.' Harold jokingly put in.

'Don't you mean jetlag Harold?' Richard asked, moving his head frantically from side-to-side like a demented shopkeeper whose Value Added Tax return forms had just been pushed through the letter box.

'No, no, a jetslag is a woman who is a member of the 'Five-Mile-High Club'.

'And what does one have to do to qualify for that?' Beryl asked naively and sounding very much like the Queen.

'Go into Preston and buy an authentic Indian carpet with made in Bradford printed on the label.' Harold suggested.

The meal arrived by two waitresses and to open the proceedings, the *shui mai*, soft prawn and pork dumplings, torpedo king prawns and wafer paper prawns which were bursting with flavour, delicately cooked and presented with great attention to detail, namely lotus flowers made from pink wax to accentuate the decoration. What better way to showcase fish than to serve it all up in a spectacular bird's nest; an eye-catching creation of crispy noodles delicately cooked by the restaurant's chef, Michael Tang. The half-roast Vietnamese duck was a symphony of rich flavour, served on tender Cambodian greens, the meat melting in your mouth. All of the dishes were placed on top of a heated plate which rotated clockwise and anti-clockwise in the centre of the table and, like a roulette wheel, it usually came to a gradual stop with a prawn ball ending up on the floor.

'Would you like a bottle of wine to wash all of this down?' Harold asked the Patels.

'Oh, no, we are teetotal; we don't drink and we don't smoke.' Beryl replied who had more bags underneath her eyes than a Warrington coalman.

'What do members of the Indian Raj get up to when they are not drinking and smoking?' Harold began to wonder.

'We concentrate on food, mainly; chicken curries, lamb tikka, tandoori king prawn masala; that sort of thing.' Beryl said with another outburst of confidence which would have been enough to frighten Delia Smith.

'Do you have a sitar and the bongo drums playing in the background?' Harold went on.

'Harold, do shut up and eat your food because the candles are about to burn out underneath the plate-warmer.' Mabel interrupted.

'Tell me, Harold.' Beryl asked. 'Have you ever watched the Indian cookery programme, Queen of the Tiger King Prawns with Madge Jaffrey, or the send up of Delia Smith as portrayed by comedienne, Rita Longbotham alias Cecilia Crépe.'

'No, I can't say that I have.' he replied.

'Well, one of her recipes inside her book goes something like this:'

Cecilia Crépe goes Bombay
First of all do you see the Sari?
You know I look like Mata Hari
And now I am going to make a curry

So I hope you are not in any hurry
To dash out today to your favourite
                    Indian take-away
Now wash your hands before we commence
You know it makes a great deal out of sense
The curries I make are very hot
Sorry about the onions, I forgot
The sauce I have prepared comes out of a jar
You can get this from your local Spar
One can make this dish in a trice
With lots and lots of Pilau rice
And if you want to know where
                    I am coming from
This is called Poppadom
They start of round and kinda flat
I like those and so does the cat
You will find this recipe somewhere
                    In my book
So it's goodbye from Cecilia
                    And lots of good luck

'Ah, what the' *eck*, you can get all of that stuff in Freck.' Harold said
after he had listened attentively to Beryl's ramblings.

'Richard is the managing director of Mumbai Leather goods in India,
and specializes in leather jackets, don't you Richard?' Beryl had to make
quite clear.'

'I've heard about these sun-tanned leather jackets.' Harold said with
caution, being in danger of receiving another kick from underneath the
table. 'And so much for your sacred cows, they almost invariably end up
on someone's back, and the first sign of rain, and they turn white. Do
you know, Richard, if it wasn't for Queen Victoria, her long suffering
German husband, Albert, her Prince Consort, and the hook-nosed Jewish
Prime Minister, Robert Disraeli, the first Earl of Beaconsfield, India
would have missed the chance of joining forces with the British army to
go over to France and give her grandson, Wilhelm the second, an
extremely good hiding; the Kaiser was the person responsible for trying

to destroy the pub, "The Queen Victoria" in Beryl's favourite television soap opera, "East Ender's" by way of a Zeppelin flying overhead.'

'But we weren't in The First World War.' Richard so knowledgably said.

'Ah, but you were too busy in the cotton mills of Bombay, churning out calico to make into four-by-two 'pull-through's' so that they could be used as cleaning rags; to be forced down the barrel of a Tommie's .303 bolt action rifle.'

'Do you know, Harold, you could take a degree in Military History.' Beryl sarcastically put in.

'Oh, I couldn't possibly do that because I haven't the time; at the moment I am taking a correspondence course on how to become a member of the Special Investigation Branch attached to Britain's Royal Military Police, aren't I Mabel?'

'Shut up, Harold, just shut up and give your mouth a rest.'

'Now, who is going to eat the last *shui mai*, the soft prawn and pork dumpling?' Harold asked around the table.

'Me.' Richard and Beryl said speedily in unison.

'I rather suspected it would be you.'

'They are irresistible.' Richard continued to speak, stabbing a small rubbery parcel which could have been mistaken for '*Heinz*' ravioli.

'You and Beryl seem to have done remarkably well taking into account Indians don't eat pork.' Harold said with a big grin on his face.'

'Tell me Harold; how does one eat a full-Monty English breakfast in a five-star Mumbai hotel if one doesn't like pork sausages, fried bread, bacon, eggs, potatoes, mushrooms, Italian peeled tomatoes, baked beans and black pudding?' Richard asked.

'By opening one's mouth like everyone else.' Harold replied.

'You are now on the same wave-length as me, Harold; if the company pays for it, you eat it.'

'Yes, we had a similar thing going in Saudi Arabia.' Harold continued to put in. 'We were forced to eat sheep's eyeballs at a Bedouin feast evening which was organised by the Saudi Arabian Government; they tasted like squelchy multi-coloured interwoven elastic bands, but one could live on them; the eyeballs I mean. There was rumour afoot that the sheep's eyeballs could make one see a registration number plate better at thirty paces in the dark, especially when one was either sitting on the back of a camel or in the front seat of a Typhoon multi-roll jet fighter aircraft.'

'Well, that was a lovely meal.' Beryl said in all honesty, leaving the chewy bits around the side of her plate to create a decorative creation to give to the restaurants cat. Shall we have a pot of China tea; it works wonders for the digestion.' She suggested, 'I think it is something to do with the perfume fragrance attributed from the lotus petals which float around on the top.' she so wisely explained.

'No, I think Mabel and I shall give this one a miss and we will have a coffee and a brandy instead. I can recall a time,' he went on,' when Mabel and I stayed at a guest house in France on our way to Bad Aachen in Germany, and the landlady had the audacity to serve us with an assortment of fresh flowers for our breakfast; I wouldn't have minded but after we had munched our way through several slices of bread, a baguette which must have measured at least six-feet long, we saw a cat sitting on the flower beds and using it as a public convenience.'

'Really.' Beryl said with concern.

'Yes, and if that wasn't enough, Mabel was attacked by a stray '*Stuka*' Dive Bomber in the courtyard when a low flying pigeon decided to dump some of its load off on to her recently purchased white cotton blouse.'

'Oh, how awful, you must have been devastated, Mabel.'

'Yes, I bloody well was, and Harold did try to claim the money back from our travel insurance, but unfortunately they said it was an Act of God. Harold, however, called it something else which came as no great surprise; he said pigeons, except for them being placed underneath a layer of puff pastry in the kitchen of the 'Derby Arms' at Trailles, and like useless grass and snow, the birds are no good to man nor beast, except when four and twenty are baked in a pie, he went on. They are all God's creature, I said to him, but it made no difference, Harold made a point of taking it out on one of the German guests, telling him if it wasn't for them, our beloved 'Fray Bentos' corned beef and tins of 'SPAM' would definitely have gone out of business. And do you know, Beryl, it was a wonder we got to Germany in one piece and, when we visited Monchau, the cuckoo clock village where they make gingerbread men, peach and banana liquors and serve *Bratwurst* sausages as long as your arm, he complained at having to wait for at least half-an-hour inside a *guesthof* before we finally got served. We realized later that when one goes into a pub in the village one is supposed to be shown to a table and not barge in looking like one owned the place, Harold.' Mabel went on. 'It was after we had returned from Germany Harold penned a poem, didn't you dear?' Undaunted by not receiving any response from him, she divulged to the Patels, giving them an idea of what to expect from a place where it is quite common to see candy floss stuck on to a jacket displayed inside a Burton's window in the ancient city of Rouen in Northern France.

A City of a Thousand Baguettes
Everyone here seems to be having a feast
Filling their mouths full of carbohydrates and yeast
Munching their way around ten thousand clocks
It's no wonder why they all look like an ox
In Supermarkets there is a danger
That they may bump into a disparaging stranger
They walk backward, sometimes forward, they talk
                                        to themselves
As produce start falling off from the shelves
One has to be aware of the unexpected pram
From behind a medieval battering ram
They weave their way round with shopping trolleys
With a point of a finger, it's up with their brolleys
Still eating away in the busy street
A pain au chocolat is a real treat
In a Boutique stands a fine looking dress
As someone with sticky fingers makes it a fine looking
                                        mess
Then a friend appears looking rather chic
Slaps a dollop of cream upon your cheek

Not once, but twice, and if that's not enough
Your face is then covered with a whole load of stuff
After smoothing down her expensive lingerie
Then it's back to the Boulangerie
Bent over the counter oooh la la...
She fancies another pain au chocolat
Where is this place, you will never know
I'm looking through a glass of Bordeaux

'Well, we really must be getting along.' Richard said with a real understanding for modern contemporary poetry.

'Yes, it's been really nice, and we must do it again sometime.' Beryl suggested, diverting her attention by looking at Harold in the mirror.

'Do what?' Harold asked.

'Harold!' Mabel said angrily, if only looks could kill.

'Well, I will see you, Mabel at the 'Bring and Buy' sale on Saturday.' Beryl uttered.

'Tell me Beryl.' Harold asked. 'Will you be in the sale?'

'Of course, I will, Harold, I will be stood on one of the tables with a B&Q garden chain wrapped around my ankles.'

'How much do you think you will realize, Beryl?'

'Oh, quite a substantial amount.' she replied cheekily.

'Well, in that case, I will bring along quite a lot of my loose change.'

'Harold, what did I tell you?'

'Yes dear.'

'I think I would like to go home now.' she demanded.

'As you wish, Mabel, but not until we have looked inside the travel agent's window.'

Thompson's, the travel agent was just a few doors down from the 'Wooden Gong' restaurant and staring them in the face was an advertisement in the window depicting a four-day mini break to Amsterdam, put together by British Airways, departing the first week in September.

'What do you think Mabel? The Dutch are such hospitable people, and they have the most remarkable cuisine in the world; everything seems to be done with cheese. They also have the *Bloemenmarkt*, the only floating flower market in the world.'

'So long as there aren't any *bloemen* flowers ending up on my breakfast plate; I don't think I could stand any more of that.' Mabel said, diverting her attention to two other posters; one offering a six day cruise, following in the wake of Agatha Christie on the River Nile, and another offering a six-month camel ride in Saudi Arabia, taking in wonderful views of the desert wastes, countless oasis, wrecked steam trains and blown-up railway tracks at Hejas ; you can even have your photograph taken standing next to Colonel T.E Lawrence, a Lawrence of Arabia look-a-like, that is providing the traveller reaches, Cairo, the Jordan Valley, Akaba, Damascus, and the Mediterranean Sea, just in time.'

'Well, what do you think, Mabel?

'I don't think sitting on a camel for six months is quite up my street, Harold, but after today, I will be game for anything.'

Chapter Nineteen

The golden opportunity had arisen when Mabel was forced to speak to her husband, reminding him of a lucky charm bracelet she had not received as a present that day.

'It may, or may not have escaped your attention, Harold, you were going to buy me a lucky charm bracelet in Morecambe; this was to be the highlight of my day trip.'

'Ah, but that was before I was threatened with wheel clamping and had to put up with a hefty fifty pounds fine.'

'Yes, I know Harold, but you should be more careful where you park the car in future.'

'Anyhow, these bracelets are a big con; one has to keep adding on with a variety of different charms, and the range is endless; one begins the collection with a cat and then, after several visits to H. Samuel and 'Argos' the catalogue people, one ends up with a teddy bear, a monkey, and a nine-carat banana.'

'Must you put the dampener on everything, it wasn't so long ago I bought you an engraved sterling silver propelling pencil from John Menzies for your birthday, it laid rather heavily on my housekeeping money, but I bought it for you, nonetheless.'

'It's no use having lead in your pencil, Mabel, if you have no one to write to.'

'You can always use it to write postcards when we go to Amsterdam, Harold, but I seem to recall that when we returned to Matt Jollies Middleton Towers holiday camp in Morecambe during the early nineteen-seventies, you wrote them on the bus coming home.'

'So, we have decided on flowers, cheese and hurdy-gurdy men turning the handles of barrel organs in Dam Square instead of camel rides in a war-torn Syria desert where the British Foreign Office are still allowing tourists to visit providing they buy a bullet-proof flak jacket before they go.'

'Well, most people get away with it, so why shouldn't we.' Mabel said, still looking at an E flyer in the window with what looked like Kate Adie in the background.

'Fine looking woman, that Kate Adie, she has got what most men haven't.'

'And, what would that be, Harold?'

'A machine-pistol strapped down her leg.'

'I suppose you think that is funny, Harold; if it wasn't for the foreign correspondents, we wouldn't get any news from the front line.'

'Are you talking about Afghanistan where George went into action against the '*Taliban*' rebel tribesmen?' Harold replied out of respect for his son.

'Yes, if you want me to paint pictures.' Mabel insisted. 'He used to write to Abigail every week and kept us regularly informed which is more than I can say for our SKY satellite television set which allowed more football matches to enter into our house than David Lineham's programme "World of Sport" on Saturday afternoons.'

'Well, it wasn't my fault, Mabel, I bought the wrong television package, and we found it difficult to find John Simpson, Kate Adie and Sue Lloyd Roberts crouching down underneath a hail of bullets; the danger must have been quite harrowing knowing an RPG7, a rocket propelled grenade could hit you in the backside at any second.'

'I can well imagine; it wouldn't half make your eyes water.' she said concernedly, as if she knew the consequences of being in a prone unsupported dangerous position.

'Listen, Mabel, are we going to stare into this window all night or are we going to call into The Lightning Club for a nightcap before going home.'

'I think it is best if we go home, Harold because we have a big day ahead of us tomorrow, the gas man is coming at eight o'clock to read the meter, the electricity man is coming at nine and, if we are lucky, we may be able to avoid the television detector van which seems to be careering up and down the avenue as we speak; can you remember the time you had to explain to the television licensing authorities why we hadn't renewed our annual fee; you said he had to wait until the bill finally surfaced to the top of the pile. And, if that wasn't enough, you were threatened with prosecution because you said the old 'Grundig' black and white set needed to be fixed and it was temporarily placed in the attic; the truth of the matter was, Harold, our Dixon's 'Top-of-the-Range' 'Phillips' flat screen television with its 'State-of-the-Art' hand set and integral DVD player was hidden away in the loft.'

'Well, it gave us a little bit of leeway, Mabel, by not having to pay the BBC exorbitant amounts of money to keep Dawn French and Jennifer Saunders in a job.'

'And, can you remember the time you had to attend a tribunal in Preston to stop you from going to gaol.'

'I know, but anything is better than watching "The Vicars of Sibley".'

'The programme is called "The Vicar of Dibley", and like you Harold, there is only one.'

'Ah, that's nice of you Mabel; would you like some cocoa before we hit the sack?'

'Richard Patel is going back to Mumbai tomorrow.' Mabel said trying to change the subject to a much lighter one.

'Nowhere is safe these days, my dearest, and not so long ago the hotel Richard stays in was attacked by terrorists; let's face it, Mabel, one can't go on bloody holiday these days without being accosted by some faction or another. Take for instance, when we visited Edinburgh during the festival and a transsexual 'jumper ooter' *hoots man*, who nearly frightened us to death when he leapt out from the bottom of the castle steps wearing a white luminous bra, stockings, suspender belt and a pair of four-inch high-heeled chisel shoes; rumour had it he was the star caber tosser at the Braemar Highland Games.'

'I see Tommy Snape has lost his driving licence again because of clocking up far too many points.' Mabel said, feeling sorry for the dog next door who has to put up with shit seven days a week. He won't be delivering his meals on wheels around the village anymore,' she added.' and by the time he gets his plastic card back we may all have different ones because of our leaving the European Community; there are rumours afoot in the House of Commons, according to ex-councillor, Tommy Turton, the one who knows everything, that if David Cameron and Boris

Johnson get their way, the country will be broke by next Christmas.'

'Well, points make prizes.' Harold said trying to imitate Bruce Forsythe rather badly when he kicked one foot several times in the air, giving the impression he had become a Greek Adonis after placing a fist underneath his untrimmed salt and pepper beard. 'Didn't he do well?' he added.

'Bernadette Cartmell will just have to put up with eating salads for a while.' Mabel commented. 'She is always complaining about having to eat fish practically every day.' she went on.

'She never complained when Joseph Maitland, the local fishmonger drove up every Thursday in his van.' Harold had to mention. He made sure that she and Cuddles, her pet cat, never went short during the 'Cod War'.'

As one warily drives through the village of Freckleton, it is not uncommon to see a poster prominently displayed in the churchyard which reads, "Caution" If you go off the road, the hand of God will point you in the right direction, namely 'The dickens', The Pickwick Tavern in Warton, or the police station at Kirkham, where they lock you up and throw away the keys for five minutes; this being a token of their low key authoritarianism and intellect before referring you to higher authorities in Lytham where they take away your means of transportation, and without compassion force you to join the ranks of the unemployed.

The village also boasts an Anglican vicar who enjoys exhuming bodies from his graveyard all because someone called his mother-in-law by the wrong name, and to be buried in the church grounds is like asking a polar bear to unwrap a Fox's glacier mint. The crypt which lay beneath the Holy Trinity, is not exempt from this macabre distastefulness when the reverend William Burke, the reverend Thomas's successor, was accused along with his verger, Archibald Bradley Airey of body-snatching; it was told that a skeleton which looked like the late footballer, Georgie Best, and the late ace "Pot Black" snooker player, Alex Higgins were hanging up inside a medical school in Manchester.

Suddenly, it is Sunday, and on Sundays one can hear the sound of the church bells ringing out from the top of the building; the knell from the bells being played from a seventy-eight revolutions per minute record which was produced sometime during the Second World War; the older inhabitants say the loudspeaker was the same one which was used in the film "Casablanca" to alert the people of Paris, the German army was fast approaching, but in Freckleton's case it was America.

I, being a big fan of God and a big defender of the faith, cannot exonerate the organist and choir master, Denny Lane, who doubles-up as a Mexican *Groucho* every Sunday when he sits down in front of his piano wearing a poncho wrapped around his neck to make himself look like Clint Eastwood. To begin the service Denny plays, "A whiter shade of pale"; a catchy tune popularized in the 1960s by an American band called, "Procal Harlem" and this is when the vicar and his entourage appear on the starting line facing the pews at the back of the church. And the choristers are just something else, dressed-up in robes, cassocks and surpluses to resemble a collection of ecclesiastical angels drifting down the aisle, headed by a slow-moving vicar, gesticulating to the congregation like the Pope, indicating to the masses that he was definitely in charge of the proceedings. It was during a choir practice one of the sopranos, a Miss Melanie Woodruff, was called Miss 'Head and Shoulders' because of an acute scalp problem which added to the festive appearance on top of the Christmas tree. Melanie however, was not amused when she was presented with a 'Betterware' dustpan and brush after the snowflakes had fallen on to the floor next to the crib.

When everyone has been chucked out of church following the evening song service, and after the door is secured on Sundays by the local AA man, Archibald Airey, the reverend William Burke disrobes in his vestry to don a rather loud Tahitian shirt with an abundance of palm trees and garland-clad hoola-hoola girls cavorting all around him; this is the time he goes to the pub, throws a few darts, hits the 'Boddingtons' and dreams up another slogan to fit inside his roadside display cabinet. "The end of the world is nigh" was uttered by one of the local customers when the pub had sold out of 'Walkers' salt and vinegar crisps and lost playing a game of dominoes.

It was during a purposeful series of renovations to a duck pond in the centre of one of Britain's best kept villages, Wray Green, that controversy unfolded when a flotilla of ducks and a flight and gaggle of geese disappeared forever after a tragic detour in Freckleton; rumour has it they ended up one Christmas on the menu in the 'Bombay Mix' Indian take-away, and on Boxing Day inside 'Wong's Lucky House' kitchen.

I can remember festively being held prisoner in Freckleton when one Christmas I visited my late Auntie Maud, who had the misfortune to live in Rydal Water Avenue. It was during that dreaded Christmas Eve; the weather was extremely cold and it began to snow heavily. The flickering lights inside all the bungalows were systematically switched off, leaving only an orange glow to reflect up from the pavements outside. I can vividly recall Freckleton's 'Prize Band' playing "Silent Night" in a nearby street, and Auntie Maud making it seem like the 'black-out' after she had switched off the lights in the front room lest a stray trumpet player knocked on her door holding a converted Cadbury's cocoa tin.

Oh, those were the days when on Christmas day I had to have my stomach pumped in order to find a silver three penny bit which I swallowed eating a piece of plum pudding together with a lashing of 'Tate and Lyle' syrup. How I missed those tinned peaches with 'Carnation' evaporated milk, and especially the walnuts which had been gathered-up sometime between the third and fourth centuries BC.

Oh, how I do feel for Harold and Mabel, and it is not for the want of trying to escape this picturesque den of iniquity to a land full of better fields, of the type which don't get water-logged during heavy rain falls, and where dairy farmers don't have to be rescued from their homesteads in rowing boats, supplied by courtesy of 'The Royal National Lifeboat Institute' from Lytham St. Anne's. And, wherever the Rigby's chose to live, they would just be passing through, and where else away from the hearts of Freckleton could one find so much entertainment contained within fifteen-hundred square metres of consecrated ground.

'Would you like me to make a cocoa supper before we hit the sack, Mabel?'

'Yes, I would like that very much, Harold.' she replied before he had the chance to change his mind.

'And by the way, Harold, the cocoa tin in the kitchen looks very familiar; it has a narrow slot on top of the lid.'

'Oh, that may have had something to do with when I volunteered to bang on the big bass drum one Christmas Eve because Peter Hogarth, the regular bandsman, suddenly went off sick with chronic earache.'

'I don't think I will bother having the cocoa supper, Harold, because of the sell-by-date which reads the fifteenth of December nineteen eighty-seven.'

'As you wish my nearest and dearest darling wife.'

'You sound as if you have more than one wife, Harold.'

'Now, let's get one thing straight.' Harold said with a vengeance. 'It's a bit like your 'Shredded Wheat'; one is enough and two, is two too many.'

'I'm sorry Harold, I was only joking.'

'And, what are we going to do about your charm bracelet; it is your birthday on Sunday and we don't want to miss that, do we?' Harold lovingly enquired.

'What don't you want to miss, Harold, me or the nine-carat gold charm bracelet with an assortment of dangly bits attached to its chain?'

'Don't you worry Mabel, H. Samuel still has a sale in its window and I'm sure we will find something suitable.'

'And, if you think we are going to return to that Samlesbury Hall, to put that confounded poem back inside its *hidy-hole*, then you can forget it.' she said in all seriousness.

'Ah, the eighteenth century walnut bureau will probably be bought by an affluent antique collector from Germany.' Harold made to comment. 'The item of furniture, will I'm sure, be cosily wrapped up inside a container bound for Munich the following Monday, and it is of little wonder how our telephone and Post Office letter boxes have remained at the side of the road because the Bavarians like that sort of thing; it reminds them of the Yorkshire Dales and Nora Batty.'

'What a load of cod's wallop.' Mabel replied putting on a pink negligee to make her look like her literary heroine, the late Barbara Cartland. 'Surely, they have their own telephone and letter boxes up the mountains?'

'Yes, a couple were given to the Reich Chancellor, Adolf Hitler and his girlfriend, Eva Braun by the Duke of Windsor and his American wife, Mrs Wallace Simpson during the Second World War; they were subsequently buried in an avalanche to be never seen again.' Harold said, continuing with his stories which were completely untrue.

'Who or what was buried in an avalanche, the Duke of Windsor, Wallace Simpson, the telephone or the red-letter box?' she so genuinely wanted to know.

'There was a tale that a skier once heard the sound of a telephone ringing underneath the snow.' Harold went on, bringing that conversation to an abrupt close when he said: 'He immediately put his ear to the ground to listen and consequently suffered severe frostbite.'

'And just what are we going to do for your birthday, Harold? It is of little significance that your birthday falls on the same day as Guy Fawkes Night on the fifth of November, commemorating the Gun Powder Plot in 1605 when he tried to blow up the Houses of Parliament in Westminster.'

'It's a great pity Guy Fawkes didn't succeed last year, because if he had, David Cameron, our so-called Prime Minister, would have been joining the ranks of the unemployed. He is like a crow on a washing line, listening to peoples' comments, and then he takes on board everything they say and implements their wishes; he must go down as the worst decision-maker since the Italian World War Two leader, Benito Mussolini. Cameron's total inability to make decisions will, I'm sure, call for a referendum to pull Britain out of Europe and he will then pass the buck on to someone else to sweep up the debris he has left behind. And, to return to your question, Mabel, why don't we celebrate my birthday by going on a trip to London, taking in the sights and to do some Christmas shopping; we could then join in with the Festival of Remembrance in Whitehall, and that will be fun won't it?'

'Oh, yes, Harold, that would be wonderful, and perhaps we could go and knock on David Cameron's door in No 10 Downing Street to ask him if he would like to accompany us for a 'Steak and Kidney Pudding' and a free drink in "The Lord Moon of the Mall", the flagship of Britain's better roadside soup kitchens.'

'You know, last night, I had a nasty dream, Mabel; I dreamt the Brazilian *bossanova* singer, Astrid Gilberto was singing, "The Girl from Ipanema" in a Wetherspoon's pub.'

'Now, that wasn't a nasty dream, Harold; it was a nightmare.'

Chapter Twenty

Those eventful days preceding Mabel Rigby's sixty-seventh Birthday, Sunday 23rd August 2015.

Tuesday began with the digging up of the road in front of the Rigby's dormer bungalow. The pneumatic drilling being enough to interfere with one's nervous system and to force one out of bed, open the windows and shout 'shut up.....' at the top of one's voice; this was the prelude to Harold and Mabel's day.

'What on earth are you doing making all this noise at eight o'clock in the morning?' Harold asked a representative from the Council, who just so happened to be wearing a hard hat and dispensing coffee from a thermos flask, and at the same time, attempting to eat an egg and bacon roll purchased from Brown's sandwich bar in the village.

'We're digging up the road because there are large pot-holes in it caused by subterranean channels of water running parallel along your front and back garden; it begins at the stream and ends somewhere on the banks of the River Ribble.' Mr Kelly, the Irish born bringer of bad news said.

'You mean to tell me our houses have been built in the middle of a lake and every time it rains we move closer and closer to Belfast.'

'Ah, I wouldn't worry Mr Rigby, just plant a handful of shrubs and a few trees, and that will contain your problem for a number of years until the global warming affects the level of water in the estuary and envelops the whole village. Everything these days comes back full circle, Mr Rigby and your bungalow is no exception.' he added speaking in a language which was barely recognisable.

'And, just what do you mean by that little statement?'

'Well, it is like this, Mr Rigby, you cannot help nature from taking its course; for example, your bungalow wasn't in existence fifty years ago, and if things were different the Council could have put the land to better use by turning it into a duck pond.'

'Why didn't you go the whole hog and turn it into a boating lake, you know, similar to the one in Fairhaven.' Harold retaliated not knowing

Brendon Kelly became a mature student at the age of sixty and was studying local history.

'No, that is further down the village, beginning at the old quayside pub, the "Ship" at 'Freck', and you will never know that one day, it will once again, have sea water running along one side, and be a docking area for cruise liners from all around the world to tie-up.' Mr Kelly said, believing his own personal predictions which had probably been derived from inside a County Mayo teacup.

'Well, I hope there are no Russians coming to visit because we have had quite enough of that 'Aeroflot' lot who periodically fly overhead jettisoning blocks of ice, giant snow balls and discarded pickled to death Polish onions which fall to the ground after either sliding-off from the wings, or being thrown out through the galley window.'

'Oh, for sure, for sure, Russian cruise liners will arrive in Freckleton.' Mr Kelly said. 'Those floating hotels are so big, villagers will be able to look up and see passengers observing military aircraft on the runway using powerful binoculars, and that will put Philip Bassett's nose out of joint, won't it?' he added.

'Yes, that's if he's still alive and not boring the pants off everyone in 'The Coach & Horses'.' Harold replied. 'I really must be going now, my lady wife is cooking an English breakfast; it really has been quite an experience talking to you, Brendon, and be careful not to dig too deep because you might discover the French underwater frogman, Jack Cousteau, and give him a headache with your pneumatic drill.'

'Ah, there's no danger of that, Mr Rigby, he's dead already after being attacked by a fourteen foot hammer-head shark.'

Meanwhile, back at the ranch, Harold said to Mabel:

'I have just been told by the council worker that in years to come there will be huge cruise liners sailing out from the Baltic heading for Freckleton where they can tie-up and buy souvenir postcards from Fiddler's Newsagent's shop.'

'What a load of unadulterated rubbish you speak, Harold; it makes me wonder just what you are going to dream up next?'

'He also told me that it won't be uncommon, because of global warming, to see rogue icebergs floating down the River Ribble and parking themselves up by the 'Waterfront' pub on Preston dock.'

'I suggest that before you go to bed, Harold, you should take a little more water with your cocoa instead of Jameson's Irish whiskey because penguins may decide to jump off from the floating glacier to try and find their mates sitting on top of the bar which dispenses beer.'

'Don't be silly, Mabel, the brewers 'Hind Coope', the southern maker of fine ales, don't extend their distribution to pubs in Preston, their dray horses wouldn't be able to cope and they would be completely knackered by the time they reached the Dartford fly-over.'

'Here's your breakfast.' she said, giving him the chance to glance at the newspaper before the contents became illegible due to him splattering the third page with several thumpings of tomato sauce. 'And, I hope you are going to change from wearing your 'Rob Roy' tartan dressing gown and pyjamas and put on something more in keeping with respectability; I don't know how you have got the nerve to venture out into the street looking like "Brave heart" or someone who has just crawled out of his bed.'

'Well, I don't suppose Caroline Cartwright was complaining I could see her out from the corner of my eye; she was wearing.....'

'Harold, unless you want to take up camping outside in the back garden tonight, I would suggest you buck your ideas up and become more civilized.'

'Ah, that's a good idea, I may get more sense by talking to Arnold.' he said underneath his breath.

'What did you say Harold?'

'I didn't say anything dear, absolutely nothing. And, if I were to camp in the back garden, there would be a danger of being accosted by Arthur Wigglesworth, or worse still, having to deal with his queer dog Poo Poo.'

'Well, you could have a party and take some chicken and stuffing sandwiches, cheese and onion flavoured crisps, order a bottle of pop from Andrew Whittle, and then when you turn the lighting off around the fish pond, you wouldn't know who is who, which is which and what belongs to whom, and that will be fun won't it?' Mabel said, and continuing to say that: 'Jack Cousteau used a primitive yellow submarine to observe his marine life; it is now a permanent feature parked outside the aquarium in Monaco.' she who, Harold says, knows everything and very little.

'What on earth was a Frenchman doing locked inside a submarine in South America?' Harold said using his wealth of knowledge to its maximum.

'The principality of Monaco is situated next to Southern France and bordering on Northern Italy; its capital is Monte Carlo and it is by the Mediterranean, you know.' she pointed out by shoving a plastic globe underneath his nose.

'Well its close enough Mabel because, from where I'm sitting, the Atlantic Ocean is only two and a half inches wide.'

'Let's be honest, you don't know where Monaco is, do you?'

'Well, put it this way, I've never been to Bury, but I've eaten one of their pies.'

'You always have an answer to everything, don't you Harold.'

'Can you remember those two scuba-divers, Hans and Lottie Ass?' he said, continuing with his sub-aqua theme; 'they were swimming around making our television look like a fish tank on Sunday afternoons before the actor, Roger Moore who played 'The Saint" made his appearance looking like a bent pipe cleaner with a halo above his head.'

'I hope you don't get yourself into any mischief while I'm having my hair styled, and my nails manicured before doing the shopping at Morrison's supermarket in Preston.' Mabel said as she clocked Caroline Cartwright standing on the top rung of a set of step ladders to clean her windows.'

'No, I will just be a good boy, read my newspaper, circle one or two horses and assist Arnold to pull in a couple of fish.'

'I'm going now, and I shan't be long.' she said as she made her way out into the drive to open the overhead garage door.

'Take care, dear, and watch out for those rogue icebergs, Polish pickled onions, and stray penguins doing their shopping in Morrison's.'

'I will, and thanks for opening the garage door for me Harold, it was a real treat for me to find it open.'

'No worries, Mabel, I will do anything to help around the house; you know that.'

'Well, in that case you can continue with the dishes, polish the brass ornaments and clean the inside of the windows before Bert Cookson descends on the area to clean the outside.' she said, manoeuvring her body with great difficulty into the driver's side of the car hoping the door wouldn't become scratched in the process.

'What does she think, that Bert Cookson is going to drop in by parachute in order to clean our windows, and how many outsides does she think we all have?; one, two, three; in line, one in front of the other?' Harold said, muttering incoherently underneath his breath, so she couldn't detect his words by her lip-reading which she had perfected during the past forty-four years of marriage.

The impressive Ford Môndial crunched its way along the drive backwards towards the wrought-iron front gates which had been opened earlier by Harold after talking to his new friend, Brendon Kelly from Fylde Borough Council.

It was when the cat had disappeared out of sight from Calder Vale Avenue into Beechnut Drive; the mouse began to play beginning with a visit up to the attic to find the diaries left behind by Harold's late father and mother, Roland and Margery Rigby.

Following on from where Harold had left off, in between the horse racing at York and at Kempton Park on the Saturday afternoon of the previous week, he rummaged around inside a trunk to find countless artefacts of worthless unimportance, such as a pair of unwashed red translucent frilly knickers, a blackened silk handkerchief with the initials 'BR' embroidered in one corner, which he presumed belonged to Auntie Brenda Redman , a highly polished piece of Parkside Colliery coal made into an item of priceless jewellery, and an oily flat cap which looked as if it had just been run over by Fred Dibnah's steam roller; his first reaction to this was that his father may have been involved in a relationship with a British Rail fireman, or he unknowingly belonged to an Industrial Archaeology Society or a 'PE' teacher based in Lancashire.

Meanwhile, the Physical Exercise teacher cum-receptionist, with specialities, 'Jolly Baby' Pauline Evans wasn't to be exonerated from all of this nostalgic junk found up in the attic at No 23 Calder Vale Avenue that morning. There was a photograph of her basking naked in a shallow rock pool next to a bottle of 'Quick tan' bronzing cream, a discarded turquoise Licra low-back swimsuit, and a saturated copy of a pictorial "Tit-Bits" periodical floating on top of the water. She was wearing a flowing black wig which looked similar to a clump of slimy seaweed to disguise her natural blonde hair; it was plonked untidily on the top of her head to create the "Kiss me Quick" seaside headgear, and would not have been out of place served up in the "Wooden Gong" Vietnamese Restaurant in Lytham Saint Annes.

This was to become the last straw of Harold's little adventure up to the attic and it was at this point he wondered why he hadn't thought about rummaging through his father's things years ago. Again Harold realized why the intrepid Herbert-Cyril Birtwistle had extremely bad eyesight and was always looking for some loose change inside his trouser pocket to put into the wide-lens static telescope which was firmly fixed to the ground, and commanded an excellent view of the beach and wind protected sand hills.

Harold, having closed the trunk which had somehow managed to escape the 'Titanic' disaster, snapped it shut for the very last time, lest Mabel had designs on climbing up the ladder to excavate the contents of the attic. He again, had found the 'Boots' scribbling diary and autograph book which contained the names, addresses and telephone numbers of several people at 'Matt Jollies' Middleton Towers Holiday Camp in Morecambe in August 1958.

In particular, there was Jillian Beadmore's address in Bangor, North Wales, Herbert-Cyril Birtwistle's from the Wirral, Alan Hayes's from Darlington, and the ducking and diving Margaret Hogarth's from Freckleton; her house, just a stone's throw away from 'The Coach & Horses' pub in the village.

The first attempt to get in contact with Jillian Beadmore after all this time fell on stony ground when Harold phoned the number which was given to him all those years ago.

A woman, who sounded as though she was on her way out, or on her last legs, answered the phone at No 63 Tennyson Crescent, Bangor, Gwynedd, North Wales. As well as dishing out the "Fruit & Fibre" to ensure a healthy lifestyle at breakfast time, she had been left in charge of answering the phone which was placed high on a wall, making it difficult for her to reach from a nineteen-fifties wheelchair; these were just two of her daily duties at the 'Wallasey' Nursing Home on the Bridge north Estate.

'Oh, I think I've phoned the wrong number.' Harold said when a man called Mr Rumba, a Filipino businessman seemed to have snatched the phone out of Lilly's hand.

'My name is Mr Rumba, the Nursing Home proprietor, can I help you in any way; I must, first of all tell you, we don't care for incontinent patients because of us having too few bathrooms, but we make special provision for invalids in wheelchairs; they are accommodated on the ground floor next to the fire door because the stairs are totally inadequate to take them up to the rooms, and the smoke detectors are inactive because someone keeps removing the batteries; don't they Lilly?' he added, giving her another gentle nudge in her ribcage.

Harold made it quite clear to the proprietor, that he wasn't a geriatric and didn't want to surrender his pension book to a total stranger, supplementing Rumba's personal fortune, enhancing his cigarette smoking, and contributing towards the upkeep of his fine collection of classic cars parked up on a nearby farm. He suggested to Freddie Rumba, that if he didn't make plans to alter his nursing home, he would report him to the Health. If Bangor wasn't such a long distance away from Freckleton, Harold could have sworn he could hear the sound of a match being struck and could smell smoke which may have been wafting all around the building from an American "Lucky Strike" cigarette.

The proprietor, Freddie Rumba, who was as much use as a chocolate fireguard suggested that Harold make enquiries with the matron, a Mrs Shirley Powell, who proved to be excellent at window-dressing and nothing else.

'Hello.' Mrs Powell said in a Welsh accent which was enough to make sheep emigrate from Wales to New Zealand, and Snowdonian farmers to put on their Wellington boots and join them. 'And before you start, we are not in the business of removals, only if you are personally on your way out and you need some assistance by way of an undertaker; the firm is cheap and the director is called Heap; that sounds funny doesn't it?'

Rellies in Wellies
"Little 'Bo Peep' lost her sheep
And didn't know where to go
A farmer took her by the hand
She found them in New Zealand"

'I would like to put out an 'SOS' to look for a missing person; a Miss Jillian Beadmore who used to live at the 'Wallasey' Nursing Home's address.' Harold said giving her an instant headache before saying:'

'When I was in the Carmarthen Philharmonic Orchestra Choir, I sung "Songs of Sardou".' The matriarch of the staff tried to impress on Harold. 'Maybe, I will be able to find the person you are looking for, Mr Rigby. Now, let me see, this fine looking Edwardian house used to belong to the Beadmore Family way back, but they don't own it anymore.'

'And, why don't they own it anymore?'

'It's because they moved away from Bangor to live in Australia, didn't they Lilly?' Powell said after conferring with "Lilly the Pink" who, in the words of the Scaffold was not of this so-called human race.

'Well, thank you very much Mrs Powell, you have been most helpful and give my regards to Uriah Heap this evening when he arrives in the early hours to perform his take-away service, because I'm sure your residents will need a chapel of rest after having had the privilege of staying at the 'Wallasey' Nursing Home for a number of years.'

Harold's feelings and aspirations were dashed, knowing he would have to either get in touch with the detective, Sam Spades, or the Salvation Army's World-Wide People Finding Mission, that is, providing they don't visit the house rattling an empty tin.

The next person on Harold's to-do list was to try and find the intrepid Herbert-Cyril Birwistle, who was believed to have lived at No 47 Turnbull Street, Birkenhead. This was not to be, because shortly after his mother Rosemary died he married a school teacher and went to live in Skelmersdale, Lancashire where he became a Major in the Salvation Army and editor of their local newspaper. Further enquiries led him to Outer Mongolia where he and his missus were participating in voluntary service with the WVS, teaching descendants of Genghis Khan, how to make tambourines from pliable wood and untreated goatskins. Harold was not having much luck in trying to track down his distant friends, and what was the use of using the 'Internet' or a 'Smart Phone' when the only means of communication comes out from a clockwork radio.

'That is it.' Harold said, until he picked up his mobile phone for the umpteenth time in an attempt to contact one of his father's holiday camp friends, the eighty-five year old Middleton Towers 'Jolly Baby' Auntie Brenda Redman, who could be still living at No 3 Crab Apple Avenue, Wythenshawe; Manchester.

Again, this was to be an absolute no-no because the lady, a once high-kicking dancer in her twenties, would have been eighty five years of age in 2015 had it not been for a dodgy vegetable *samosa* she ate on a flight from Calcutta to Leeds. Apparently, Brenda was suitably impressed by her husband, an Indian gentleman who she met after he had won the limbo-dancing competition in the ballroom at Middleton Towers Holiday Camp where the splitting of the trousers bore no significance as to why she became married to a sixty-five year-old fitness fanatic and Yoga expert from Huddersfield. Rumour had it, Rudyard Cumin Seed, a cotton weaver by trade, was double-jointed and had the ability to bend backwards, put his head between his legs while he enjoyed the Pakistani cricket team being beaten by England on a water-logged crease during a test match at Edgbaston.

At this point, Mabel came home and after parking the car in the driveway said:

'Had a busy morning my dearest husband.'

'Well, I might have, if it wasn't for the telephone which continually kept on ringing.'

'I see, you have been failing in your duties once again, Harold; the dishes haven't been washed, the brass ornaments haven't been polished and the inside of the windows haven't been cleaned, also, Prince needs to be taken for his walkies.'

'Was there anything else you would have liked me to do while you were sitting comfortably having your hair done at 'Waves Emporium', and your talons clipped at 'Nails'. Tell me Mabel, did they use gas or electricity when they decided to plug you in; either way you were reprieved for another two weeks.'

'Harold.'

'Yes dear?'

'Just keep your mouth firmly shut, will you?'

'Well, I'll try.'

Moments later there was a loud yell from the top of the stairs, it was Mabel again.

'Harold.'

'Yes dear.....'

'Get your backside up here right now.'

Not knowing just what to expect, Harold warily made his way up to the top of the stairs.

'What is this laying on our marital bed?'

'It's a black and white photograph.' Harold replied stammering for the second time in his life; the first was when he had to say, 'I do' at the Church of the Holy Trinity in Freckleton several years ago.

'Yes, I can see what it is.' she replied. 'Who is it, where did you get it from, and more importantly, what are you doing with it?'

'Oh. I was searching through a few things in the attic and discovered it inside a box, hence the particles of dust covering one side of the bed.' Harold said convincingly.

'Who is she, Harold, and couldn't she afford to buy any clothes, and do you know Harold, if it wasn't for her wearing that awful wig, I could swear she looks like that artificial sun-tanned 'Jolly Baby', Pauline Evans who was part of the participating staff at Middleton Towers when we first met.'

Chapter Twenty-one

The first visit to Thompson's travel agents in Lytham that afternoon

The engine in the car hadn't been given the chance to cool down when Harold said to Mabel:

'Come on get your glad-rags on because we're going to Thomson's travel agents to book a short break to Amsterdam.'

'But, I am wearing my glad-rags, lest you haven't noticed, Harold; you don't seem to pay much attention to what I wear these days.'

'Well, you look very nice anyway.' he replied nonchalantly. 'I will do the driving this afternoon and you can sit in the back seat because we don't want your hair to fall out of place when I open the window to allow some fresh air to enter into the car; the hair spray they use at 'Waves Hair Emporium' brings back memories of the tiny bottle of scent I used to give to my mum when I returned home from the school trip to 'Heysham Head', the fun village, on the outskirts of Morecambe.'

'That was a long time ago, Harold, way before my time, and a long time before you and I met.'

'I know, but, it still smells the same.' Harold reiterated, looking now at a manicured set of French nails, pink in the middle and white around the edges, which initially, were stuck on with a 'Super glue' type substance similar to 'Araldite', and before being varnished with OPI lacquer, part of the Fiji collection, and blow-dried in a machine that makes a noise like an electronic hand dryer on Preston bus station.

'What smells the same Harold; Heysham Head, or my perfume; I would have thought the fragrance from a Nina Ricci bottle would smell much better than taking in intoxicating fumes from by-products produced in a nearby oil refinery in Middleton.'

'It is your perfume that smells the same.' Harold said. 'I can remember coming home from school having been dropped off from a Premier Coach and then presenting a small unidentified cardboard box to my mother, who immediately took one whiff before placing it inside the bottom drawer of her dressing table; it was still there when she died.'

'I have bought you something nice for you evening meal, Harold, and I hope you will enjoy every bit of it?'

'Not Sirloin steak again, Mabel, can you not diversify and prepare something simple to ring the changes; for example, a simple dish consisting of honeycomb tripe and onions with a delicious '*Béchamal*' sauce, followed by tinned Ambrosia Rice Pudding and strawberry jam.'

'No it isn't Sirloin steak, Harold, it is a dish made from Poisonous mushrooms, garlic bread, and a broth made from bat droppings.'

'The food sounds remarkably like the stuff John Ashworth and I ate and drank all those years ago when we were abducted from our tent in the middle of the night.'

'I know, Harold, incredible isn't it? How time flies by so quickly, especially if you're sitting on the back seat of a broomstick drugged-up to the eyeballs on 'Ecstasy', hallucinatory 'LSD' and 'Speed'.

'And, what is that supposed to mean, Mabel?'

'Well, with all the cavorting which was going on, it's a wonder you didn't catch your death of cold.' she said without compassion.

'I was wearing my pyjamas and an anorak and a scarf at the time.' Harold made clear.

'And, apart from when you wrestled with a fourteen-foot crocodile in Queensland, made friends with a Great White Shark in Melbourne, and charmed the pants off a Suzie Wong in Hong Kong, I suppose that was the fastest you've ever moved in your life.'

'No, Mabel, the fastest time was when I was chased off a farm in Pemberton for nicking a sack of onions; I used to disguise myself as a 'Jonny Onions', purporting to be French, and ride my bone-shaker of a bicycle with the merchandise strung together on either side of the forks.

'Do you know Harold, not only am I married to a fibber, I have a tea-leaf on my hand as well.'

'Did you know Mabel, the breakfast cereal, 'Cocoa Pops' are by appointment to Her Majesty Queen Elizabeth the Second?' he said looking at a fake box of the said product which was produced by a Belgium manufacturer called "Ever been had Supplies", distributing to retail outlets in France, Germany, Great Britain and all around the World.

'No, I didn't know that.' Mabel said disbelievingly until she read the inscription on the front of the box. 'And I don't suppose the Office of Fair Trading or the Race Relations Board know that either; I can't see her majesty eating 'Cocoa Pops' for breakfast, not with an Al Jolson look-alike on the back, and I will bet, she doesn't clear up after breakfast, polish the brass and clean the inside of the windows.'

'I will agree to that, Mabel; that's my job, and, did you know,' he added. 'The Queen eats 'Heinz' Baked Beans?'

'Don't be silly, Harold; the Queen would never eat baked beans for health and safety reasons.'

'Well, she does, and that is why she has lots of ladies in waiting; remember, Queen Elizabeth the First?'

'I can't say that I do Harold, I wasn't in existence at the time.'

'It is important to note, Mabel, that in 1581, Sir Walter Raleigh brought Haricot Beans and Black-eyed Peas back from South America, the Spanish Main and Guyana, and with the aid of some Heinz tomato ketchup he presented a large plateful to her having gone over the top with Caribbean chilli peppers, regardless to say he was beheaded several months later in 1592 for giving the Queen of England the idea he was a smart arse; far too clever for her. His cloak is still in the dry cleaners after he had thrown it down on to the mud for Elizabeth to walk upon.'

'Oh how awful.' Mabel said with great sadness before Harold continued telling her about how Sir Walter Raleigh introduced King Edward potatoes to Ireland, and how they became part of the country's staple diet, but that was before bottles of Guinness came along,' he continued, 'and instigated a catastrophic potato famine which lasted until nineteen sixty-four; the advent of the Anglo British Turkish kebab. He also brought back pot plants too, hallucinatory by-products of the marijuana family.' Harold went on. 'It is of little wonder why Queen Elizabeth the First was as bald as a coot and had ruthless barbaric tendencies and I can understand why she wanted to remain a virgin; it is because if she had children they would have all been drugged-up to the eyeballs.'

'Are we going to go now, Harold, or are you going to give me another lecture on sixteenth- century outlandish behaviour, most of it stemming from the Royal Court, written by Neville Williams and edited by Antonia Fraser. I sincerely want to get back home to see a repeat episode of the "Antiques Road Show", it's coming from a place called Samlesbury Hall, near Preston; I don't suppose you've ever heard of it, have you Harold?'

'Well, I never did'

'Well, you never did what Harold?'

'Well fancy that.' he replied before falling into the realms of incoherence.

'Fancy what? she said puzzlingly.

'Just fancy, we will be seeing Samlebury Hall on our television set; it was only yesterday we were there.' he said, with a muffled voice that sounded like a vicar inside a Gothic church with acoustics echoing all around the walls.

'Yes.' Mabel said with dismay. 'And, it was only yesterday we went to that Conundrum Lane in the Trough, the Forest of Bowland, and met up with that stupid witch, Louise Hubbard; I smelt a rat as soon as we knocked on her door.'

'You know dear, I felt the same way and for me, it was as if the past was returning to the present making the hairs on the back of my neck stand up.'

'That reminds me. Harold, you are in desperate need of a haircut.'

'All in good time my dear, all in good time.'

'And, at the same time, Harold, you can perhaps tell the barber to shave off that stupid beard; it looks like you have just arrived from the "Planet of the Apes".'

'Tell me Mabel, where are we going to eat at lunchtime because Thomson's travel agents don't open until two o'clock, and you know how you get angry if you don't eat at regular intervals; I suppose that's why they invented the 'Milky Way' chocolate bar because it's the only sweet you can eat without ruining your appetite.'

'I can remember the mini Hovis.' Mabel said, reminiscing of her school days in Southport. 'They were miniature wholemeal brown loaves, chewy, wholesome and fresh, ideal for eating between meals and they only cost two pence. 'The Grapes' at Wray Green do lunches, that's if you can stand listening to those back seat drivers of multi-million pound jet fighter aircraft talking about how they can take-off from the aerodrome at Warton at three o'clock in the afternoon, circumnavigate the Orkney's and still be back home for afternoon tea and biscuits at four-twenty-five.'

'These jet fighter aircraft must travel very fast, Mabel, to go down to the Falkland Islands in less than one and a half hours because in nineteen eight-two it took the British Task Force two weeks to get down there; how times have changed.'

'I just want to put the record straight.' Mabel said shaking her head in total despair. 'The Orkneys are in the Outer Hebrides, to the North of Scotland.'

'Oh, now I remember, it is that God forsaken place in the Northern hemisphere where everyone wield axes, eat reindeer meat, and live like bears, and during the cold winter months these centrally heated Vikings set fire to long ships after the Northern lights have been put on to dimmer.'

'Do you know, Harold, you are truly amazing because your extensive range of geographical knowledge holds no boundaries.'

'Why don't we go to the *"Dickins"*, the 'Pickwick Tavern'?' Harold enthusiastically suggested. 'The pub serves food all day, and I believe the steak and kidney pie will be an excellent choice; the dish is served with all the trimmings, new potatoes, baby carrots and fresh garden peas and the 'Bisto' gravy is just something else, similar to Wincanton axle grease.'

'Okay, that sounds good to me.' she replied knowing that Harold's plans for him to drive the car had completely changed. 'I think, perhaps, I will box clever and just have a Mexican chilli burger and chips, you cannot go wrong with that kind of food, can you?'

'The restaurant also serves *'Chicken Kiev'.'* Harold graphically pointed out. 'This dish is served with a choice of chips, roast or mash potatoes and Harry Ramsden's mushy peas. The main part of the course arrives at the table with a slight difference; it is a succulent half-roast chicken with green stuff oozing out from its backside.'

The time was nearing one o'clock when Harold and Mabel walked into the 'Pickwick Tavern' by way of one of the two entrances at the front of the building. It is applicable to note that only ten minutes earlier a huge crowd of British Aerospace Systems employees had systematically made their way out of the pub and cavalry-charged through the gates in a wild attempt to beat the digital clocks which are commonplace throughout the plant.

Every second counts when lunchtime revellers leave a trail of debris behind in their wake; plastic sandwich containers, fish and chip wrapping paper, empty Burton's 'Wagon Wheel' packets, and recycled polystyrene burger boxes which had the same characteristic similarity to highly inflammable ceiling tiles or cavity wall insulation; both of which would be a BAE Systems fireman's nightmare if someone was careless with either a blow lamp or a box of matches.

Harold and Mabel chose a seat underneath an original eighteenth century window where the afternoon light shone in on to a dark wood table which had probably been wiped more times than David Cameron's bottom.

The food was ordered by Harold at a desk in a separate part of the dining area where they were given a time of ten minutes to wait for the food to arrive at their table. This was all reminiscent of the days when he used to frequent the pub after repetitively replacing avionic equipment in multi-million pound aircraft inside one of the hangars at the *"dooin's"*. Sometimes, there would be a rare leisurely moment when he would pretend to be one of the test pilots, sitting cosily in the front seat of the cockpit, and after pulling 'G', the joy-stick would be again pulled back to its maximum in the hope that in his dreams he could raise the roof, which over a number of years dealing with unwavering bosses, became his favourite occupation. Many workers throughout British Industry are seduced by promises of stardom; allusions of grandeur; others are left alienated by so-called leaders who seem to be unwilling or unable to take the decisive action that is so desperately needed. Gone are the days of instant decision making skills and qualities; it is like the old adage "Send reinforcements we're going to advance, and by the time the issue in question had finally reached the end of the line, it was "Send three and four pence we're going to a dance.

'Nice in here, isn't it Mabel; makes a change from 'The Coach & Horses' doesn't it?'

'Yes, I quite like the fire place and the chimney breast; it gives you an idea of how the pub really was like way back in the early nineteenth century when it was called the 'Clifton Arms', I have a couple of Christmas cards in the drawer back home showing you how it looked in the days of Queen Victoria. Stage coaches used to come by here on their way to Lytham St Annes and Blackpool.'

'The only stage coaches and horses you will see tethering up outside the 'Pickwick Tavern' nowadays are covered wagons and ponies from the 'Ponderosa', the Country & Western Club on Lytham Road. I believe the 'hoe down' on Saturday nights is a real hoot when they bring Roy Rogers, Gene Autry, Merle Haggard, Tammy Wynette and Patsy Cline back to life again, and then shoot the living daylights out of the compere with a Colt forty-five handgun.

'I would like to join the line-dancing club; they say it's good for your figure, and to wear one of those colourful western hats with a drawstring, that would be equally nice, wouldn't it Harold?'

'Oh yes, really nice, and I could dress up looking like a Native American; a Red Indian complete with feathers, and furthermore, I could do a war dance and prance around the stage similar to Jimmy Summerville.'

'You see the barmaid behind the bar?' Mabel said, and now beginning to feel hungry for the first time.'

'You mean Carol Rutledge?'

'Yes, if that's what you want to call her.'

'Well, she used to work in the 'Queen's' pub in Lytham and had a reputation of turning up late on Sunday lunchtimes because she had another job.'

'And what job was that, if I may ask without being rude?'

'She was the goalkeeper for the "Tangerinies", the ladies football team in Blackpool and they used to have a knees-up every Saturday evening in Bloomfield Road, especially when they played Burnley "Pathetics" in the ladies premier league.

'Do you know Mabel; I have often wondered why she has knobbly knees, sports a 'Number One' haircut, and is blessed with a broken nose.'

'That's not by playing football.' Mabel said, folding her arms and looking up towards the ceiling.

'Oh, I get it, she fumbles around on her hands and knees in the dark, has chemotherapy once a week and as well as being in a ladies football team, she's into kick boxing too.'

'Harold, please be sensible, I'm only trying to tell you what extra mural activities these people from Warton get up to on a day-to-day basis, our barman, for instance, being a prime example.'

'Okay then, what does he do when he's not serving *ooch*, 'Desperado' Sangria, 'Smirnoff Vodka Ice' and 'Tequila Bonanzas' with lime wedges poking out from the neck of the bottles.'

'Alison told me he is called Mark Turley and is sub-contracted to BAE Systems, works incognito, and is into information technology, computers, that sort of thing. He spends most of his time fishing and snooping around, hacking into people's desk tops and reporting any budding computer chess champions or 'Snake' experts to his or her manager; that's why he's got a black eye.'

'My word, Mabel, you seem to know everyone around here.' he sighed.

'Well, it doesn't take a great deal of brain power to get to know the regulars, they come in all different guises, the rough and the smooth; the rough mainly. Take, for instance, the guy with the much lived-in face sitting on the stool in the corner, he is a regular and has been coming into the 'Pickwick Tavern' for years; you can always tell when he's in evidence because he leaves a trail of muddy footprints on the floor when he walks in.'

'His father used to come in here, apparently, and sit by the old log fire on cold winters evenings when the snow was piled up high on either side of the front door; those were the days when they served parched peas, pigeon pie and jacket potatoes for supper; these days, its eight ounce rib-eye steaks, a half-roast chicken and chips, Beef Madras Curry or a spicy Mexican chilli Burger.'

'Talking about food, Harold, we have been here for over half an hour and there is still no sign of it.'

'If you will be patient, Mabel, I will go and find out just how much longer we will have to wait for our meal.' Harold said concernedly.

'By the way our table is number two, Harold, not number twenty two, which is at the other end of the pub's restaurant.' Mabel said to him when the waitress said she couldn't find the person who had ordered the food and apologised for it being cold.

'Enjoy your meal.' she said with an apprehensive look. 'The condiments are over there on top of the cabinet and if you want any more chilli, madam, I will be more than pleased to get you some from the kitchen to bring your burger back to life again.'

'Two; twenty-two, what does it matter, she could have easily gone around all the tables and asked if it was ours; people don't use the intelligence rule these days.' he said doing his best to exonerate himself from any blame.

'Listen, Harold, if it wasn't for you giving the restaurant staff the wrong table number we could have been eating our dessert; two scoops of strawberry and vanilla ice cream, instead of you beginning to dissect a half roast chicken, and me munching my way through a Mexican chilli burger which could be mistaken for a 'cantina' well-trodden door mat in El Paso. I think I will take up Alison's offer of having more chilli sauce brought to our table to add a little more spice to my so-called hot chilli burger which is in desperate need of chucking back onto the char grill; and just where did she say the English mustard, the tomato and 'HP' sauce is located Harold?'

'Oh, about two miles down the road, past the traffic lights and they are in a mobile home park on the left-hand side of the road.'

'You will have your little joke, won't you Harold.'

'I'm not joking, it was only last week the dustbin men found a whole stack of books with "Harris Library" embossed on the first and last pages and judging by the covers, they had been loaned out to someone who was heavily into criminology and should be locked up.'

Chapter Twenty-two

"I ho..... I ho

    I ho, I ho, it's off to town they go

    To book a trip where they make egg-flip

    I ho, I ho, I ho, I ho....."

'This place is very popular, Mabel; there still seems to be a great deal of money sloshing around this neck of the woods; they must be paying them too much.' Harold would insist in saying loudly when a queue was formed just inside the door of Thompson's, the travel agents.

'Who is paying them too much, Harold?'

'The people who they work for, Mabel; you can always tell when there has been a big pay settlement at the Winter Gardens in Blackpool; the employees from BAE Systems in particular, all walk around with wide beams on their faces having got what they wanted and before diving into the first bucket shop they can find to look for cheap flights to Jersey, the Isle of Man, or to book an all-inclusive two-week holiday in a half-built hotel in Benidorm.'

'If you had played your cards right and behaved yourself, Harold, you could still have been there, working your cotton socks off until you are seventy, and in that way you would have been able to join them in Blackpool.'

'Are you, or are you not, the full box of matches, Mabel? As you very well know, we are now in receipt of a very good pension from Aerospace and, it's about time some of the 'hangers-on', hung their boots up to give the younger generation a chance to have a go at their bosses.'

'Do you know Harold, I didn't know you cared so much; I'm greatly impressed.' she said with extreme reverence knowing what he was going to say next.

'Well, some of us had to work for a living, and you haven't done too badly from the proceeds, have you Mabel, which is why we are standing at the back of a queue waiting to be attended to, and by my estimation we should still be here two weeks on Tuesday.'

'Harold, you do seem to exaggerate; it won't be long now until we are at the front of the queue because from where I am standing and from what I can see by just looking around, most of the customers are tyre-kickers and only want to browse through the tour operator brochures; can you just imagine if it was raining, the place would be packed to the gunnels?'

'Yes, I can well imagine, you never know, Mabel, we may get back in time to watch the "Antiques Road show' after all, and we don't want to miss that, do we my dear?'

'Next.'

'We will be next, Harold,' she, more hopefully said to him when a woman in her eighties plonked a Saga Holiday brochure down on the desk in front of the travel agent, Mrs Janice Pickering.

'I want to go to Minorca.' the woman said to her forcibly. 'I want to go to one of those over-sixties 'Beach Clubs' and soak up the sun; I would prefer one that has an indoor pool just in case the weather decides to take a turn for the worse, and preferably, I would like to stay in one of those holiday complexes that doesn't tag you like a cancer patient in the Royal Victoria Hospital in Blackpool.' she added.

'Well, in that case.' Mrs Pickering said. 'How about a three months Saga extravaganza holiday in Malta, the climate is very good there, but in February it can be a wee bit inclement and you will need your rain-mate to stop your hair from falling out. You can also save on your fuel bills back home, and where the hotel is situated, the sea comes over the wall on to the road; it was only last year when two of our clients were walking along the promenade in the picturesque seaside town of Sliema and haven't been seen since.'

'Is she, or is she not, going to book this bloody holiday because time is getting on and the way things are going the tulips, daffodils and hyacinths will be in bloom before we ever get to Amsterdam.' Harold complained, looking in front and at the back of the woman who was wearing Nora Batty type stockings which were twisted around her ankles; her thunderous anatomy having the hallmarks of her being related to the late Liberal Member of Parliament for Rochdale, Cyril Smith.

'I have a two-week holiday in Bournemouth Mrs Boardman, and the

"Ravens Brook" hotel is near to the centre of the town, next to the British Gas offices.'

'The woman looks as though she's stroking a parrot, Harold.' Mabel said, when she observed a heavily-veined hand crawling over the back of one of Mrs Boardman's shoulders.'

'No, no, Mabel.' Harold said, regaining his confidence, knowing that they would be served within the next forty-eight hours. 'The woman is obviously practicing yoga and is limbering up prior to her wading into the sea in Bournemouth to cause a '*Satsuma*', an enormous tidal wave stretching as far as the Isle of White; can you remember those saucy seaside postcards one could buy in the souvenir shop on Boscombe pier; those with shapely bathing belles, and women with bosoms the size of basket balls, and enormous behinds which could easily be used to park a three-speed 'Raleigh' bicycle?'

'Yes, I do remember those, especially the black and white ones you bought showing Brigitte Bardot climbing into a bath; you should be more careful where you choose to hide things because I have the ability to spot certain things at forty paces. And, please lower the tone of your voice Harold; people can hear what you're saying.'

'You haven't seen what is hidden inside the roll of lino in the garage, have you Mabel? You missed that didn't you?'

'Don't worry Harold; I will get there before you to see what has been placed inside, and if it is what I think it is, I shan't talk to you for a week.'

'A week; is that all?' he said hoping she was going to extend the embargo to another few days. 'I wouldn't have thought a copy of 'Jane's' weekly was enough to silence you, Mabel; Ingrid Bergman was a fine looking woman, especially when she played Ilsa in the classic 1940s film "Casablanca".

'Well,' Mabel said, 'I suppose, the situation could have been worse.'

'What do you mean?' he replied.

'For instance, you could have taken a shine to Rock Hudson when he starred in "Pillow Talk".'

'It is in Rock Hudson's wildest dreams.' Harold said, with a cheeky Cheshire cat grin on his face.

'Rock Hudson; he was one of them.' Mabel said. 'You know, one of those that Mother Nature played a nasty trick on; these unfortunate people have the ability to entertain the public when they walk along the pavements, and it's as if something or someone could be responsible for causing their affliction; shame in it?' she added with the utmost compassion.

'Everyone thought he was macho, but that was until the pathologist found him to be wearing pink frilly knickers.' Harold said, knowing full well the story wasn't true.

Meanwhile, the holiday of a lifetime had been booked for the woman in front who had as much charm as a soggy chip and, looking at the elasticised support bandages which were swathed around her legs, she could have easily been mistaken for an Egyptian mummy. The holiday, apparently was a fortnight in Torquay, staying at the famous 'Gleneagles Hotel' where people say, the general comfort is on a par with "Fawlty Towers".

'Next, please.....' Mrs Pickering said with a tired expression upon her face having just said goodbye to a fourth dynasty Queen Nefertiti.

The Rigby's sat down while Mrs Pickering got up from her seat to make a beeline to look for a couple of aspirins inside her handbag.

It was when she had composed herself, the travel agent asked: 'And, where would you two like to go to this weekend, China, Tibet, the Himalayas, Outer Mongolia, Clacton-on-Sea or Bognor Regis?'

'We would just like to book a holiday which is advertised in your window Mrs Pickering; you know the British Airways trip to Holland.' Mabel said to begin an enquiry.

'Oh, you won't like Amsterdam, The Haag or Haarlem.' Janice Pickering said. 'The city itself smells of Edam cheese and rotting cabbage leaves which have been thrown into the canals from steam-driven barges and bridges; the nightlife is not that special either, at night the district is transformed into dens of iniquity and there isn't a Methodist Church in sight. I went to Amsterdam once with a female friend of mine,' Janice would insist on telling us. 'We went into a bar on the salubrious and notorious *Canal Straat*, where the manageress was a man and smoked

Dutch Maritime 'Shag' tobacco; he would insist on showing us his stocking-clad legs which he kept on bending backwards and forwards until someone who had the misfortune to sit in front of the bar fell off their stool.'

'We are only going to visit the libraries, museums and places of historical importance, aren't we Harold?'

'Yes dear, that's right, that's right.'

'Take for instance, the famous Amsterdam Diamond Centre.' Mabel put in. 'You could perhaps, buy me a diamond eternity ring instead of the charm bracelet, and which would be in keeping with my wedding ring.'

'Yes dear, have you got anything else you could possibly tempt me with; a large bottle of export Heineken, a block of 'Moroccan Black' cannabis or a Malaysian tart hanging out from one of those red-light windows.'

'Don't worry, Harold, you will be safe with me; no one will get the chance to go anywhere near you, not even the chamber maid, can you remember.....?'

'Yes, I can remember it all too well, Mabel; it was when we were going through France.'

'You mean when *you* were going through France, Harold, and I'm sure Mrs Pickering doesn't want to hear any of that.'

'No, no, please do go on Mrs Rigby, it's not often I get to know the autopsies and stories from clients after they have returned from their holidays; some of them never return, they either die of sun-stroke or buy a villa in Spain.'

'Well, that's a comforting thought, Mrs Pickering; tell me, did any of them work for BAE Systems at Warton?'

'It was like this, Mrs Pickering.' Mabel said. 'It was when Harold and I were staying at a hotel in Rheims I decided to go out on my own to do some shopping. I came back to find Nell Gwynn, the chamber maid trying to part with her oranges in our bedroom; she was having a bit of trouble with her basket which had been left in the corridor inside a pram, hadn't it Harold?'

'Yes, Mabel, she was distraught and needed someone to talk to.'

'You mean to someone who wasn't wearing any shoes?'

'I think Amsterdam should be a good choice, after all, Mr, Mrs Rigby; just sign on the dotted line and don't forget when you return from your holiday, I will want to know all the juicy bits.'

'We'll do our very best.' Harold said to her with a sense of enthusiasm like a ringmaster inside a circus tent when he was about to introduce the next act.

'Come on Harold, let's go home and watch the "Antiques Road show" because I'm dying to know what the well-known antiques expert, Eric Knowles has to show us this week?' Mabel said giving him the impression Knowles had something that Harold lacked.

'Maybe, you could call in and see him because he was born in Nelson near Pendle Hill.' Harold sarcastically put in.

'Oh, we're off back to Pendle again, are we; it's a pity you didn't stay up there when you were just a slip of a lad cavorting with those so-called witches; nymphomaniacs more like.' she said.

'Well, put it this way.' Harold replied. 'If John Ashworth and I had stayed up there in the Forest of Bowland, no one would have noticed back home because my mum and dad were far too busy swigging pints of beer back in the 'Coach & Horses' pub, and you wouldn't have had the privilege of meeting me all those years ago.'

'And what about your sister, Veronica; where was she in all of this?'

'Oh, apart from a wet cuddly toy, she was probably alone in her bed sobbing her heart out; things were like that in those days.'

'How awful,' Mabel said with tears in her eyes.

'Yes, things were a lot different then, but nowadays, parents would be locked-up for leaving their kids unattended.' he emphasised.

"Silent Nights"

Glancing at Shadows around four bedroom Walls
The gas mantle is dimmed as night time falls
Down to the depths of the bed we would slide
An idyllic place where one can still hide
Away from the dark and dismal atmosphere

That induced evil thoughts
And brought unwanted cheer
It was a place where we would be
In a dream world beyond reality
The snow was melting from white into grey
As a drunk passed our window to make it our day
When on Christmas Eve, the last knell of the bell
The drunk fell down a hole, and said bloody hell
It was back into a bed with a blanket so thick
We had to lie down next to an Accrington brick
Wrapped in white linen to add to the heat
It was a shame it couldn't have been extended
to an outside toilet seat
Our parents came back sometime in the morning
When the cock crowed
And the milk maids were yawning
They sneaked into our room smelling of booze
To hang up our stockings while we were trying to snooze
And when we got up my sister would say
Not nuts, tangerines and fruit gums again
"Merry Christmas" Harold,
And have a nice day

'Put the kettle on, Mabel; we can have a nice cup of tea and a piece of that strawberry flan you painstakingly made at the weekend. We can also have some crème fresh; the stuff that one shakes-up and then instantly disappears in front of your very eyes. The programme will be starting in fifteen minutes, and one has to allow time for a handle or a spout to be glued on to a china tea pot which was probably manufactured inside a Staffordshire pottery and sold during the Pot Fair on Preston market.'

'Yes dear.' Mabel said with air of foreboding knowing their 'Willow Pattern' tea service was bought from a Stoke-on-Trent auctioneer who was an expert with a hammer.

'It's like being at the cinema, isn't it Mabel?'

'Just shut up and eat your cake, Harold, you might miss something.'

'The show is just about to start, Mabel, are you sitting comfortably?' he said looking at a bird's eye view of Samlesbury Hall from a helicopter which had followed the M6 motorway all the way up from Manchester's 'Ringway' Airport via the "Little Chef" Diner at Knutsford in Cheshire.

'Ah, doesn't it look lovely.' Mabel said nostalgically, as if the place had changed dramatically by some strange metamorphosis from yesterday morning's visit.

Following the introduction which included yet another mentioning of the notorious Lancashire Witches, Harold saw what looked like the bureaux which belonged to the late Lady Geraldine Harkness and suggested it could be possible that the phantom white lady of Samlesbury Hall who was ultimately responsible for taking two German Daimler Benz Chrysler articulated trucks off the road, was indeed her.

'At what time does the usherette come round with the choc ices, Mabel, because there is more to this item of furniture than what you think?' Harold said when Eric Knowles looked underneath the desk to find a piece of paper fixed on to its base with four rusty old staples and showing the manufacturer's name, the date, where it was made and how much it cost.

The faded information became clear that the drab Victorian desk was made by a George Woodbine in the Kings Road, London during the late nineteen century at a cost of fifty-four pounds and ninety-five pence halfpenny; the latter denomination being the price of the four staples.

'We have a piece of paper stuck on the bottom of our Hi-fi cabinet, Harold; it has been there ever since we bought it from MFI.'

'I will have a look and see what it says, Mabel, and you never know it could have been made by a well-known cabinet-maker in Bond Street.'

'I wouldn't have thought so, Harold, because it is made from plywood and was probably knocked up by a Joe Blogs on an industrial estate in Coventry for the same price.'

Chapter Twenty-three

A series of hilarious events continued and recalled at breakfast the following day.

'I am so pleased we have booked the mini-break to Amsterdam, Harold; it will be just like old times again, going around the street markets and looking for bargains while listening to traditional barrel organ music.'

'You mean when we visited Rheims in France, Mabel, and we listened to a barrel organ playing 'Queen's' "It's a kind of Magic" followed by "La vie en Rose", popularised by the French singer, the late Edith Piaf, also commonly known as the 'Little Sparrow'.'

'Yes, Harold, and can you also remember the time we were sitting outside a street café during the carnival, and a clown who was walking on a pair of stilts hit you on the head with an enormous plastic hammer?'

'And, I can also vividly remember, the Rottweiler inside the cafe going crazy having just seen a red-head of a buffoon towering at least seven-feet high above the brassiere's canopy.' Harold said, trying to avoid opening up an old wound on the top of his head. 'It is of little wonder why it shot out from the establishment and took a chunk out of the clown's wooden leg.'

'Well, it was carnival time, and one is allowed to go a little wild for a few hours.' she said benevolently.

'A few hours, Mabel; the festivities lasted for two days, and it took the coach driver five hours during the first afternoon trying to find his huge state-of-the art wing mirrors.'

'Anyway, anything goes and is negotiable in Rheims, Harold, even you.'

'Is this why the mirrors were found positioned on either side of a fourth-floor bedroom window, Mabel, so that the occupants would know if the *Police*, the *'Gendarmerie'* or the *CRS* were about to arrive on their doorstep?'

'That was a hoot, wasn't it, dear when the local constabulary arrived outside the hotel 'Des Arts' in rue de Cool, and an entire French family were lined up in order of size and misdemeanours'.' reminding him of the more sleazy aspects of their holidaying in France.

'And, can you also remember, Mabel when the local populous, mainly Portuguese, were hanging over the railings of their balconies cheering with excitement hoping things would hot up and someone would get shot in a failed attempt to escape apprehension; it was "West Side Story" all over again. Remember that awful woman, the village busybody who must have been in her late seventies conducting the proceedings; the police had the misfortune to have her interfere when a motor scooter rode at speed on to the pavement to avoid a set of traffic lights, and to add to the frivolity, the pillion rider snatched her wicker basket containing three loaves and five fishes having just visited the Saturday morning market after being given the opportunity to say three hail Mary's in front of a Roman Catholic priest to convince him she wasn't an urban terrorist.'

'Could you please bring me the breadknife from the kitchen drawer, Harold; it is the one we bought from a departmental store in Brussels when we were travelling en route to Germany; the famous breadknife with a serrated edge concealed inside a wooden sheath to emulate a freshly baked French baguette, and it is also the one that nearly got us arrested at the Port of Dover when it fell out of your day-bag on to a rubber conveyor belt as we walked poker-faced through the customs and excise building; that was the time the coach driver came back with enough cheese and wine in his hold to open up an auxiliary Morrison's supermarket on Preston Docks.'

'The final straw was when I opened up a brand-new pack of playing cards which I bought from an 'Alcon' Hypermarket near Calais.' Harold said miserably. 'I was hoping to benefit by seeing the French 'bimbo', Brigit Bardot, posing in various frames of undress but, unfortunately the packaging had been wrongly put together, and when we played 'Poker' I had to contend with the American horn player, Louis Armstrong acting as the "Ace of Spades".'

'Ah, Sambo, he played a wonderful trumpet; you must admit Harold.'

'His stage name was "Satchmo", not "Sambo", Mabel, and I didn't expect to find fifty-two picture cards with him trying to blow his brains out from two heavily-suntanned bulbous cheeks.'

'We still have those playing cards in the sideboard; I tell you what Harold, I will shuffle them, and afterwards we can both cut for who goes into the village this morning to do the shopping.'

'Okay, Mabel, but don't blame me if you pick up my most hated card, the two of diamonds; not only as it cost me a fortune in the past but, it also depicts Louis on the reverse singing with Ella Fitzgerald which is enough to stop one, and to try one's 'Patience' for life.'

'Ah, very funny Harold, and the only fortune you have ever lost at cards, is a two hundred gramme bag of 'Duty Free' chocolate 'Minstrels' you bought on a British Rail Ferry. It was a good thing we didn't bet on the magazine you had stashed away in the garage, Harold, because you would have lost; I don't suppose Lou Hefner would be very pleased to hear that one of his top-shelf magazines had ended up inside a roll of surplus kitchen linoleum.'

'Do you know, Mabel, you have missed your calling; you should have been a detective and I am beginning to wonder what other things of insignificant non-importance you have found lying around the house?'

'Well, now you have bothered to mention it, I did find a pair of frilly knickers in the attic, Harold, and here was me thinking you were on the turn.'

'They belonged to my father.'

'He wasn't on the turn as well, was he?'

'Oh, come on Mabel, give me a break, and as you know, he liked the ladies, especially the ones who wore white short pleated skirts, uplifting bras, ankle socks and trainers; remember the floozy who entered into the sack race at Middleton Towers Holiday Camp? Every time she jumped up and down inside the sandbag, she was nearly knocked unconscious by the simultaneous movement of her boobs.'

'Yes, I can remember it all too well; the highlight of the afternoon's entertainment was when your father came to her aid by helping her out of the sack having fallen flat on what looked like a pair of over-inflated balloons.'

'It was this; amongst other things which contributed to my dad becoming the runner-up in the 'Man of the Week' award ceremony at

Morecambe, and no one can take that away from him.'

'I don't suppose anyone would want to.' Mabel said when she looked at the plaque deliberately placed high and askew on the wall inside the hall.

'It is now ladies before gentlemen.' Harold said after he had shuffled to death the pack of highly desirable playing cards. 'You cut first, Mabel; I feel this is going to be my lucky day.' he added, pre-empting her going out to do the shopping by placing her Burberry raincoat on one of the fireside chairs.

'Bloody hell, it's that Sam Spades again; that Louis Armstrong fellow blowing his heart out, and of all the cards in the pack, you would have to choose him.'

'Now, it's your turn, Harold.'

'Two of diamonds, it is just my luck to pick Ella Fitzgerald.'

'Would you mind putting my coat back in the hall, Harold; I think you had better find your umbrella because it looks like it is going to rain.'

'That's what the hangman said when he took a prisoner outside to be hanged.'

'Ah, very funny Harold.' she quickly put in.

'What was funny Mabel?' the prisoner, or the hangman having to keep on going outside in the rain?'

'Will you be long at the Co-Operative 'Late Shop', Harold, because I'm hoping to make a Lancashire Hot Pot with red cabbage for lunch and I don't want to end up collecting you from the 'Coach & Horses' in a worse for wear state of repair.'

'Don't worry, Mabel, I have my fingers firmly placed on the pulse.'

'Ah, that's what I thought when the Irish Doctor, O' Flannigan, died of a heart attack inside his surgery.' she said laughingly.

'Well, he should have known better than to take on a Jewish patient who is suffering from severe brain-damage, an injury to the lower part of her left arm, and wears a patch to cover her right eye, all of which were caused by her involvement in the Arab, Israeli war in 1967; it is of little wonder why the residents in Kirkham find it difficult to tell the difference between her, Long John Silver and the late General, Moshe Dayan, the

Israeli Commander-in-Chief, who was then one of the most famous desert rats of them all.'

'Is this the reason why she works in the dry-cleaning shop on Lytham Road and always asks if you can return the coat hangers and plastic bags?' Mabel replied, puzzlingly.

'Yes, she has a good business there; she is the only person I know who can sell sand to an Arab, and ice cream to an Eskimo.' Harold said with an unwanted smile.

'It wasn't her fault Harold that she found herself in Britain, looking for the Promised Land.'

'Well she wouldn't have found it in Freckleton; that's for sure.' Harold said, glancing at an old Sunday school prize depicting Jesus surf-boarding on the River Galilee. Do you know, I was told Barbara Zimmer-frame sucks 'Polo Mints' down to a slither, and then sells them to Aerospace Systems to be used as electrical washers.'

'And, do you know, Harold; you talk the biggest load of rubbish. And by the way she is called Zimmermann, and not something you hold on to whilst walking along the pavement.'

'Well, how come, her husband Lionel, made a fortune by selling second-hand Austin Rover cars in Blackpool, and now, is the largest manufacturer of Kosher Bagels in the North West, on a par with Jack Rubenstein's original Cornish pasties he sells in his shop on the Golden Mile.'

'Remember when we used to go to Blackpool, Harold? We would go dancing in the Tower Ballroom and then eat fish and chips out of newspaper; the salt and vinegar which ran down your arm before taking a smoky bus ride back to Freckleton.'

'Yes, I can remember it all too well; Doris Day singing "Kiss my Arse, my Arse, Whatever Will Be, Will Be", and Johnnie Ray singing "When your bums on fire, you will be a liar, Smoke gets up your Nose".'

'Somehow, I don't think you've got the words quite right, Harold; the American actress and singer, Doris Day sang, "*Que Sera, Sera*" and Johnnie Ray sang "Smoke gets in your Eyes"

'Anyway, Johnnie Ray was deaf and wouldn't have been able to hear the difference.'

'Remember David Whitfield singing with "Mantovani and his Orchestra", Harold? He sang "Answer Me"; they were very popular in those days.'

'Do you mean the guy who made you feel like throwing up every time he made an appearance on Sunday Night at the London Palladium?'

'And that American country singer who sang, "It's Only Make Believe", Conway Twitter; I can remember as if it were only yesterday, I always pressed the number fifteen button on the juke box which was firmly fixed on to the wall in Joey's cafe on Lords Street, Southport to hear his lovely voice.'

'Don't you mean, Conway Twitty, Mabel because I don't think he was into mobile phones in the nineteen-fifties?'

'Of course they used mobile phones, Harold; I saw Michael Caine using one in the classic World War Two film called "A Bridge too Far".' she said, recalling the actor portraying a British army officer poking his head out from the turret of an armoured car. 'He would have been twittering all the way to Nijmegen Bridge in Holland.'

'Do you know, Mabel, I once saw Michael Caine playing the part of a British army officer in the block-buster film, "Zulu"; his classic line was "follow me chaps", but when he turned around, half of the cast, who were supposed to be red-coats in the South Welsh Border Regiment, had buggered off for '*Camp*' coffee and a custard cream biscuit at Jack Hawkins's chuck wagon. Ah, how I remember the charmer, the actor with the boyish grin was often seen in East Berlin, spying over walls and barbed wire fences, using binoculars with extra strong lenses. In a film he caused a sensation when he came up against the entire Zulu nation; "follow me chaps" he would say in the end they'd had enough and went away. The man with the blond hair and lots of chat, the charmer who goes by the name of Harry Palmer, there's not a lot of people know that; I will go down to the shop now.' Harold said giving Arthur Wigglesworth time to walk along Calder Vale Avenue before turning into Beechnut Drive with his dog Poo Poo, his only closest friend and confidant.

'Yes, Harold, and if you hurry up you may just see your girlfriend,

Caroline Cartwright, getting up from her bed; it is her day-off today, and don't forget to make an appointment to see the optician on Lytham Road.' she added.

'Do you know, Mabel, Caroline must be sick and tired of assessing people's furniture.'

'Yea, I bet she is.'

The car slid stealthily out from the drive with Harold patronising the steering wheel; "Speedy Gonzales" had nothing on this man when he returned home in record-breaking time to drool over a woman with a body which could only be found mounted on a pedestal either in Greece, or in Rome.

'Ah, Caroline Cartwright, oh, how I remember happiness.' Harold uttered while putting his well-used plastic binoculars back inside their case which was now showing signs of decay around the edges and had definitely seen better days.

'You've been in the loo a long time, Harold; I was beginning to wonder if you had flushed yourself down the toilet, but I suppose chance would be a fine thing.'

'Now, now, Mabel and why is it that our conversations always seem to be relegated to the lavatory?'

'And, by the way, I must emphasise Harold.' Mabel interrupted. 'It isn't Caroline's day-off today; it is tomorrow, and it was a good thing you visited the optician this morning because the person you would have seen through her window would have been Mr Cartwright flexing his muscles in front of their new six-foot mirror.'

'Well, how is it, he has long blonde hair and wears stockings, suspenders and black patent leather high-heeled shoes?' Harold said, and at the same time picking up an optical lens cloth he'd inadvertently dropped on to the bedroom floor.

'Oh, he was probably rehearsing his lines for this year's amateur dramatic society review which is to be held in the church hall at Christmas.' Mabel replied with absolute diplomacy.

'And what part do you think he will be playing this year, Mabel? It won't be "Keeping up Appearances" that's for sure.'

'Remember when you used to frequent the "Arse and Clinker" pub in Preston Harold after your karate sessions; I didn't mind you disappearing every Wednesday evening, but the last straw was when you came home with a broken nose, a sprained ankle and a dislocated right hand.'

'I had to sort my opponent out once and for all because he nicked my chocolate biscuit during the tea break, and don't you mean the "Plough and Anchor" Mabel?'

'No dear, I was correct the first time; they all have broken noses and are a load of assholes that drink in there.'

'Can you remember, all those years ago, Mabel, when the church hall put on a review and all the stage lights were systematically put out by a Boy Scout who was sitting in the audience terrorising the cast of "Annie get your Gun" with a pea shooter; Margaret Hogarth was never the same after that performance.

'Yes, and I can remember it was your friend John Ashworth who was responsible, and after several ticking's off from a rather disgruntled Scout Master who was unconvincingly playing the part of a Red Indian Chief, he was asked to hand over his implement of destruction and to leave the hall.'

'I have to tell you Mabel, that I wasn't at all surprised to find four extra aces in the pack of cards; one of them was of Brigit Bardot stepping out of the bath, another was of her climbing up a ladder, and one of her bending down in front of Sacha Distel, and the fourth of her breast-feeding a long-haired Persian cat; how very fortuitous, and I think this calls for a re-shuffle and for you to go into the village and buy me a couple of beers.'

Chapter Twenty-four

Mabel Rigby's celebratory birthday party, Sunday afternoon, 23rd August 2015

'Happy birthday, Mabel, and here goes another expensive *artisan* cake which, during the course of the afternoon's celebratory proceedings, will be clinically dissected into twelve equal pieces before being offered to our family guests; it's a bit like the twelve disciples who are mentioned in the Holy Bible, all sitting at a table eating the last supper, and at the same time watching the omnibus edition of "East Enders" on television.'

'Tell me, Harold, and where does Jesus come into all of this?'

'Oh, he'll be with us this afternoon; he is everywhere, he's my mate you know.'

'But, you haven't got any mates, Harold. I wonder what Herbert-Cyril from the Wirral is doing now. It seems such a long time ago you and he were pals at the holiday camp in Morecambe; it was way before you and I met and it's a wonder there was any camp left after you both decided to set fire to the flotsam and jetsam you both found lying on the beach.'

'Flotsam and jetsam; does that come with cream Mabel?'

'It is the stuff that one finds when one looks for messages inside bottles which have been jettisoned by sailors from ships out at sea in order to find the person of their dreams.' Mabel replied knowledgably.

'But you did find the man of your dreams in the holiday camp, Mabel, and if it wasn't for that ludicrous progressive barn dance, you would still be riding around that famous ghost train in Southport.'

'Do you know Harold, you really are the pits, and it's a wonder you weren't arrested by the camp security for bending the glass on the fruit machines inside the amusement arcade so you could win a few pennies. I can also remember you turning the crazy golf course into something even crazier than what it was after you filled the holes up with sand, and an adhesive additive called cement; you know, Harold, why I ever fell for you at Middleton Towers still puzzles me.'

'It's because you love me, that's why, Mabel.'

'Yes, that may have something to do with it; more's the pity.'

'Herbert-Cyril Birtwistle and his Missus are busy bible-punching somewhere in Outer Mongolia, Mabel; on Tuesday last, I took the liberty of phoning his office in Skelmersdale, and they informed me that Major Birtwistle was on a mission.'

'Don't tell me he joined the SAS, and from what you have been telling me, I always thought he was a bit peculiar.' she commented.

'No, Mabel, he is a member of 'The Salvation Army' and is the editor of the local 'War Cry' in Skelmersdale, that's when he's not trying to induce a hip operation by banging a tambourine on his backside.'

'Who else have you been trying to contact while I've been away trying to make inroads to feed you.' Mabel said.

'No one in particular my nearest and dearest; there was absolutely no one else to consider.'

'That means, yes, and you are lying to me, Harold.'

'Now, would I do a thing like that, Mabel?'

'Yes, and who is Jillian Beadmore, Harold? I found this piece of paper on the floor inside our bedroom when I returned home from Preston, and I do hope you have not been phoning Queensland in Australia, because if you have, and I discover you are deceiving me, then you can say goodbye to our trip to Amsterdam.'

'I didn't know the Queen was visiting Australia, Mabel, she seems to get everywhere these days, now she has fallen-out with Scotland.'

'Do you know, Harold, I can't make my mind up to decide whether you are deaf or just plain stupid.'

'And, while we are still on the subject of reminiscing to places in history, where I would much prefer to forget,' Harold emphatically maintained. 'I can remember Herbert-Cyril as if it were only yesterday; he always had a runny nose which dripped like a tap, and can you remember the poem I penned not long after my escape from the camp.' he added.

The Dewdrop
A dewdrop dripped from Cyril's nose
Where it came from, God only knows
Cold as an icicle, ever so brittle

Water ran down it, little by little
There was to be a sigh of relief
When it broke off and fell into
A handkerchief
Now squidgy and wet around the edges
It had dog-end stains, care of 'Benson & Hedges'
For his mum it became an exceptional issue
When he asked to borrow a '*Kleenex*' tissue
She said you really must be quite insane
To go out naked in the rain
Late at night he rose from his bed
To have a smoke inside the bike shed
He said, 'how did you know, mum, I get up from my bed?'
She said, 'I didn't think it was a tyre-kicker from Birkenhead'
At last his wet nose began to stop
To make way for another unsuspected dewdrop

'Well, Harold, you didn't answer my question who is Jillian Beadmore? I promise you I will not talk to you ever again unless you explain who she is.'

'Ah, she was just an old flame I met at Middleton Towers Holiday Camp; it was a few years before we met and unfortunately I ended up playing second fiddle to her boyfriend who lived in Bangor, North Wales.'

'It was a blessing the flame went out, Harold, because you could have set yourself on fire, and that would have solved some of our problems years ago.'

'And, if it wasn't for your father, Mabel, I could be basking in the sun somewhere in the South of France.'

'You mean like one of those sharks that lurk off the coast of San Tropez, waiting to take a bite out of someone's leg.'

'Well, I wouldn't be averse to lying on the beach next to Julia Roberts; she played a good part in the film "Notting Hill", and it was strange he wasn't given the chance to take a bite out of one of her legs because he was far too busy giving her cups of tea and feeding her with fruits of the forest.'

'The only beaches you are likely to see Harold, are those in Blackpool and Southport, and furthermore, when you visited my family all those years ago, I couldn't tell the difference between you and Harry Corbett's two hand puppets, "Sooty and Sweep".'

'Oh, come on Mabel, give me a break, it wasn't my fault we didn't have a proper bathroom, and Veronica and I had to contend with using the same water.'

'You see, there you go again, Harold; Veronica was always in the firing line and was blamed for everything that went wrong in the family, no wonder she now enjoys living in America.'

'Having read her last communication, it sounds like she has put on a few pounds since I last saw her; it is probably due to her eating far too many "*Big Mac*" beef burgers, and bucket upon bucket of popcorn and greasy Kentucky Fried Chicken.'

'She has an over-active thyroid problem, Harold; you have no idea have you?'

'I suppose she, like everyone who live in America, Mabel, is over-active and needs to lose weight by not eating junk food; those potato sticks which purport to be chips, and look like they have just passed through a paper shredding machine are positively disgusting; they would never get away with it in Freckleton.'

'Get away with what, Harold?'

'By not having to travel twenty miles down the route sixty-six highway just to find a diner where they serve cow pie and buffalo steaks which have to be dusted down before they are eaten.'

'Do you know, Harold, I think you are jealous of your sister because she is able to enjoy a lifestyle far better than you traipsing back from the "Coach & Horses" on Saturday evenings, and calling in at 'Wong's Lucky House', 'Something Fishy' or the 'Bombay Mix' on your way home.'

'Well, you don't complain, Mabel; those complementary vegetable spring rolls given to us by May Wong are exceptionally good, especially with the curry sauce.'

'Tell me Harold, what can I get you for your lunch before the family arrive to eat us out of house and home?'

'Oh, I think I would prefer to eat a triple beef burger with chips; that sounds pretty good to me.'

'You are joking, of course?'

'Yes Mabel, I'm joking, I only want the one.'

'And I shall be doing the baking and cooking while you are in the pub this lunchtime, it is of great relief to me, Harold to get rid of you for a few hours because then, I can concentrate on things a lot better when you're not here.'

'You mean like gathering up a few tips from Jamie Oliver on how to prematurely get rid of your dinner guests by feeding them with rat poison.'

'What do you mean, Harold, Jamie Oliver is an excellent television presenter, and his culinary expertise in making Welsh rarebit leaves your toad-in-the-hole somewhat way behind in the field of cooking.'

'The only Welsh rarebit I know, Mabel, is Bonnie Tyler, and from what I have heard she is pretty good in a field.'

'Go and put your jacket on Harold; the crowd will be arriving at three o'clock and promise me you won't come back until a week on Tuesday.'

'That all depends on me meeting Bonnie Tyler.'

'My father will be arriving from Southport and will be delivered at two-thirty.' Mabel reiterated.'

'You sound as if he is going to arrive disguised as a DHL parcel; he deserves to be treated with more reverence.'

'Well, in that case, I will redirect him to the 'Coach and Horses', and you can both get sloshed together; it won't be the first time.' Mabel said, reminding him of the time Liverpool won against Manchester United in the Football Association Cup Final at Wembley Stadium.

'I can remember that Saturday afternoon all too well.' she continued to say. 'When you and your father-in-law ate so many free chip butties in the pub, you were both not able to eat your dinner that evening, and furthermore, you both had an argument over the referee's behaviour when he called for extra time because he lost the pea in his whistle.'

'You're dad carries the stigma of being an Anfield supporter and has had the audacity to wear a Liverpool scarf inside the pub where the customers are predominantly Manchester United fans, and you wonder why hardly anyone ever talks to me.'

'It's not because of that Harold; the real reason is that no one likes you because you keep on missing the dartboard. It was only last week that Elaine Jordan mentioned that she had to replace more bulbs in the spotlight before Michael Bobbly and Blackpool Borough Council switched on the illuminations.'

'His name is Michael Bublé, my dear; he is an Anglo French Canadian.'

'I like a bit of fuzz.' Mabel said unbuttoning Harold's shirt for the first time in years to examine his chest.

'Well, at least I'm leaving my mark in the village.' Harold said with pride and prejudice.

'Yes, you can say that again; most of them are all on the pub walls.' Mabel retaliated.

'Tell me Mabel, who is transporting your father from Southport to Freckleton?'

'He is being brought by his next door neighbour, Stanley Mann.'

'And will 'Stan the Man' be participating in the refreshments and confections which will be on offer this afternoon because the pie-chart is becoming less and less in size and proportion.'

'There will be enough for everyone, Harold, and if push comes to shove I'm sure Prince will be quite willing to give up some of his dog biscuits.'

'I don't think 'Stan the Man' will approve of eating pink dog biscuits in the shape of a bone.'

'I wasn't thinking about him, Harold, it is you who will be eating them if you don't stop whinging; whinge, whinge, whinge, that's all you do from the moment you get up in the morning until you decide to go to bed, and when it's time for you to get up, you start all over again.'

'Oh, you do exaggerate Mabel.'

'Alison will be arriving shortly to give me a hand with the catering.' she said looking at a pile of dishes in the sink waiting to be washed.

'That bloody birthday cake seems to be getting smaller and smaller by the minute.' Harold replied with a drawl not dissimilar to Jeremy Clarkson's.

The kitchen door leading into the drive was opened allowing the baking smells to penetrate into the dank morning atmosphere; apple pies, Bakewell tarts and delicious home-made scones were enough to render Mr Kipling, and his exceedingly good cakes, redundant. Harold said to Mabel on his way out, he would be back just after one to witness the distinctive yellow DHL van arriving outside No 23 Calder Vale Avenue carrying his father-in-law, Bert Hatton. It was then Mabel said to him that if he didn't conduct himself properly, someone would be carrying him out inside a box.

Harold's leisurely, albeit missionary stroll down to the pub seemed a lot longer that Sunday morning because of a sighting in the shape of Margaret Hogarth, his girlfriend of long standing who on Smith's farm seems to suffer from constant hay fever, and has a fetish for muck spreading; most of it circulating around the village. The necessary diversion which led Harold towards a Medical Centre where patients are issued with raffle tickets in order to see a doctor was it seemed the only escape route to avoid a woman who should be confined to a stable in Horse guard's Parade in London.

Having escaped a series of complications which could have led to Harold's immediate downfall, he entered into the pub and confronted by.....

Boss-eyed Fred

The 'Littlewoods' rep with eyes that stray
Stands at the bar every single day
He keeps his coupons in his pocket
Already to give one to Miss Lucy Locket
Lucy, who sports an hour-glass figure
Has a chest that seems to get bigger and bigger
A regular said she looks like Bet Middler
Who tries to latch on to another Fiddler?

Fred's Jewish eyes are those one could say
Are one at home and one away
And in his dreams, it is an illusion
For him to be an Institution
In a village where there are lots of minders
Who call you names that sound like spiders?
And on Saturday afternoon's
Just to add to the fun
One sits down to see if one has won
And, if they're lucky, they can't disparage
Moving to a house with a double garage
A greenhouse, a shed, mini-golf, and of course
A kennel for the dog and a stable for the horse
Boss-eyed Fred is very reliant
When he keeps an eye on a prospective client
Who is handed a form to enter into a riddle
To save-up and buy a second-hand fiddle

Harold, just to add to his non-existent importance said to Fred:
'What do you call a Jewish raincoat?'

'I don't know; what do you call a Jewish raincoat?' Frederick Green replied with an air of caution.

'It is called a 'Shmack'. And,' he added, 'what do you call a Jew wearing a raincoat?', and helping towards the village ethnic cleansing programme.

'I don't know; what do you call 'The chosen people' who wear raincoats?'

'You call them 'Schmucks'. Harold replied.

'Do you know, Harold, that when I depart from Freckleton and I arrive in 'The promised Land', I will send you a dirty postcard.'

'I didn't know they sold dirty postcards in heaven and furthermore, Fred, I will buy you the train fare; that's if I can afford to buy a British Rail ticket.'

'Tell me Harold, how much did you pay for your 'Schmack'?'

'I think it cost forty-nine pounds and ninety-nine pence from Burton's

Gent's Outfitters in Preston.' Harold replied with exceptionally good recall.

'My raincoat was bought from 'Marks and Spencer' in Blackpool. I took the original one to a dry-cleaning shop in Lytham St. Anne's and during the process it became lost. I told the manageress in the shop that it was a '*Burbury*', and it cost two-hundred and fifty pounds from an exclusive store in Regent's Street London, and furthermore, I was entitled to compensation. The manageress soon coughed up the money and now I am able to periodically take my replacement raincoat back to Marks and Spencer to avoid having to pay for it to be dry-cleaned.'

'It is of little wonder why you drive a twelve year-old 'Skoda'; you know Fred, people have only got money when they are seen to be spending it.'

'Is this why you are always at the back of the queue when it is your turn to buy a round of drinks, Harold?' Fred cleverly put in.

'Can I buy you a drink Fred? Harold said when he felt embarrassed at Fred's last statement. 'How about a large glass of arsenic?' he added. 'And that should do you and the world a great deal of good.'

'Do you realize, my family came over from France to Britain in nineteen thirty-nine, just before the Second World War, and set up shop on the Isle-of-Man?'

'Those shops wouldn't be on a par with the Royal Bank of Scotland would they?'

'No, no; I was only speaking metaphorically.' Fred said cautiously. 'And, years later my father made a fortune buying, repairing and selling '*Singer*' sewing machines in Blackpool; I have to contend with restoring old violins in the hope that someone has the money to buy one that sounds very much like a '*Stradivarius*'.'

'Have you ever listened to a Stradivarius violin being played, Fred?'

'No, but I can imagine.'

'I once had the pleasure of listening to the virtuoso, Nigel Kennedy playing Gypsy music on BBC's Radio Four; he was one of Hoodie Ammonium's prodigies.'

'Don't you mean Yehudi Menuhin?' Fred said with a sense of shock.

'And which football team did he play for, Fred?'

'It may be of interest to some that Phil Collins was a personal friend of Nigel Kennedy when they were attending the music academy in London.' Fred continued to say.

'You mean it was a "Groovy kind of Love".'

'Do you know Harold; if whit was shit you would be constipated.'

'Yes, I've heard all of this before Frederick, and that is why I carry a toilet roll around in one of my deep pockets.'

'Never mind the quality just feel the width; that's what my grandfather said to my brother when he measured him up for a new suit to celebrate his coming of age.'

'You mean when they all dance around tables and smash-up the crockery; it all sounds like '*Yates Wine Lodge*' in Blackpool on a Saturday night.'

'As usual Harold, I think you've got your geography wrong; it is the Greeks who dance around tables and smash-up dinner plates in the fireplace not the Jewish people. It wasn't so long ago you were seen heading home in the wrong direction having had a skin-full of '*Boddingtons*' beer.'

'Ah, that was because I had an offer I couldn't refuse.'

'And what, may I ask was the offer, and who made it?' Frederick hesitantly asked.

'If I said Bombay potatoes and chicken Madras curry, who do you think made me an offer?' Harold replied with a cheeky boy look.

'Oh, that will be Raman Chaterjie in 'The Bombay Mix' take-away on Lytham Road.'

'It's not often you're right, but you are wrong again Fred; it was Beryl Patel, Freckleton's answer to Mata Hari; her husband was on business in Mumbai and she was left to tend to the elephants in Crofts Butts Lane.'

'But, there aren't any elephant in Croft Butts Lane.'

'There will be, Fred, there will. And just before you go, give me one of those football coupons; I feel lucky this week. "Oh, we were such mucky kids, dirty as dustbin lids, and someday we'll have a splash when Littlewoods provide the cash"; that's what our Cilla used to sing.'

'I always thought your sister's name was Veronica, Harold.'

'She was Fred, she was.'

'Well, just look at the time, I must depart.' Frederick Green said disparagingly. 'The missus has got the *bagels* on.'

'I didn't know she wore glasses.' Harold replied.

Chapter Twenty-five

'Hello, fancy seeing you here.' Harold said to Bert Hatton, his father-in-law, who had a reputation to be an expert in wheeling and dealing in Southport. He was to make his fortune by selling second-hand cars and replacement batteries after surreptitiously popping effervescent '*Alka Seltzer*' tablets into their cells during obligatory, albeit unnecessary MOT inspections during the hours of darkness.

'*Hi...a*; is you all right *den dare* our kid.' Bert Hatton said in his eloquent *Scouse* accent which could be equated to an adenoidal dock worker from Liverpool.

Ah, Harold's father-in-law, the man with the golden bollocks, and the only person in Merseyside to need an electronically controlled voice box fitted to his throat so that people could comprehend what he was talking about, also, the need for an interpreter to put his words into a language which everyone should be capable of understanding.

'Have you sold any of those American Willis Jeeps this week Bert; you know the type which mysteriously disappeared from military bases at Burtonwood and Warton during The Second World War.' Harold asked when he metaphorically acted as a wind-up vehicle to raise Bert's hackles up from the back of his long scrawny neck. 'It was some time ago I read in a newspaper that one of those jeeps had been sold to an American army veteran in Southport for the sum of ten-thousand pounds. It was when he tried to transport the vehicle over to Nashville, Tennessee; he was confronted by the British Customs and Excise authorities who asked him for a certificate of ownership and his export licence. It transpired that the jeep had done the rounds more than once and that the short wheel-base metal chassis had come from an old Ford Prefect.'

'Ah, ya can't trust anyone, these days.' Bert said tongue in cheek. 'The "Yankee doodle dandy" was probably Elvis Presley.' Bert went on. 'He became one of those 'ENSA' guys who travelled on British Leyland buses entertaining the troops.'

'But the American troops weren't here during the early nineteen seventies.' Harold made absolutely clear.

'Ah, you can't believe everything you read in the newspapers, Harold.'

'Yes, I will go along with that dad, because after all the article was in the "Liverpool Echo" I was reading.'

'Hi dad, had a safe journey from home, have you?' Mabel said, as her father adjusted his seat belt which was fitted to his mobility chair to enable him to move safely down the drive for the umpteenth time since Harold and Mabel moved from their nostalgic humble abode in Naze Lane, to a semi-detached dormer bungalow in Calder Stone Avenue.

'Well, I am still here gal, and I am chuffed that I've got my trusty driver, Stanley Mann to take me everywhere.'

'He doesn't work for DHL parcel carriers by any chance, does he?' Harold asked looking at a yellow Ford Transit van with mauve letters embossed on one side.

'I wouldn't say no to a whisky, Harold.' Bert said looking at his over-the-top H. Samuel 'Casio' chronograph wrist watch which displayed the time around a set of luminous dials, and unless you were a formula-one racing driver or an over-enthusiastic train spotter standing on platform two on Preston railway station, the timepiece was as vulgar as Julian Clary.

'It seemed a long journey to Freckleton this time our kid; why can't the Ministry of Transport get their heads together and build a bridge across the estuary from Lytham St Anne's to Southport, not only would it shorten the journey by two thirds, but Blackpool would be more attractive to the people living in Merseyside.'

'That's what 'Fylde Borough Council' are scared of dad.'

'What have they got to be scared of, Harold?'

'Wheels, wing mirrors and hub caps disappearing from their vans.'

'Here you are, dad a large Irish whiskey to keep you going, but keep your voice down because they'll all want one, especially her next door, Mrs Cartmell; she's probably got her ear trumpet to the wall as we speak.'

'Will she be coming to the party?' Bert curiously asked.

'Fortunately no, it is only the family who are attending and the birthday cake will not be able to take any more dissecting. Bernadette will insist on singing "When Irish Eyes are smiling", after swigging back several glasses of my 'Jameson's' Irish whiskey.'

'Well, I must say *la* she has good taste.' Bert said smiling.

'It's funny you should say that, dad; the milkman used to say that too.'

'I've got a good joke for you la.' his father-in-law would insist on telling. 'What do you call a homosexual snake that's good at maths?'

'Do you know dad; I haven't a clue.'

'They are called 'Puff Adders'.' Bert was quick to reveal.

'And, what do you call homosexual dandy lion spores?' Harold asked, trying to go one better than his father-in-law.

'Go on our kid; stuff it to me.'

'They are called 'Puff balls'.' Harold retaliated with a sense of one-upmanship knowing the frivolity could extend well into the afternoon.

'You will be pleased to hear, Harold that your favourite dental practitioner from Blackpool, Doctor S.R Wilson, our daughter Jean and two granddaughters, Janet and Susan won't be arriving until four, they are currently visiting some friends who live in Mildew Lane, Burnley.' Mabel explained having just received a call on her mobile phone.

'Is that the road next to Gasometer Street and Oil drum Road?' Harold inquisitively asked.

'Yes, that's right, Harold; your geography is improving at last.' Mabel replied.

'Do you know Burnley has a reputation for having such exotic names to call their dwelling places?' Harold said, continuing with his inverted snobbery. 'One can almost imagine being on a desert island with palm trees waving softly in a light sea breeze, and coconuts hanging down underneath the leaves just waiting to drop on top of one of those skimpily-clad Swedish tourists lying down on the golden sands beneath.'

'You've been eating far too many 'Bounty Bars' Harold; that's your trouble.' Mabel said turning round to go back into the kitchen.

'The way you describe Manchester Road in Burnley, Harold, makes Scottie Road in Liverpool sound like Sunset Boulevard in Los Angeles.' Bert Hatton said with long term experience of wearing down the cobbles on one of Bootle's more famous streets.

The next person to arrive on the Rigby's doorstep was their daughter,

Emily, the thirty-eight year-old long lost family no-hoper from Garstang who brings happiness to everybody's lives, especially unruly school children when they find themselves in range of a British Athletic Association hammer-throwing champion.

Completely dedicated to her job as a gym teacher at Saint Bartholomew's Church of England Junior School, Emily is still looking for the perfect doormat of a man who she can twirl around inside her humble flat and then toss him into a coal bunker several streets away.

'Hi Emily,' Harold said as he looked down on his daughter who momentarily appeared to be a few feet shorter than him, but that was until she stepped inside the bungalow to reveal her true height.

"What does a Pakistani do when he visits the Highland Games? Harold asked her before she had time to sit down.

'I don't know dad, please tell me, and I hope it's not going to be another one of your attempts to join the Diplomatic Corps.'

'He tosses the Kaiber.' he replied.

'That wasn't in the least bit funny, dad; it took me a long time to develop my muscles and then go on to win a bronze medal in the Commonwealth Games.'

'Yes, we were all very proud of you Emily, especially when an African road runner won the silver and a Kiwi fruit picker won the gold.'

'You never let up, do you dad; it was a good thing you had to prematurely come home from Saudi Arabia because the government out there would have had your head placed high on top of a pole.

'Hi granddad,' Emily said, before going into the kitchen to join her mother.

'Hi...a, are you alright den dare our kid.'

'Oh, for Pete's sake granddad, can't you talk properly; you sound like a demented buffoon from Kirkby.'

'That reminds me.' Bert said with a chuckle. 'Did you hear the one about the 'Lion'?'

The Lion
A lion escaped from Blackpool zoo

And said to-day what shall I do
Maybe a stroll along the Promenade
And then stop off to buy a card
Maybe to 'Yates' for a drink and some 'Coke'
Then take in a show for a laugh and a joke
He had a chat with a legless Buffoon
And said it was quiet for a Saturday afternoon

'It was a good thing granddad you didn't give up your daytime job to become a poet because you may have had to join the ranks of the unemployed.'

'Ah, but you see Emily, your great grandfather had a gift for making money and passed all his knowledge onto me; he bought a garage and began selling second-hand cars after being a tick-tack man on Aintree Race Course where horses, unfortunately fell at the first fence.

'Where do you go for a good pint, a good read, and to shelter from the rain dad?'

'I go to the pub on the corner of our road; it's called the 'Black Bull'.' Bert replied.

'Well, I go to 'Weatherstones'.'

'Ah, very funny, Harold, and don't give up your daytime job to become a comedian.'

At around three pm, the Garston family arrived. There was Doreen and Barry, Howard and Raymond to set the party going around the dining room table after a bowl of monkey nuts accidently fell onto the floor.

'How is my big sister Doreen?' Emily said when she came back into the lounge wearing one of her mother's aprons with the words "Let me Entertain You" emblazoned on the front.

'And, if I may ask, where is my favourite brother-in-law, police sergeant Barry Garston and my nephews, Raymond and Howard?'

'They are underneath the table scooping-up monkey nuts.' Doreen replied as an item of baggage rose to his feet and said good afternoon.

'Well, Barry will know all about monkeys having served as a copper in

Her Majesties Royal Military Police.' Emily knowledgably implied.

'I will have you know that Barry has devoted his life to law and order, and both Howard and Raymond want to follow on in their father's footsteps; they are police cadets at Hutton and will, I'm sure, turn out to be pillars of the community.'

'Is this the reason why they are *dare* on the floor picking up nuts?' Bert said with a big grin on his face.

'Now granddad, that was uncalled for.' Doreen said.

'The truth of the matter, our kid, is that because of all the cut-backs there are no coppers on the beat; they are all keeping warm inside panda cars and their headquarters watching "Brookside" on close circuit monitors and television.'.

'Oh, get a life, granddad.' Doreen retaliated. The police are doing a great job; they no longer have panda cars, but have helicopters and powerful motorcycles, and as for watching "Brookside", the television series was phased out long ago and so was "Dixon of Dock Green".'

'Tell me Emily, just where did you get that pinafore from? Bert asked knowing what he was going to say next.

'I borrowed it from my mum; she said it would be perfect for the party and would raise a few eyebrows when I circulated with the champagne glasses.'

'I didn't know you were into entertaining; life is full of surprises, isn't it?' her grandfather replied with a curiousness like figuring out the life and times of Betty Grable.

'When I organise wild 'Tupperware' parties for some of the lady teachers in Garstang, I seem to excel at entertaining.'

'Is that when they inspect the goods thoroughly before the windows get steamed-up?' Bert said, grinning at her white rolled down and twisted ankle socks.

The afternoon continued with Harold having his belated lunch in the kitchen accompanied by Mabel bending his ear every two minutes to pay more attention to eating his food than drooling over a stocking-clad pair of legs which stretched to the adjoining page of a *'Sunday Times'* supplement.

'It's a pity George, Abigail and the kids won't be able to come to the party because my family would have been all together this afternoon.' Mabel said with a sadness which brought tears to her eyes. Even the dog became emotional when his artificial bone was kicked away from under his nose by Emily as she rushed in through the door as if it was a way into the kitchen from a busy restaurant.

'Yes, it's a bit like Christmas when one comes out from the midnight service to find the pub has just closed.' Harold replied bringing back memories from the previous year when he had to make do with going round twice to drink the communion wine; the vicar thought he was hallucinating and had to sniff the chalice to find out just what the hell was in there.

It was around four when the Rigby's son-in-law, Doctor James S.R Wilson arrived with their daughter Jean, and grandchildren Janet and Susan.

'How was Burnley, is it still there?' Harold asked in jest.

'Of course it is dad.' Jean quickly replied. 'The town has a thriving tourist industry and is visited by thousands of people each year including His Royal Highness, Prince Charles.'

'Oh, he's the guy who appears to be a quick-change artist and fiddles with his lose change in his jacket pockets.' Harold went on, continuing with his nonsensical style of wit.

'He is going to be the next king of England, Northern Ireland, Scotland and Wales.' Janet said reassuringly.

'Well, in my estimation, he will be at least a hundred years of age when he ascends to the throne, because like those "Carry On" films, Her Majesty will go on, and on, and on.' Harold inferred.

'You know, Harold that when I extracted that wisdom tooth some years ago, I would have expected you to retain at least a modicum of intelligence inside that brain of yours.' James said knowing that one cannot put little grey cells and matter into a skull with limited capacity.

'I can remember taking a cake to the Christiana Hartley Nursing home in Southport where Mabel was born.' Bert Hatton said with pride just before the candles on her birthday cake were deliberately blown out.

'The only Hartley's I knew were on the side of a jar of jam, and the bandleader, a national hero from Colne in Lancashire who was unfortunate to be on the ill-fated '*Titanic*' when it sank.' Harold said to James, trying unsuccessfully to convince him he wasn't entirely an absolute idiot. 'Wallace Hartley's body was found during the same month on the thirtieth of April, nineteen hundred and twelve, and although his violin case was strapped to his back and served to identify him, there was no trace of the violin.' Harold continued to explain. 'And, six weeks later the families of the heroic musicians who owed money for their uniforms were being constantly pressurized for payment; the "White Star Line" seemingly uninterested in getting involved; the wooden coat hangers which had been deeply branded with the company's name were of free benefit to the players but could have been used to hook some of the passengers and crew out from the water before being winched up by a Royal Navy Wessex helicopter.

The poem I am about to show you.' Harold went on. 'Was written with something in mind; it is about ships that flounder and lie beneath and have nothing to do with a new set of teeth.'

"Titanic"
No one can hear the voices from a silent grave
But just a ripple from an incoming wave
Where the 'rouges' lurk and echoes sound
In a silent grave two and a half miles down

'But helicopters weren't put into operation until the nineteen-fifty's granddad.' Howard had reason to point out, knowing that someday he would become a pilot in a police force who are hell-bent in peering into bedroom windows from a dizzy height.

'I was only trying to make light of it all.' Harold said undiplomatically before adding a few more arms and legs to the story. 'Would anyone like more ice to go with your drinks?'

'Do you know, dad?' James said emphatically. 'That when you and my mother-in-law go on this trip to Amsterdam, you will have to make sure there aren't any icebergs floating in those canals.'

'Don't worry, James, Mabel and I always avoid disaster situations; take for instance the time we flew to the Isle of Man from Blackpool Airport; I insisted on sitting at the rear of the plane because have you ever heard of an aircraft to back into a mountain?'

Raymond said to keep up with his brother, and to point out that some of the contents of Harold's stories were not exactly true.

'Well, we could have made a detour over Snowdonia in North Wales; the weather was a bit inclement and the windows kept steaming up.' Harold said swinging the conversation around three hundred and sixty degrees.

'The windows kept steaming up, Harold because of a couple sitting on two adjoining seats over the aisle were having a late breakfast.' Mabel outwardly explained.

'On the way here, we stopped off at Samlesbury Hall, didn't we, dad?' Susan said bringing the story to a close.

'Yes, we sat in during the antique auction and we bought a bureau.' James put in.

'And, where may I ask is this much sought-after item of furniture now?' Harold asked.

'It's in the back of the off-roader which is parked directly in front of your house.' Jean said totally oblivious to its history.

'It has saved you a trip back to Samlesbury Hall, hasn't it Harold?' Mabel said realizing he had only a few yards to walk and put Lieutenant Percival Hywel Owens's letter and poem addressed to Lady Geraldine Harkness, back where it belongs, and for the Wilson family to resume and begin the investigation all over again.

'I'm sorry to have to tell you, dad.' Emily said removing her apron in preparation to run quickly out through the door.

'What's the matter now, Emily?' Harold asked, thinking by some miracle she may not have been taking precautions.

'Prince has just eaten your slice of the cake.'

'Typical isn't it? I turn my back and the dog runs away with my only means of happiness.'

Other titles by Michael Alty:

The Guildford Boys – ISBN 978 1 84549 428 5

The Ghost of Latchford Hall – ISBN 978 1 84540 528 2

The Bells of Saint Clements – ISBN 978 1 84549 620 3

27 rue Mortain – ISBN 978 1 84549 686 9

Published by arima Publishing.